PRAISE FOR T

MW00641542

ONE OF THE BEST ROMANCE NOVELS OF THE YEAR. "A powerful, honest look at love as both a motivation and a risk."

THE WASHINGTON POST

"*Thirsty* held me captivated from its first page to its last. A singular reading experience."

USA TODAY

"*Thirsty* offers readers a powerful redemption arc while avoiding the casually racist escape narrative. Sal and Vanessa don't want to leave their neighborhood; they want to make it stronger. The book is unusual for being from a hero's-only point of view, but Hopkins' portrayal of Sal and Vanessa's love story is fully satisfying."

KIRKUS REVIEWS

"A brilliant read. There are good writers, and then there are writers that just leave you in awe. And Hopkins has definitely left me in awe."

HYPABLE

"Sexy and soul-wrenching, with Sal's irresistible voice luring you through a living, breathing Los Angeles."

USA TODAY BESTSELLING AUTHOR SIERRA SIMONE

"An amazing read! I stayed up way too late to finish and haven't stopped thinking about the characters. Highly recommended!"

USA TODAY BESTSELLING AUTHOR MOLLY O'KEEFE

PRAISE FOR TRASHED BY MIA HOPKINS

ONE OF THE BEST ROMANCE NOVELS OF THE YEAR. "A beautiful portrait of a vibrant community replete with compelling messages of forgiveness and redemption, a heart-shattering reminder of how love in all its forms can be the ultimate salvation."

ENTERTAINMENT WEEKLY

"At times such as these, reading a book like this, it feels important to choose words with care. The word I most want to use about this absolute masterpiece of a contemporary romance is: *visionary*."

SEATTLE REVIEW OF BOOKS

"Whip-smart progressive romance with a whole lot of sizzle."

THE ALLITERATES

"Mia Hopkins keeps it sexy in *Trashed*, wrapping Eddie and Carmen's romance in a story that's ultimately about culture, community, and the happily ever after we all deserve."

THE DAILY WAFFLE

"Delightfully raunchy, yet tender and loving. Hopkins does a great job of capturing both the vulnerability and the passion of sex in her writing."

BUSTLE

PRAISE FOR TANKED BY MIA HOPKINS

ONE OF THE BEST ROMANCE NOVELS OF THE YEAR. "Gorgeous and emotionally bruising, this story of a former underground fighter and a social worker out of work will wring you out in the best way....One of my top contemporary series of all time."

THE NEW YORK TIMES

"A moving, poignant look at the struggles we all face as human beings and the way we survive and persevere....I absolutely adored this book (and this whole series). I can't recommend it enough."

SMEXY BOOKS

"*Tanked* has so much heart and was a delight to read. I stayed up too late, I read while I was supposed to be doing other things. I could not put it down."

EMMALITA, CANNONBALL READ

"Hats off to the author for writing a third book in this series that is just as captivating as the first two! The whole series is going on my re-read shelf."

ALL ABOUT ROMANCE

THIRSTY

AN EASTSIDE BREWERY NOVEL

MIA HOPKINS

Copyright © 2018 by Mia Hopkins

Excerpt from *Trashed* copyright © 2019 by Mia Hopkins

All rights reserved.

No part of this book may be reproduced in any form or by any electronic or mechanical means, including information storage and retrieval systems, without written permission from the author, except for the use of brief quotations in a book review.

Digital ISBN 978-0-9996306-5-5

Print ISBN 978-0-9996306-6-2

Originally published as an ebook in 2018 by Loveswept, an imprint of Random House, a division of Penguin Random House LLC, New York.

First trade paperback edition: April 2024

Cover by Natasha Snow Designs

Thirsty is a work of fiction. Names, places, and incidents either are products of the author's imagination or are used fictitiously. Any resemblance to actual events, locales, or persons, living or dead, is entirely coincidental.

AUTHOR'S NOTE

Thirsty is a standalone contemporary high-heat romance novel with a happily ever after. This book is for mature readers only. It mentions explicit sex, violence, homelessness, poverty, child and domestic abuse, substance abuse, anxiety and self-harm. Please exercise caution if these are sensitive topics for you.

ONE

YOU WANT A HERO.

Before we start, you should know—I'm not him.

I'm not your hero.

A hero is a Prince Charming, a firefighter, a cowboy. He's handsome and perfect. He's probably white. He has his shit together.

None of that is me.

For example, would a hero be standing barefoot and half-asleep on a sidewalk in his *chones,* holding all his belongings in a backpack? Because that's what I'm doing right now. Staring at the scene in front of me.

"You lying, no good son of a bitch!"

Regina tosses another drawer full of clothes out the second-story bedroom window. The clothes are followed by a wrestling trophy, which falls gently on a pile of T-shirts.

"You're a fucking liar!"

Next, a PlayStation controller, followed by a grip of games. Some land on the grass and others on the concrete driveway with an ugly crash.

"You wanna live with that *puta*? Fine! Go be with that whore! Go!"

The neighbors are coming out now. Some of them are holding coffee mugs. Kids in pajamas appear, pointing and laughing.

I might be the one standing here in my underwear, but luckily I'm not the one they're looking at. I put my bag down and pull out a clean T-shirt and basketball shorts. I get dressed, right here in the street.

My buddy Spider stands on the lawn. He's shouting up at his old lady like some kind of opposite-day Romeo. "Regina! Listen to me!"

"Go to hell."

And down comes the PlayStation itself. It doesn't land on the grass or on a soft pile of clothing, but on the driveway. It crashes nasty, parts flying, and all I can see are dollar signs, floating away like little butterflies.

Oof. Ice cold.

"Regina!"

This goes on for a few minutes. Some of the kids are pulled back inside, some neighbors get in their cars and drive off. The neighborhood *chismosas* are all out, though—gossipy old ladies, grandmas and *tías*. And they're not going anywhere until this plays out. They're looking for a fresh scandal. This is good stuff.

I sit on the curb and get my socks and shoes on. I tie the laces, rub my face, and fold my arms. It's August, so the cool morning air is already heating up.

Spider is wearing shorts and a wifebeater shirt. He's halfway between pissed and heartbroken, his emotions swinging back and forth. Dumbass. I told him not to sleep around on Regina. I told him that she knew, that she'd get fed up with him, but did he listen to me? Does anyone?

"Fuck you, and fuck your no-good friends," she shouts.

I raise my eyebrows. Wait a second. Is she referring to me?

"Hey, that's not fair," I murmur.

I've been crashing on Spider and Regina's couch since I got out of prison six months ago, but I've been a good houseguest. Regina's even told me so. I clean their living room every day, bathroom and kitchen too. Regina and Spider have three kids and between the five of them, before I got there, the house looked like a hurricane hit a rat's nest.

Every evening before I'd leave for work, she'd cook for all of us and I'd do the dishes without being asked. Once she even told me, "You're gonna make a woman super happy someday, Ghost."

Me?

Doubt it.

I look down at the sidewalk. Something is written there. I clear away a little of the grit with my hand. I see it, scratched into the surface. Old graffiti, sixty, seventy years old. A cross with three lines. Pachuco cross. Below it, four letters. ESHB, East Side Hollenbeck.

My grandfather's gang. My father's gang. My gang.

"Regina, don't be this way!"

I look up. Spider is begging now. Begging, in front of everyone. He has it bad for this woman. Why he couldn't keep his *verga* in his pants for her, I'll never know. Like a lot of homeboys, he has a problem with the females, especially the ones who are hot for gangsters. In this neighborhood, there are a lot of those.

Bang!

When she slams the window shut halfway through his speech, I know the conversation is over, at least for now. I get up, stretch, and yawn. I had been asleep for only a half hour when all this drama started up. I've been working all night. I'm so tired, I'm not even worked up. I should be. Now that Spider got us thrown out of his house, I've got nowhere to go.

As he walks toward me, I can see the hurt on his face. He tries to hide it. "Fuck." He blinks away the pain. "This bitch is crazy."

I want to say, "I told you not to sleep around," but that would make me an asshole, particularly at this moment, so I just shrug.

"Where will you go now?" I say, even though I know the answer. The other girl's door is open, at least for now. Unlike me, Spider has a bed to sleep in tonight if he wants it.

"I'll be around." He looks up at me apologetically, knowing he's fucked up for both of us. "I'm sorry, man. Ruben said the crash pad has space."

"I'll check it out," I say, even though I won't. That dump is overcrowded, and there's always shit there—drugs, guns. I need to stay away for now. My parole officer has a hard-on to get me back inside. "I'll find someplace. Don't worry about me."

I watch as Spider leaves all his stuff on the lawn, walks to his car and starts it up. He's never gotten in serious trouble with the law, so he still has his car and driver's license. I don't have those things anymore. These days all I drive are my socks and shoes. Where should I go now? Another homie's house? Crash with a booty call? I'm too tired to brainstorm. I pick up my bag, turn, and shuffle for the park. I've slept there before. It's not the best thing in the world, but I need to get some sleep before my shift tonight. I feel like a zombie.

Now that the show's over, everyone goes back inside. The only one who doesn't is Chinita, Spider's neighbor. One of the *chismosas,* she's a little old lady from the neighborhood, church-going and respectable now, but who used to raise hell back in the day, or so I've been told. Chinita's sitting on her porch smoking a cigarette. I nod to her. "Señora."

As I walk by, her dog dives off the porch and rushes me, snarling and furious. He bashes the gate with his head over and over again until it clicks open and now I'm being attacked by a furious wiener dog who chomps at my shoelaces and whips me with his skinny brown tail.

I pick up the dog. The little fucker snaps at me. His teeth are sharp. He's got fight in him, which I suppose I admire. I'm too tired to react anyway.

Chinita walks over. She's wearing blue jeans and a Dodgers sweatshirt. She's got curlers tucked underneath her kerchief, and I notice her glasses have rhinestones all over the frames.

"Bad dog. Chancla! Bad dog."

I smile. Chancla—it means "flip-flop." Sandal. A good name for this dog. I hand him over to Chinita and he immediately stops growling and squirming. Instead he mad-dogs me. If you've ever been mad-dogged by a mad dog, you know what I mean.

"Sal." Chinita calls me by my real name because she remembers a time when Salvador was my only name, a time before Ghost. "How are you doing, mi'jo? Staying out of trouble?"

"Trying, señora. Trying hard." It's true—I am. I yawn again. "Just tired is all."

"You worked last night?"

She's just making conversation. The chismosas already know all our ins and outs. They know everything. They know who's sleeping with who, and when we change shifts at work, and how we like our hot dogs. "I worked last night," I say. "And again tonight."

"Night shift. I used to do that. At the bottling plant. No fun." She kisses Chancla's head and the dog wiggles against her. "So where are you going now?"

I shrug. "To find a place to sleep."

"Where?"

"Park, probably."

"¿*Con los borrachos?* With the drunks? No, you need good sleep. You need to keep your job." She looks me up and down and narrows her eyes. "Were you paying rent at Regina's?"

"Not really. I gave Spider fifty a week to add to their groceries. And I cleaned the house a little. That was it."

It was a good arrangement. With two part-time jobs, I'm saving up for an apartment, but with first and last month's rent and a cleaning deposit, it'll be a hot minute before I've banked enough cash. I've been out of the *pinta* since February, and at the moment, I'm still on my own. The family house is long gone, mortgage payments shot up a junkie's arm. My younger brother Trouble is still locked up but he'll be paroled in two months. The apartment is really for him. He's a troublemaker and he needs a good place to land, somewhere I can keep an eye on him. Our youngest brother Angel still lives in Salinas, where we sent him to keep him safe. As for our dad?

Well.

Let's just say Dreamer Rosas is a ghost story for another day.

Chinita stares at me over her glasses. "Fifty a week, huh? Tell you what, *mi'jo*. Pay me fifty a week and you'll have your own room here. Your own entrance even, so you can come and go as you please."

"What?" Los Angeles rent is sky-high. Two hundred a month for my own room is a crazy price. "Are you serious?" If she doesn't ask for a deposit, I could keep saving money at the same rate I've been saving it.

She opens the gate and Chancla starts growling at me again. "*Ya, calmate,*" she says softly to the dog. It whines. She puts it back in the house and shuts the door. "Come 'round back," she tells me.

I follow the old lady past the flowerbeds and lemon tree.

Like the other houses on the block, this one is an old one. Maybe a hundred years old or so, a two-story clapboard mess, falling apart, repaired here and there with duct tape and cheap nails. We walk up the driveway and she unlocks another gate.

"I didn't know you had a guesthouse back here." I maneuver around a big aloe vera plant and pots of fresh Mexican herbs that smell like old memories: *yerba buena* and cilantro. *Epazote. Hoja santa,* with its big dark green leaves. My mom taught me their names a long time ago. Everything is growing wild.

"Guesthouse? That's a good one." Chinita finishes her cigarette and puts it in a big ashtray on the back porch. It's full of butts. She lowers her voice. "Vanessa doesn't want me smoking inside."

Her granddaughter. I don't say anything, because everyone knows who Vanessa is, and no one in their right mind would cross that woman.

"Come on," Chinita says with a smoky exhale.

I follow her past a half-assembled swing set and an enormous patch of overgrown grass. Rosebushes of every color line one side of the backyard, and a tall avocado tree throws a dark shadow on a small ivy-covered garage. The old lady unlocks a side door and tries to open it. Paint flakes fall to the ground as she pulls hard on the knob. Two big yanks and the door pops open. I follow her inside. My eyes struggle to adjust. She snaps a switch and a few fluorescent light tubes tap on. One of them flickers like a horror movie.

"Ta-da!" says Chinita, and I look at what she's offering me.

Crumbling cardboard boxes and yellow stacks of newspapers. An ancient Chevy pickup truck, rusty and cobwebbed, its bed stacked high with more boxes and weird junk like plastic tubes and steel pots. Spiderwebs everywhere. Enough dust to choke a camel.

Smiling like a used-car salesman, Chinita yanks a folded-up

bedframe from the corner and unstraps the mattress. She unfolds the tiny twin bed until it clicks open. There's a deep and dusty crease in the middle. I can see metal springs through the pale yellow fabric.

"Huh? What do you think? Nice bed, right?" Chinita pats the mattress, raising more dust. She coughs a little bit. "I'll get you some sheets from inside, *mi'jo*. Then, no problem, right?"

Before I can answer, something scratches in a dark corner of the garage. Little claws. So the garage comes with previous occupants. Maybe that's a good thing. My case manager says I should try to make new friends.

Chinita studies my face. I look skeptical, I'm sure. I'm not a princess or anything. I've slept in gutters and in fields, on hard prison beds and on cement floors next to drains. But after being spoiled on Spider and Regina's couch, I'm wondering if this housing situation is really the best I can find.

"*Mi'jo*," Chinita says, "I know what you're thinking. But look. Look!" She points to an outlet in the wall. "For a reading lamp. And to charge your phone." She clears a few boxes off the workbench and reveals the smallest, dustiest window I've ever seen. We had bigger ones in prison. "A little sunshine." She takes a couple keys off her Ensenada bottle opener keychain and hands them to me. "A lock on the door. A safe place to keep your stuff." She pushes the door open and gestures toward the house. "That other key—the bathroom is right through the back door, through the kitchen. Plus, you can keep food in the fridge."

Red flag. "Vanessa wouldn't mind me in the house?" I ask.

Chinita waves her hand. "Vanessa don't spend any time in the kitchen. She won't care."

I have my doubts.

"No one will bother you here, Sal," Chinita says. "All of this was Ben's old stuff. Do you remember him?"

"Yeah." Ben—her husband. An old Okie, the only white man in the neighborhood. He was always nice to me when I was little and wild as a weed.

Chinita sits down on the bed and looks around, slowly nodding to herself. "To be honest, I should've taken better care of this garage. Years pass and, you know, everything just gets away from you. It all just gets away."

I run my hand over the curving wheel well of the truck and I try to remember what this place looked like when I was a kid. Clean and orderly. The truck was in tip-top shape, shiny and well maintained. This was Ben's place. I imagine him here in his coveralls, always building something, always fixing something. I must have been six or seven. He let me watch everything he did. I was fascinated by his tools and materials, by his big clever hands, all stained and beat-up. Workingman hands.

As if she can read my mind, Chinita says, "Twelve years he's been gone already. You remember his funeral, don't you?"

I was thirteen. Ben's funeral was the first of too many funerals I attended that year. I nod. "Sure. I remember."

"What a character. My old man."

Maybe this garage is already haunted. Maybe there's no more room in here for me. I'm about to thank Chinita for the opportunity when she catches the expression on my face and cuts me a deal.

"Listen, *mi'jo*. I've got an idea. Clean this place up and I'll charge you two hundred for the first two months' rent."

"Clean it up?"

"Yeah. Clean it up." She smiles. "Sort out the boxes and see what's inside. We'll figure out what we can sell and what we can give away. This place has been neglected for a long time—too long. It's time to discover what kind of treasures are hiding in here." She pauses. "Might be junk. Might be worth a million dollars. Who knows unless we look, right? Plus, two months for two hundred dollars? Who else is going to charge you rent like that?"

A month of free rent—an extra two hundred dollars to put toward a real apartment. Plus privacy. It's no palace, but when I look closer, it's not bad. A little sweeping. A little soap and water. A little time. I could live with this.

"Okay. Deal." I hold out my hand. Chinita shakes it. I reach into my backpack for my wallet and count out ten twenties. After that, I've got two fives for the next three days until I get paid again. I hold back a sigh as I hand over the bills. Maybe Ben hid a cheeseburger somewhere in here for me.

"Excellent." Chinita stands up and tucks the money into the back pocket of her jeans. "See? I knew we could work something out."

I put my backpack down. While Chinita goes into the house to get some bedsheets, I pick the thin mattress off the rickety frame. I take it into the backyard and shake the dust out of it. I look at it in the sunlight and realize that the dust is just that— dust. No bedbugs. No fleas. No critters.

Chinita comes out of the house and hands me a pillow and a set of pink sheets. They're covered with fairies. I look at her with my eyebrows raised. "Really?"

"Suck it up. These are the only twin sheets we have."

They belong to Vanessa's daughter. I take the sheets and make the bed. By the time I tuck the old flat pillow into the pillowcase, I can barely keep my eyes open. I settle down on the bed to take off my shoes and the springs whine under my weight.

Chinita taps my forehead with her finger. "One more thing. Ground rules. No drugs. No guns. No shenanigans. None of your troublemaking friends or girls from the neighborhood in here, okay? I got a great-grandbaby, and she doesn't need to see none of that garbage. Understood?"

I nod and lie down. "Understood."

"I need your word, Salvador Rosas."

"I promise, señora."

"Okay. As long as we're clear." Chinita turns off the lights and drags the crumbling door shut. My eyes are already closed when I hear her say, "Sweet dreams, kiddo."

WHEN THE ALARM on my phone goes off, I take a second to get my bearings. It's warm in the garage, and the air is still. It smells like old wood, grease, and gasoline. There's a dusty shaft of sunlight that starts at the window and lands on the back wall. Black paper peels away from the wood. I look up. The bare rafters are coated with fine dust, like ash from a volcano.

I turn off my alarm and sit up. It's six o'clock.

Now there's one thought in my head—food.

Feeling like a bear getting ready to leave its cave, I get dressed for the night. Jeans, a T-shirt, my one pair of sneakers. I find the keys that Chinita gave me for the house. I need to clean up a little before dinner and the bus ride to work.

I put my hand on the doorknob, but the door is stuck. I bash my shoulder against the wood just like I saw Chinita do it. The door gives way on my first try and I explode out of the garage.

Before I can do anything else, a woman is screaming at me and a blast of cold water hits my face. It doesn't let up. I try to cover my head with my hands but the water moves downward, soaking my clothes. It's ice cold.

"Hold up," I blubber. "Stop, stop!"

At last, the water turns off. "What the hell?" I say. There's water up my nose. I'm coughing. I take off my soaked shirt.

When I stop drowning, I look up to see Chinita's grand-daughter standing next to the rosebushes. She's wearing an office skirt and blouse. Her dark hair is pulled back tight. I see pearls and pretty red lipstick. Her mouth is wide open. Instead of high heels, she's wearing old Converse tennis shoes with the backs smashed down. She's little but curvy in all the right places and I can't help it. I rub the water from my eyes and stare.

Goddamn.

She's fine.

Almost fine enough to make me forget that she just tried to put me out like a fire.

"Ghost?" A confused look crosses her face as she grips the hose. "You scared me. What the hell are you doing in my garage?"

I wipe my face with my T-shirt. I try to come up with something cool to say and fail. "Hey, Vanessa."

TWO

"EXPLAIN," Vanessa says, "and talk fast. I've had a long day."

To buy time, I shake out my wet shirt and hang it on the fence. How to explain to this angry woman that she now has a tatted-up ex-con living in her garage for the next eight weeks? "Your grandmother rented the garage out to me because I needed a place to stay," I say. "She didn't tell you?"

Vanessa glares at me like an eagle. "No, Ghost. She didn't tell me, as you can probably guess from my reaction just now."

"Yeah, okay. I see your point." There's water in my ear. I turn my head to the side and knock on my temple to get it out. "We agreed on two months. I paid her up front."

"Up front? How much?"

"Two hundred."

"Two hundred a month for rent? That's ridiculous."

I clear my throat. "Uh, two hundred for two months."

"Say what?"

"Two hundred for two months. And she told me to clean out the garage. While I lived here."

"To clean out the garage?"

"Yeah." I look at her face, which seems to be turning redder with each word I say. "She said . . . she said you would be okay with it."

"She did?" Vanessa rubs the bridge of her nose and takes a deep breath. "Well, she was wrong. I have to talk to her. This is not going to work out."

But this—whatever this is—has to work out. I need a place to sleep, and I need to keep saving money for an apartment. Just like Chinita had to sell me the broken-down garage as a place to live, I find myself in the weird position of having to sell myself to Vanessa. I have to convince her that I'm a good idea. Tall order.

I narrow my eyes at Vanessa to make it look like I think she's crazy. In reality, I'm trying to check out her boobs without her noticing. The top buttons of her blouse are holding on for dear life. If I squint, I can see the outline of her lace bra through the cotton.

Okay, focus.

"But this is a good deal for both of us," I say, as if I really believe it.

She looks up and, even though she doesn't mean to, her eyes drag up and down my chest. She blinks away the heat I'm pretty sure I see there, and suddenly I feel aware of myself. I'm half-naked.

A pretty girl just checked me out.

I can work with that.

"I'm a hard worker," I say quickly. "I'll get this garage all cleaned up. Find out what you can sell and what you can keep. You can make a little cash. I'm sure this stuff has been sitting here for years. You've just been too busy working and taking care of business to go through it. Let me take care of it."

"But—"

"I saw a lawnmower in the garage." I scan the yard. "I could cut the grass back here. Trim up the tree." I look at the swing set, new but half-assembled. "I saw your grandpa's old tools back there. I could get the swings put up too."

"I don't need a live-in handyman," Vanessa says.

"It won't be permanent. I just need to finish saving up for my own place. Two months. That's it."

Thank God, Chinita comes out of the back door and walks down the porch steps. She lights up a cigarette and winks at me. "Why aren't you wearing a shirt, *mi'jo*? Are you already trying to seduce my granddaughter with all those muscles and tattoos *o que*?"

"*¡Abuelita!*" Vanessa says, turning around. She switches to Spanish as if I can't understand. "How could you make this arrangement without me? This is not a good idea."

"Why not?" Chinita reaches into her back pocket and hands Vanessa the wad of twenties I gave her earlier. She speaks English and nods at me. "Look. Back-to-school money for Muñeca. Haircut, new shoes, backpack. All the tissues and wipes and school supplies she needs, right there."

Vanessa takes the money. She looks at it and looks at me. "Where did this money come from?"

I try not to be defensive. She's right to be careful. She's got a kid. I understand. "It's totally legit. I have two part-time jobs. At night. I have the check stubs if you want to see them."

"I do. I do want to see them."

"He's paying rent to live in the garage and clean it. Are you telling me that's not a good deal? You look at numbers all day long. Are going to tell me that you don't want someone to pay for the pleasure of looking through all that *basura* and cleaning it up? What kind of an accountant are you?" Chinita laughs. The ha-ha's come out as coughs. "It's a good deal, Vanessa."

Vanessa looks at the money again and looks at me. I can see she's struggling not to look at my body. I fold my arms. I flex, just a little. Her beautiful dark eyes dart down to my biceps before snapping back up to my face like pinballs.

"Check stubs," she says, and her drill-sergeant tone scares away my self-confidence.

"Fine, fine," I say.

I turn around and go back into the garage. My backpack has a pocket where I keep my paperwork, all the forms my parole officer makes me cart around, plus the stubs I kept from the check cashing office. I don't have a bank account yet. I pull out the stubs and bring them over to Vanessa, who has her hand out like a first-grade teacher who wants my slingshot.

"Give it here." With a frown, she looks each one over. "Defiance. What's that?"

"The gym where I work."

An eyebrow goes up. "What do you do there?"

"Janitor. Four nights a week, eleven to seven."

"And what's this one?"

"Serenity Day Spa. I clean up there too. Three nights a week."

"You work every night?" she asks.

The clockwork schedule keeps me out of trouble. "Yes. Two part-time jobs. I'm saving up for my own place. I'm almost there."

"So you'll be asleep here during the day—"

"Both places are in Santa Monica. Two-hour bus and train trip, each way. I'll barely be here." I do some quick math in my head. "Your daughter's in kindergarten. Her summer vacation just ended, right? While I sleep, you'll be at work and your daughter will be at school." I search her face and give her a little smile. "Ghost. Like my name."

She looks at the money once more, then at her grandmother. "You gave him keys? To the house?" She says it like she can't believe her grandmother could be so stupid.

"Of course I did. Where's he gonna shit? The bushes?"

"¡Abuelita!"

"Salvador's not all bad, Vanessa. Will you lighten up?"

"No, I will not 'lighten up.' This is our home," Vanessa says. And even though Chinita's on my side, I feel a little bit of pride in Vanessa. She's not going to get bullied into anything. She's not going to be pushed around. There's fire in her. I can feel it from here. God help the poor motherfucker who underestimates this woman. When she turns her glare on me, I have to fight the urge to step back.

"I'm going to say a word you probably know really well," she says. "Probation."

I laugh. "Probation? Yes. Yes, I know that word."

She hands back my check stubs. When she comes close, I can smell her perfume. Strawberries and vanilla. Something sweet—something to crave. "You're on probation. We'll see how it goes. If for any reason I, or my daughter, or my grandmother feel uncomfortable with you living here, with you being on our property, you are out. Like that. You clear out as soon as I say."

"And I get my money back?" I ask.

"Minus the days you slept here, yes."

I watch her face, the small adjustments and movements that secretly broadcast what she's thinking. I fold my arms again to see if I get another rise. "So what would make you feel uncomfortable, Vanessa?"

I can tell she's fighting to ignore the move. "It's a long, long list," she says. "Too long to tell you right now. I'll just let you know when you cross the line."

"If that's the way it's gonna be."

"That's the way it's gonna be."

"All right. Deal."

With a sigh, she picks up the hose again and heads to the faucet. She tightens the spigot and carefully coils the hose. I watch her manicured hands getting muddy and dirty, and for some reason, I feel something move inside me. A deep-down ache, a longing. Something about her hands—clean touching dirty. For a moment, I wonder if she'd ever touch me like that.

"I gotta wash up." My voice is kind of scratchy and rough, and I can't get the words out properly.

Chinita stands aside and nods at me. "Go ahead, *mi'jo*. I think we tamed the beast for now."

Vanessa shoots her grandmother a silent, furious glare and I feel that blast of heat again. It's strong. I try to shake it off—I can't.

"Thank you, señora," I say quietly, and go inside.

Before we go on, you should know a few things about Vanessa.

First off, she's a good girl.

Always has been.

When I was in middle school, things started happening. I don't mean the usual things, like the girls getting titties. Obviously, that stuff is pretty interesting but not exactly what I mean.

In my neighborhood, in addition to going through puberty, kids in my school split into two species.

You could watch it happening.

One group of kids just kept doing what they were doing, going to school or playing sports. Their lives were about grades, school dances, marching band. Some of them worked in their parents' shops and had nice *quinceañeras* where there were no fistfights and the cops didn't get called.

The second group of kids took the gangster track. They began dressing different, acting up in school, running errands for the older homies, and getting into minor trouble—smoking weed, shoplifting, shit like that.

The girls who went that way usually had parents or older

siblings in gangs. The transformation would happen over a long period of time or it would happen overnight, but it would happen, sure as shit. Caterpillars to butterflies. Before long, the girl would arrive at school wearing her makeup a certain way. Her clothes would be different, she'd stand taller, smile less. One day she'd get jumped in and just like that, she was a *chola*. A homegirl.

Vanessa was never a *chola*. She was just a quiet girl from the neighborhood who lived with her grandparents. I never knew what happened to her parents, but for as long as I remember she and Chinita and Ben lived in that rickety house by the park.

She never called attention to herself, except when it came to grades. She was a good student.

I was already skipping school by the time I started to notice Vanessa. Who didn't notice her? Two years younger than me, pretty and smart. She wasn't talkative. When she talked, it mattered, and when she made a joke, it wasn't a silly ha-ha, it was the kind of laugh that made you bend over and laugh your ass off. She made it count. Back then, I'd flirt with her because I was a *travieso* and what little troublemaker didn't like to flirt? It didn't matter anyway. I knew the truth. She was off-limits to me, hidden behind the high wall of her good grades and no-BS attitude. So I crushed on her from a distance.

Later, while I was in jail awaiting trial, I heard the news. Vanessa didn't make it out of the neighborhood like we'd all thought she would.

She'd gotten with a homeboy from the grade above me. Got herself pregnant. A quick wedding. No fancy university far away for her. Instead, she had to stay at home with her new husband and her grandmother.

Locked up, I had lots of time to wonder about her, this untouchable girl who got touched. Her path ended up so different from the one we had imagined for her.

The thing that ate at me? I'd known the father. He was another kid in ESHB, a soldier like me, nothing special. Sleepy was his name.

Lying awake in my metal bunk bed, I'd think about Vanessa's situation. Why'd she fall for Sleepy? She could've fallen for me. It should've been me.

I should've been the one.

Holding her.

Being her man.

Going to bed with her—I thought about that a lot.

Putting a ring on her finger when I learned she was having my kid.

I had a lot of time to think about these things. What did Sleepy have that I didn't? I couldn't figure it out. Instead, alone on those cold nights, I imagined coming home to her, climbing into her bed at night, and lifting up her nightgown. She'd reach for me too—she'd want me as much as I wanted her. At least in my dreams.

Wet dreams, I guess.

My trial date kept getting pushed back. Meanwhile, the Organization was getting more aggressive. Ruben, our leader, passed down messages from the shot-callers in the *pinta* that ESHB had to secure our territory, to push out any dealers who didn't pay taxes to do business within Hollenbeck's boundaries. Sleepy became part of the group sent out to intimidate them.

When a lowlife small-time dealer turned up dead in an alley with a bullet through his left eye, the cops were all over it. Ruben said to hold steady, be polite, don't give up any information, but don't trip. The heat slowly died down and after a few months, it was back to business as usual.

One problem—the job had affected Sleepy.

He started drinking. Then he started using. From what I

heard, he wasn't showing up at home or at meetings with Ruben or his crew. He'd disappear for days.

For all the shit I've done, I've never killed anyone. I knew some homeboys, both in and out of prison, who had multiple kills under their belt. Whether they were convicted or not, each death was a sentence. A silent punishment. A weight to carry forever.

Once, in a quiet moment, I asked Ruben, "How does it not make you crazy, thinking about all this crazy shit?"

He told me, "You have to disconnect. It's not violence to be violent. This is business. This is what we do."

And those words became the thing that kept pushing me forward. Kept me steady when I had to beat someone down or intimidate people.

This is business. This is what we do.

When Sleepy turned up dead, we were surprised, but not really. Ruben said the kid had been fading, becoming less of himself, distant and twitchy. A heroin overdose. It didn't look like an accident but no one said suicide out loud. Whatever the case, Sleepy was gone. The gang sent a little money to Vanessa and that was it. She was left alone, a widow and a single mother even before her baby was born.

Eventually, Trouble and I were tried and given our time. I started my sentence just before Sleepy was laid to rest. I imagined the funeral, the group of homies posted up at the church and drinking beer at the house. Vanessa dressed in black.

I thought about her.

But this time I wondered what it was like to *be* her, a good person who fell in love with the wrong person, fast and hot. A widow with a baby.

Now her life would be forever different. Forever changed, because of this turn she'd taken in her road when she was young.

A few years later, I heard she graduated with a degree from the local college. Of course—that's what people like her do. Her grandmother retired and watched the kid while she studied and worked. Bookkeeper, I think.

I wonder if she misses Sleepy. I wonder if she regrets the choices she's made.

I ask myself that question all the time. Do I? Do I regret my choices?

After I wash up and put on a fresh T-shirt, I grab my hoodie and my backpack from the garage and head out into the night. Vanessa and her grandmother are upstairs. I can hear a TV and a little kid laughing. I lock the back door and the gates when I leave.

First off, a taco dinner. The owner of the truck sees me counting out quarters to pay him and gives me two more on the house. I tell him no, no, no and he says in Spanish, "Pay me a little extra when you can." I fist-bump him through the window of the truck.

The thing with our neighborhood that outsiders can't see is the pride we have in it. The way we take care of each other. Yes, I'm kind of a lowlife. Yes, I come from a long line of lowlifes, and yes, I'm an ex-con who can't get work except night shifts as a janitor, but this is my hood. I know the people in it, and I would throw down for them as they would for me.

Poor looks after poor.

Believe that.

I finish my tacos and throw the paper plate in the trash.

Off to work.

The two-hour trip from East L.A. to Santa Monica is an epic journey. First, I catch a bus downtown and walk to the 7th Street Metro station. I catch the Expo Line to Santa Monica, eighteen stops. I get off at the ocean and take one final bus to Main Street.

My favorite part of the trip is the train. That's my quiet time.

I take a deep breath and let it out. As always, the train car is almost empty except for a few misfits like me heading out into the night. It's August and the sun has just set. When winter comes, it'll be dark the entire time I'm out, which is fine by me. I prefer the dark.

Six months ago, when I first started working in Santa Monica, my case manager handed me a Metro map and drew out my route. I thought, *No problem. I can do this.* But as soon as I stepped out onto the crowded train platform at 7th Street, something happened to me.

I couldn't understand it.

People crowded up against me, moving like water, this way and that. All of them going in a different direction, all of them rushing. The noise of the trains and the echoing of the high ceilings in the station filled my ears.

I got dizzy. I couldn't breathe.

When I leaned against a trash can to get my balance, a sheriff's deputy approached me, his eyes wary, his hand on his gun—as almost all law enforcement approaches me. This one was older, at least. His calm voice dragged me out of the darkness.

"Son, are you all right?"

Son. He called me son.

When I was younger and the chip on my shoulder was big and hot, I would've looked him in the eye and spat, "I'm not your son, motherfucker."

But in this moment, my voice shook as I said, "Sir, I think I'm having a heart attack."

The deputy called for backup. A small group of officers arrived, followed by paramedics. They sat me down on a bench and as a crowd gathered to watch, the paramedics took my blood pressure and ran their tests. My chest was tight, tight like a fist. I felt like I was breathing through a coffee straw. I couldn't get enough air.

"Am I dying?" I asked.

One of the paramedics took my hand. "You'll be okay," she said. "You'll be okay."

I didn't believe her.

THREE

MY CASE MANAGER sent me to my doctor.

My doctor sent me to a heart specialist.

The heart specialist sent me to a therapist.

The therapist told me, "You had an anxiety attack."

"A what?" Twenty-four years old, healthy as a fucking bull, and I had an anxiety attack? Wasn't that for little, sickly nervous people? I almost stood up and left the office.

"Wait, Salvador. Let's talk about this," the therapist said. "How long were you in prison?"

"Five years," I said.

"Five years in a cell with one other guy. One hour in a yard a day. That right?"

I nodded.

"And you think you wouldn't be affected by suddenly being in the company of hundreds of people, all doing whatever they wanted, without any bars or guards to control them? You're fooling yourself. What you had? That was an anxiety attack."

His words hit me hard. Later that night, I talked to my homie Spider about it. "He said I had an anxiety attack caused by the fear I couldn't control the situation."

"You mean, like, you'd lose control? Like the Incredible Hulk?" Spider asked.

"No, no, nothing like that," I said. "Like I couldn't control the people around me. I couldn't predict what they would do. Maybe one of them might push me onto the tracks. Or another one might pull out a gun. Or all of a sudden one of them might start swinging and then there'd be a fight—"

"So, basically, a fear you couldn't control the people around you?"

I nodded. "Yeah, that's what he told me."

Spider shook his head. *"¿Y ahora, qué? ¿Estas loco?"*

Crazy. Am I really crazy? "Maybe. I don't know."

My case manager made me schedule regular appointments with the therapist. I didn't like it. The therapist wanted me to open up. To talk to him about everything that was bothering me. We had these sessions in prison but that was different, easier— group therapy. I didn't mind that so much. But sitting in a room with just one other person talking about yourself—that's weird as hell. I stopped going to my sessions three weeks in. My case manager shook her head and sighed. "You're not going to get better this way, Salvador."

The question still nags at me.

Am I broken?

Shit, isn't everybody broken?

Some people just like to touch their broken parts more than others, to rub them over and over again, like jacking off. I want to leave my broken parts alone.

I push myself to take the trip to Santa Monica again and again. I force myself to walk through the busy train station. I put myself in the middle of the biggest crowds and slowly, silently get used to the feeling of drowning in people. Whenever I get dizzy, I pinch my arm through my hoodie until the skin bruises.

I tell myself to get a grip. I call myself useless, a piece of shit, an unlovable loser.

I force myself to do this.

I pinch the same patch of muscle on my arm. The dark bruise fades. I put new ones on top.

I need to work.

As if it's afraid of me, my anxiety slowly recedes to some dark corner in my head.

The train doors open. I catch my last bus to Defiance Gym. It closes at midnight but I always get there at eleven and start on the bathrooms and offices. By the time the last clients and trainers clear out, I'm on my own and can work on the equipment in the main part of the gym.

I come in through the back door and stash my backpack in the owner's office. He's sitting in there on the phone. He's a young guy, a little bit older than me. His parents are loaded. They fronted him the money for this place. Rich takes care of rich just like poor takes care of poor. Fine by me—he always pays me on time.

I take off my hoodie, put on my Defiance T-shirt, and check the clipboard the owner and the trainers leave for me. The clipboard holds notes and special requests. Today, they want me to check the shower drains in the women's locker room. They're clogged with hair. Nothing new. They're always clogged with hair. I don't see anything else so I head off to the storage room to get my cleaning supplies.

"Hey, Sal." The owner's name is Barrett. Last name, White. He wants me to call him Barry. I'm not even kidding. Barry White puts the phone back on the receiver and leans back in his swivel chair. "How's it going?"

"Good, boss. Going good." I put on a happy face for him, like I do for all the bosses I've ever worked for. I'm a quiet guy so people tend to assume I'm gloomy. A long time ago, I learned that it pays to appear cheerful. People begin to assume you're approachable. You know, a thug, but a friendly thug. You want them to say things like, "Sal? The gangster? The ex-con? He's so *nice*. Let's give that fucker a raise."

Barry always wears designer gym clothes and the latest Nikes. He's wearing a baseball cap with his gym logo on it, the word *Defiance* with a big fat *D*. "Listen, Sal, I'm about ready to take off."

"All right, boss." I clock in and put my card back in the slot. "You have a good night."

"Actually, listen. A friend of mine just opened a bar nearby. I want to check it out. How about a drink? One or two before your shift starts?"

I look at the time. My shift starts now. If I go out with him, I'll be behind on my work for the rest of the night. "I don't know if that's a great idea—"

"Sure it is." Barry stands up and claps me on the back. He takes the expensive hoodie hanging on the back of his chair and puts it on. "Let me buy you a beer. No problem. Let's go."

I like routines. I like schedules. The boss asking me to join him for a drink is going to mess up my whole routine including my workout, but what am I supposed to say? He's already shutting down his computer and zipping up his sweater. He takes out the keys to his Raptor and holds the back door open for me. "Ready?"

I nod. "All right, boss. Sure."

The bar is just a few blocks away. Barry's truck is brand-new, fully loaded with a leather interior. Just driving to the bar feels like a luxury for someone who doesn't have a car. During the short trip, I think about how many F-Series trucks my brother and I lifted, how satisfying it felt to turn the screwdriver in the ignition and hear that engine start up. We liked Ford trucks, and we loved stealing Lexuses. Easy to chop, easy to move. We were fast. We worked clean. Never caught.

Well, just one time. That last time.

"Here we are." Barry knocks me out of my trance.

Abbot Kinney is a hip neighborhood, and tonight all the street parking is taken. Barry doesn't hesitate to drop his truck off at the $20 valet.

I nod at the puzzled valet and follow Barry into the bar. The sign above the door says BAY CITY BREWS.

"You good?" asks Barry.

"Yeah," I say.

I look around. This bar is dark and fancy, all wood. You can smell the fresh varnish on the walls. There's a long row of taps along the back of the bar—no liquor bottles, just beer.

I follow Barry to the back of the room. He's fist-bumping and waving at people. They all know him either as their trainer or as a local business owner. I notice everyone down to the last server is white. A couple of them do double takes when they see me, but hipsters love tattoos and the fact that my arms and neck are covered with them, along with the fact that I'm wearing a Defiance T-shirt and I'm with Barry, gives me a pass to their bar. If I showed up here alone, I'm one hundred percent sure I'd still be bounced in a heartbeat.

Barry slides into a booth and takes a look at the menu. It's big, a binder, pages and pages of beers. While he decides, I lean back and scan the crowded room. I see pretty Westside girls with their expensive clothes and straight white teeth. Computer nerds in glasses and plaid shirts. And some big bodybuilding monsters, a couple of whom I recognize from Barry's gym.

"Here." Barry slides the menu over to me.

"What does this place serve?"

"Local craft beers. Some made here."

I look at the binder in front of me. The beers have long

descriptions. Each beer has a fancy name, the alcohol content, and the price. None are less than eight dollars. Following each description, there's a list of items the beer supposedly tastes like. Floral. Intensely hoppy. Hints of dark chocolate and coffee. Blackberry essence. Ripe bananas.

What the hell is this?

Doesn't beer just taste like beer?

All I've ever had is Bud. A Corona or a Dos Equis or two. Whatever was in Regina and Spider's refrigerator. Whatever was in the cooler at the party. I never really thought about how it tasted.

"What are you getting?" I ask casually, trying to hide my confusion.

It's noisy inside the bar so when Barry answers something like "A fly!" I nod and say, "I'll get that too," even though I have no idea what a fly is.

A pretty waitress comes over and takes the order from Barry. Afterward, he makes a point of checking out her ass as she walks away.

"Not bad," he says.

I nod and shrug as if to agree. I wouldn't kick her out of bed. This woman looks nice but she doesn't do anything for me.

I like them shorter. Angrier. Red lipstick definitely helps.

"So there's something I need to talk to you about," Barry says.

My vision of Vanessa disappears. I blink and sit up. Immediately, my mind goes all over the place. I've screwed up somehow. Someone's complained. He's not happy with my performance. His nephew is coming in from Nebraska or some shit and needs my job. I'm on alert. "What's up?" I ask, trying to sound casual.

"You've been with us about six months now. The trainers and me, we love the work you do. Always on time, detail oriented, no drama. And you know when you started I gave you permission to use all the gym equipment when you were done with your shift."

Yeah. It's a perk I've taken full advantage of. My favorite part of the job. After I'm done cleaning up, if I rush, I've got an hour and a half to work out on my own and take a shower before I start back home. This gym is almost $150 a month for membership. As long as I finish before the first clients show up, Barry said I have full run of the equipment.

Which could mean only one thing. "Do you want me to stop working out? Has anyone complained?"

Barry laughs and waves his hand. "No, no, nothing like that. Nothing like that at all. In fact, I'd like to ask you something totally different."

"What's up?" I'm really wary now.

"I've seen how you work out. You know a thing or two."

I shrug. "I read a lot about weight lifting when I was locked up."

"Didn't you lift when you were inside?"

"No. California got rid of weight rooms in prisons a long time ago."

"Really? So how'd you stay fit?"

"Routine." Barry looks confused so I explain. "In our section, all the homeboys, we shared the same routine. Every morning, we'd make the beds, clean the cells, clean ourselves. Everything had to be spotless. After that, we had a two-hour workout. One guy called out all the exercises. Push-ups. Crunches. Lunges. Anything you could do in a five-by-eight cell, we did. I got really into it. I got books on bodybuilding and read every single one. That way, when I got out, I'd be able to start lifting."

"So you learned it all on your own?" Barry asks. "No help?"

"I guess so."

Barry nods to himself. "I've been thinking about this for a while. Tell me, how'd you like to take on some clients of your own?"

My jaw drops. "What?"

"I'm losing a trainer and another's going part-time, so we'll have some extra clients. What if I trained you to be a trainer?"

Me? A trainer? Is he joking?

I search his face. Whether he's serious or not, I have to handle this right. I know I'm not cut out to be a teacher. I don't have the patience, and I don't want to hold anyone's hand. "That's really kind of you, boss, but I can't afford to lose any wages while I learn something new. I'm saving up for—"

"I'd pay you a trainer's wages on day one." He looks at me like he can't believe I'm turning him down. A part of me can't believe it either. "It's on-the-job training," he says. "Come on—you know you'd be great at it."

I don't know what he's seen or heard about me that would make him think I'd be good at training people. He'd be disappointed if he knew how much I hate being around people. Well, maybe *hate* is not the right word. Being around people doesn't make me hate them. Being around them makes me tired. And more than that, you need to be an upbeat motherfucker to be a personal trainer. That isn't me. "I've never considered it," I say carefully. "Won't people be turned off by . . . my appearance?"

Barry snorts. "The tattoos? The fact that you're fucking yoked? No, Sal. No one will be turned off by that. The bigger, the better. These guys, these pale office-worker guys with dad bodies and minivans? They'd kill to look like you."

His words make me feel weird. It's not a strong feeling, just a deep-down shiver. I'm not like his clients. I didn't buy this body. My muscles are from five years of sit-ups and burpees in a cell. From weights lifted alone, just me trying to beat down my anxiety one repetition at a time. *They'd kill to look like you.*

Guys who look like me, they look like me because a lot of the time, they *have* killed. They *have* taken a life. They had to look like me to survive.

But my boss is looking at me like a very excited puppy dog. If this motherfucker had a tail, it would be wagging.

"Let me think about it," I say.

"Think about it?" His eyebrows shoot up. "It's a shit-ton more money, Sal."

"I know," I say quickly. "Just . . . just give me some time."

Barry leans back, takes off his hat, and scratches the back of his head. "You're breaking my heart."

"Not long. A week."

"All right. All right, bro. Think about it."

The waitress comes to our table along with a skinny white dude in a trucker cap, glasses, and a graying beard. They're carrying wooden boards, each loaded with small glasses of beer. "Gentlemen, here are your flights," she says.

Flights. Not *flies*.

Barry fist-bumps the skinny white dude after they put the boards on our table. The waitress smiles and bounces away, winking at me.

"Alan, meet Sal. He works at the gym with me." I notice Barry doesn't say whether I'm a janitor or a trainer. "Sal, meet my buddy Alan. He's the owner of Bay City Brews. We've known each other since he was my chemistry teacher at Samohi —Santa Monica High School, right down the road."

"Nice to meet you, man." Alan has a Southern accent, just a little bit.

We shake hands. I lean back as Alan sits down at the table next to Barry. They chat and laugh and ask about each other's families and I feel like I'm eavesdropping. Anxiety bubbles inside me and my knee shakes a little. I force it to be still. I don't want it to look like I don't want to be here, even though I don't.

To distract myself, I listen carefully. I learn from their conversation that the bar has been open two months. It's been Alan's dream for many years. He's been saving up money for a long time. He worked part-time at a home-brewing store. I'm not sure what home brewing is but I don't want to butt into the conversation with dumb questions so I hang back.

"So what are we drinking?" Barry asks.

Here we go. Alan starts to point out each of the little glasses, which I notice are different shades of brown, both light and dark. "We're making this all here now," he says.

He says a bunch of words I've never heard before, and more of those descriptions: coffee, hoppy, citrusy, refreshing. He uses the words *frankincense* and *myrrh,* which I kind of remember from Christmas, but I'm not sure what they mean. He talks about leather. Beer that tastes like leather? He's really excited and assumes I know the difference between a lager, an ale, and a stout. After Alan's long explanations, Barry asks, "Where should we start?" And Alan points out the first glass.

This is a lot of beer. I got drunk at my welcome-home party, of course. I got drunk at Ruben's daughter's wedding. Twice in six months. I haven't had a beer in a while. I take a sip of the first glass, and Alan is right. It's refreshing. It's good.

"That's our Dogtown IPA."

"Dogtown?" I say, impressed. "Like the gang? Out by Chinatown?"

Barry looks at me oddly. "No, Dogtown like Venice. Like *Dogtown and Z-Boys*? The Zephyr skateboard team?"

I shrug. "I'm not familiar with them." I guess just like there are two versions of Los Angeles, mine and his, there are two versions of Dogtown.

The next drink is a little bit darker. I drink it. I copy Barry, close my eyes and try to taste lemon like Alan recommends. I feel like an idiot. If anyone from the neighborhood saw me right now, I would surely get a beatdown.

"Did you taste the lemon?" Alan asks.

I nod. "Yeah. Yeah, definitely."

I take smaller and smaller sips as Barry throws the glasses back. They're small pours but they add up. For a guy who lives on chicken breasts and protein powder, the alcohol and carbs are getting to him fast. Soon he's giggly and silly. Drunk.

Eight beers in and we get to the last one. It's dark as coffee.

"This is a gingerbread stout," Alan says. "This is my newest one. Only available here, and only seasonally."

I've never had beer like this. To be honest, every single one tastes really good. But this last one tastes like a memory, although I can't remember what.

"You're tasting molasses."

I don't know what molasses is. But it's so good, I finish the glass.

Barry orders a pint of it and quickly polishes it off as Alan goes on and on about his operation. He's a nerd, but a likable one, and I enjoy his company more than I thought I would. He's into what he does.

What is that like? Being into something so much that you can't stop talking about it.

I remember dudes in the *pinta* who wouldn't shut up about cars or *jainas* or their mom's *pozole*. One *veterano* doing twenty-five to life wouldn't shut up about piñatas. I shit you not. His dad made piñatas, I suppose, and he wanted to start up the business again when he got out. Most of the time, people would tell him to shut up already about *los pinches piñatas* and what do you call a piñata full of shit because that's what you are? Me, he didn't bother me. It felt good to see sunshine shining out of some people in a place that didn't get much light.

Alan asks me, "So what do you think of these?"

"I think they're good. Really good."

"Do you drink a lot of beer?"

"Not really. When I can get it. Just regular stuff. Nothing like this."

"Do you want another? A fresh one? You didn't finish these. They'll be warm by now."

I hold up my hand. "Nah, I'm good. I gotta work later. But thank you."

Alan nods and slaps Barry on the back, causing him to splash beer on his hoodie and start giggling like a chick. It would be a funny sight to see if I didn't have the horrible feeling that now he's my responsibility.

"Barry's a lightweight," Alan says to me. He mouths *water* to the waitress and she brings two glasses over. "So tell me, which of the beers did you like best?"

I point to the last one, the dark one. "This. I really liked this."

"Feliz Navidad," he says.

"What?"

"That's what I'm calling it. Feliz Navidad. I want people to think about Christmas when they drink it."

"Do all your beers have names?"

He nods. "It helps people to remember what they're drinking and what to order again when they come back."

I get that. It's the same reason we got names when we were kids joining the gang. People remembered us. We got our new names tattooed on our skin, like a signature. Like a brand.

"That beer tastes like something I used to eat when I was a kid." I'm not sure why I say this. Maybe I'm drunk too, but I don't think so. I just feel like opening up a little, and that Alan won't judge me if I do.

"What was it?" Alan asks.

"There was a bakery near my house when I was growing

up." I look at the dark drop left in the bottom of the glass. I drink it down, and there's that memory again. An old one, from when my sister and my mother were still alive. My dad was still working at the slaughterhouse and my brothers and I were all still in school. "A Mexican bakery," I say. "They sold a type of bread . . . it was dark brown. Sweet. In the shape of a pig. It had a raisin eye." I let the flavor linger in my mouth. "This beer tastes like that. Exactly like that."

Alan adjusts his glasses and studies my face. "Is that bakery still open?"

It's in the neighborhood, but I haven't been there in years. "Yeah. I think so."

"Can you bring me one? I want to taste it for myself."

"You want a *puerquito*?" I laugh a little, thinking about how far a little brown pig from East L.A. would have to travel to get to the Westside. "Are you sure?"

"Sure I'm sure," says Alan. "Bring me one."

I like this Alan dude. "All right."

Barry has been leaning over his empty pint glass. He lifts his head. "Guys—"

And then, right before he can get the next word out, he falls out of the booth and splits his head open on a chair.

FOUR

ALAN LOOKS AT ME. "SHIT."

We pick Barry up and pull him into a nearby chair. His forehead is busted open and he looks dazed but he's laughing to himself like a deranged *payaso*.

"Oh my God," he mumbles. "Fuck."

I grab a cloth napkin and hold it to the wound.

Alan eyes are big behind his glasses. "Did he hit his head really hard? Do you think he has a concussion?"

I try to answer, but the words get caught in my throat. I'm struggling to control my breathing. My anxiety—it's rising. I know this feeling. I look around at all the people staring at us and I feel like they're crowded around me even though I know they're not.

"Is there a doctor here?" Alan calls out. A doctor in this bar full of hipsters? I doubt it. The people just keep staring at us. "How you feeling, buddy?" Alan pulls on Barry's shirt to keep him upright, but Barry can't hold himself up.

"M'all right," Barry slurs. "M'okay."

Blood runs down his face and I do my best to wipe it away.

Does this motherfucker really have a concussion? Goddamn, trouble won't leave me alone, not even on the other side of town. I can feel my heart beating hard.

Alan's face gets pale. This is his joint, his bar, and someone just got hurt in it. He takes a glass of water and makes Barry drink it. I don't know if that will solve anything, but I guess it wouldn't hurt.

"You need to take him to the hospital," Alan says. "Just to make sure he's okay."

Uh, multiple problems there. "I can't drive."

"What?"

"No license."

Alan looks at me. He's working—this is his business to oversee. But he looks back at Barry and I know he feels protective of his friend. "All right. Help me get him to my car out back."

Together we get Barry to his feet. The fucker is solid muscle and between skinny Alan and me, I'm doing most of the lifting. My old injuries start hurting again. I'm dizzy. I told Barry to hold the towel to his forehead but he's doing a bad job and now there's blood on my shirt. Thank God the shirt is black.

We stumble down a long dark hallway to the back entrance. Clumsy as fuck, we load Barry into the backseat of Alan's old Volvo and drive off.

"What's the closest emergency room?" I ask.

"UCLA Santa Monica," Alan replies. "I know it well."

"How come?"

"Teenagers and Bunsen burners. Dangerous combination."

When we arrive at the emergency room, Alan explains the situation to the staff. There are a few small groups in the waiting room, kicking it on blue plastic chairs. It looks like the visiting room back in prison, with families and little kids snoozing or running around or crying. The clerk listens to our problem and directs us to the waiting area. Barry's head's stopped bleeding, so at least there's that. We shuffle over to the blue chairs to wait our turn.

Out of the dark bar and under fluorescent lights, Alan looks a lot older than I thought he was. He's got wrinkles in the corners of his eyes.

I look over at Barry. He's leaning back with his arms crossed. Alan keeps elbowing him. "Don't fall asleep."

"Why not?"

"You might have a concussion. You might not wake up."

"Really? No shit." Barry's still drunk.

I look over at the clock. Three hours into my shift. I fight the urge to take the bus back to the gym to get my work done but I can't abandon the boss here.

"So what do you do at Defiance, Sal?" Alan asks. Conversation to make the time pass.

I look at Barry out of the corner of my eye and say, "I'm a janitor there. Six months. I work at night."

"I want him to be a trainer," Barry pipes up. "He'd be fucking good."

"I'm thinking about it," I say, even though I've already thought about it and the answer is still no.

"That's good," Alan says, brightening up. "How about before Defiance?"

Ah, here's where it gets tricky. "I was locked up. State pen. Five years."

Now, there are two ways this conversation can go, particularly with normal people who have no experience with breaking the law. First, they get uncomfortable and let the topic drop. Second, they get a weird fire in their eyes and start asking questions that ultimately lead to, "So did you do it?"

The answer of course is, yes. Yes, I did it.

But both of those reactions make me sick. Like, "Let's not talk about your past, Sal, because it makes me uncomfortable." Or, "Let's talk the hell out of your past because you fascinate me." Like those old-timey freak shows. A sheep in a jar with two heads. A woman with four legs.

I don't know which way Alan will go because Barry stands up all of a sudden and announces that he doesn't feel well. Alan takes him to the restroom where I assume Barry throws up, because when they come out, Alan looks even more tired. Even though his face is clean, Barry looks exhausted, with watery eyes, just like someone who's heaved his guts all over a toilet.

They settle back down.

"Did they call his name?" Alan asks.

I shake my head. "Nope. Not yet."

In the end, Barry is fine. Diagnosis? He got drunk and hit his goddamn head. Two stitches for the cut and that's it. Apparently, I was right. His low-carb diet makes him hypersensitive to alcohol or some shit, so the amount of beer he drank was enough to put him down. Alan was also right. He's a lightweight. A heavyweight lightweight.

After many hours at the hospital, Alan drops me off at the gym before he takes Barry home. It's five in the morning when I unlock the back door. I've got two hours to do eight hours of work. I rush through it like a crazy man, cutting corners like I hate, working until sweat is pouring off me, and I realize this is pretty good cardio, mopping and wiping like a cartoon on fast forward.

I take the fastest shower in the world and change into my clean clothes. I'm almost out just as the first trainer walks in, yawning with a Starbucks cup in her hand.

"Hey, Sal." Her name's Chantal, a little white girl from Connecticut who wants to be an actress. I'm still panting from my crazy shift. She's wearing tiny tight shorts and I can see the way the fabric hugs the curves of her ass, and the way her body hugs the fabric right back. Six months ago, that sight would've had me howling like a rabid coyote. But I've got myself under control these days, and I know better than to get tangled up with a trainer at the gym where I work.

"Looking good," she says, with a smile. "I'm going on a towel run later. Are all the hampers empty?"

I nod. "Yeah. Everything's in the two bags in the utility closet."

"Thanks, Sal." She reaches out, runs her hand down my arm, and looks up into my eyes.

Shit. I know that look.

It's a look that says, "So, your lonely ass wants me and I'm horny as hell and my first client doesn't come in for half an hour and why don't we go out back into the locker room for a quick hard fuck and get this over with?"

Yeah. That's the look.

"You haven't called me yet to get Mexican food," she says with a pout. Two weeks ago we were making conversation about tamales and I told her about a place in my neighborhood where you can get the good stuff. "You have to take me. We have to go."

"We will," I say, even though we both know this isn't true. I want to tell her that I'm not the one she wants to get with, that it would be bad news for both of us. "All right, girl. Listen, I gotta get going. Have a good one, okay?"

Her hand lingers on my forearm. She squeezes the muscle. Then she lets go. "All right, Sal. See you later."

I SLEEP like a rock but not for very long. When Chancla barks at the mail carrier, I wake up like I've been splashed with a bucket of water. Because my schedule is off, I can't get back to sleep. I feel sluggish from the beer and the long night sitting in the hospital waiting room.

No one is in the house except for an angry wiener dog that rushes me when I open the back door.

"Easy," I say.

The fucking weenie bites my ankles and my shins. Growling, scratching at me. Are wiener dogs supposed to be bastards like this? I sidestep him and walk into the bathroom. I close the door in his angry little face and take care of business.

It's Saturday morning and the neighborhood is noisy, baseball games on the radio, TVs at full blast, kids riding bikes in the street. I take the short walk to Regina's and without asking any questions, she lets me in and gives me something to eat. The kids climb all over me while I try to finish a sandwich and drink a cup of coffee.

"Have you heard from Spider?" I ask.

Regina stands at the kitchen counter in yoga pants and an old stained T-shirt. She looks like she's been crying, and I feel bad for her. "Of course not."

"He'll come around."

Regina smiles sadly at me. "I guess you're right. Just like the saying. 'What goes around comes around.' That bastard sure went around."

I don't disagree, but I don't say anything either. I stand up and take my plate to the sink. I wash the huge pile of dirty dishes, dry them, and put them away.

When I leave, Regina's parked on the couch with the kids snuggled around her. They're watching *The Little Mermaid*. I look away from the TV because of all the movies ever made, that one makes me the saddest.

"Thanks for lunch, Gina," I say, heading out the door.

"Bye, Ghost," says the littlest one.

I touch his head. His dark hair is soft. "Bye-bye, *pollito*." Little chicken. My nickname for him. He smiles big, too big for a little chicken.

A thick blanket of ivy has grown over the garage. I yank it away, find the handle, and lift the heavy wooden door.

Time to clean.

I wasn't a neat freak when I was younger, but I became one while I was locked up. Our cell block captain made us keep everything clean. Our cells, our beds, our bodies. He ran our section like a drill sergeant. We were a tight ship. If you didn't keep your shit clean, you heard from the boss. You got in trouble. As the days passed, I came to enjoy the process of cleaning things—the quiet of taking something dirty and making it new again.

I start by putting the stacks of yellowing newspapers in the recycling bin. There are empty cardboard boxes and I break them down before tying them up with twine and stacking them next to the trash cans. I figure Vanessa and Chinita don't need the dusty stack of rags next to the truck. I sweep those into an old trash bag and toss them in the bin.

I'm just scratching the surface, but cleaning the garage makes me feel like myself again. When that corner is clear, I crack into the first box to see what I can find.

It's just a regular cardboard box with loose strips of packing tape hanging from it. I take it off the stack and bring it outside into the sunlight.

The top of the box is dusty and I blow it clean. I open the top flaps of the box. Inside, there are a couple of old notebooks and binders, one marked *Stats,* the other *Accounting.* These are Vanessa's school notes. I flip through one of the spiral notebooks. It's full of notes in her neat, girly handwriting. She doesn't write outside the lines and everything is dated and numbered. But sometimes in the margins, I see where her mind begins to wander a little. A daisy. A few stars. In the corner of one page she's drawn a little cat with hearts for eyes. It makes me smile. Every schoolgirl needs to doodle. Even a straight-A student has a cartoon cat hiding in her notebook somewhere.

Carefully, I stack the notebooks and binders up on a lawn chair. Underneath that first layer I find a few medals and certificates from our high school. She cleaned up in the prize department. Service awards. Most Improved. Excellence in Mathematics.

What was I winning at the time? *Niño Travieso* of the Year. Fuck-Up Valedictorian.

I put her awards in a row on the brick planter next to the house and put the certificates on top of the binders. The sun is nice and bright and I'm feeling clearer, better. I take a deep breath and stretch out my back a little. I wish I'd been able to lift this morning, but the crazy three-hour shift made up for the workout.

At the very bottom of the box is another, smaller box, a pink shoebox. I pull it out and sit down on the other lawn chair to look through it. There's a little bit of water damage on the lid so I hope whatever's inside is still in good shape.

When I lift the lid, I see a stack of photos. A few faded rose petals. Notes from Vanessa's girlfriends, birthday cards with Hello Kitty on them.

I'm snooping.

These are Vanessa's private photos.

But I can't help myself.

On top are photos from a formal dance, probably before everything with Sleepy went down. Here she is, in the arms of some clean-cut kid, one I don't recognize, skinny in a tuxedo but trying to look hard. Here she is with her girlfriends, making funny faces for the camera. Some of her friends look like models, like grown-ups in expensive dresses, fancy hair, and tons of makeup. Vanessa is wearing a simple green dress that shows off her dark skin. Her hair is down, silky and black. She's wearing that red lipstick. She looks fresh and positive.

The anger she carries now—it hadn't reached her. It hadn't touched her. Not yet.

I search through the stack. I see photos of her with her volleyball team, photos of vacations in Mexico with her cousins. I don't see any photos of Sleepy, which makes me feel relieved, for some reason.

At the bottom of the box, there's a small envelope filled with wallet-sized pictures. Here's one: Vanessa in grade school, maybe ten or eleven, dressed like a cat. She's got black cat ears and an upside-down triangle painted on her nose. She's wearing a black T-shirt and black pants, and she's got a plastic jack-o'-lantern basket full of candy. She is smiling but she looks stiff and uncomfortable, standing next to a skinny but beautiful woman dressed like a fortune-teller. The woman has Vanessa's same dark eyes and full lips but her cheeks are sunken in. She's wearing heavy makeup and a loose dress, but she can't hide the truth.

I know a junkie when I see one.

I turn the photo in the sunlight to make sure I haven't left any fingerprints on it. I slip it back into the envelope, put the envelope back into the box, and close the lid.

Leaning back in the chair, I take a moment to take stock of where I am. What I'm doing.

I take a breath. Air whooshes quietly inside my lungs. In. Out.

The sky is open above me. Blue. Endless.

Locked up, you feel everything you can't have.

Obviously, sex.

But other things too. Smaller things. Like this, the sun on my face. A little breeze in the avocado tree. I can hear the kids playing in the street. Birds. Stupid-ass birds—I never thought I'd miss the sound of birds, but I did.

I fall asleep in the chair without meaning to. It's a gentle sleep, shallow but full of dreams.

I'm playing soccer in the park with my dad. My mom and sister are there, sitting under a tree. No one talks to me, but I can feel them all, I can feel their presence. My family—my ghosts.

So many people. Gone.

When you have to say goodbye so much, death doesn't feel like a mystery or something to be afraid of. It's the next step. A shitty one, but just a step. We will all have to take it, whether the timing is good or not.

I'm not afraid of ghosts. I'm not afraid of death.

I have lots of people on the other side, waiting for me. When I die, I'll see them again.

A LOUD CRASH. I sit up, my heart bursting.

What the fuck?

Vanessa is throwing away the old binders and notebooks. Hundreds of pages of notes. Numbers and cartoon cats. Hours of her life. She's taking one armful from where I've stacked them and just dumping each load into the trash can.

I blink. It's still afternoon. I must've dozed for just a few minutes. She's wearing jeans and a white T-shirt and those same torn-up Chucks. Her hair is tied up in some kind of messy knot. I sit there for a moment, letting myself stare. She's so pretty. Hips and a waist. Big round tits. Thick dark hair and shapely legs and I think, Man. That would be something. Being with her would be something.

She doesn't notice that I'm awake, or she ignores that I am.

When I stand up, she doesn't acknowledge me except to say, "Those piles too. We can throw those away."

She's pointing at the stacks of certificates and awards. I look at her. "Really? You really want to throw them away?"

"They're just taking up room in the garage."

I look at one on top. Dated six years ago. Vanessa Velasco. Excellence in Calculus. Awarded by the Latina Women of STEM. "What's STEM?"

"An acronym. Science, technology, engineering, mathematics."

I look at the fancy handwriting of her name, the golden seal. I've never won anything in my life. If I'd won this, it'd be in a frame on the wall. If I had a frame. Or a wall.

"It's just collecting dust." Her voice is quiet but impatient. She takes the awards and dumps them in the trash can.

"So is that how this is going to go?" I say. "I take it out of the garage, you look at it, you throw it away?"

She closes the trash can and slaps her hands together to get the dust off. "Pretty much."

"There's a lot of stuff in there."

"Most of it will go in the trash."

She pushes the trash cans back to their spot by the wall. From the way she moves, I get the sense she doesn't have time for anything. She's got energy, a lot of it. She has to move, this thing to the next. Kicking her daughter's tricycle out of the way. Using a little rake and dustpan to clean up some of Chancla's poop. She can't stand still.

I am not sure what to do with myself so I go back to the chair and sit down. The shoebox of photos sits on the grass where I left it.

"Hey." I pick up the box. "Take a look at this."

She looks up at me, impatient. "At what?"

"Just come here and see."

Vanessa walks over to me with suspicion in her eyes. I catch a little of that sweet strawberry perfume. "What is it?"

I take off the lid. "Look."

FIVE

FOR THE FIRST TIME, a ghost of a smile touches her lips. Staring at the pictures, she slowly sinks down on the grass next to me. Her leg touches mine. I stay as still as I can.

The photo on top is the one of her in the green dress. "So how long ago was that?" I ask.

Vanessa picks up the photo and looks at it closely. "Junior year, I think." She names her friends in the photo, one by one, half to herself and half to me. I look at her face. Her eyes change. They grow softer. Sweeter.

The words come out on their own. "You're really pretty," I say.

"I was seventeen." Her eyes are still on the photo. "Everyone is pretty when they're seventeen."

I didn't mean in the photo, but I don't want to scare her away. "You look like you were having fun."

"I never had fun," she says. "I was really hard on myself. I never went out, never let myself have fun. So the few times I did . . ." She trails off.

"You made sure to have as much fun as possible."

"Exactly." A pause. "Maybe too much fun."

I wonder about the kind of fun she would get up to at seventeen. Running away with a homeboy. Giving it up to him. I'm daydreaming a little bit, wishing I were that kid, taking her out in a borrowed car, holding her close. She squints at the picture and I notice fine lines at the corners of her eyes. Her cheekbones are sharper. She's far more beautiful now than she was at seventeen.

"So when did you leave Roosevelt?" she asks.

"You mean drop out?"

She shrugs. "'Leave' seemed more polite."

"Tenth grade." I was able to keep my family together for three years following the accident. And then it all went to hell. "I left right before the end of sophomore year."

"And you went to . . . ?"

"California Youth Authority. Chino." I had gotten into a street fight with a member of Las Palmas. The kid came after me with a knife. I broke his jaw with a brick and sent him to the hospital. That plus my gang affiliation and record of stealing cars got me a one-way ticket to the state's largest youth prison. I stayed there until I turned eighteen. The beatings I got back then—that's where I got my bad knee. I still can't hear so great out of my left ear. My front teeth got knocked out. Luckily, Ruben hooked me up with his dentist when I got out. "When did you start going with Sleepy?" I ask.

She gives me a slow blink, as if she can't believe I just brought him up. She looks back down at the photos and gently closes the lid. The ghost of a smile evaporates. "Not long after this dance." She stands up with the box, and I fight the fear I've scared her off.

"Are you going to throw them away?" I ask in disbelief. No pictures exist of me when I was younger. The prints, the digital cameras, the old phones that had any photos of me are long gone. It's like I'm a real ghost. Erased. "Don't."

Challenge flashes in her eyes. I like her fire, but I'm not sure why she's on the defensive when it comes to me. It's not like we didn't grow up in the same hood. It's not like she hasn't lived around gangsters her whole life. I wonder for a moment if she faces off with strangers like this. If so, I know that feeling. It's a fire that burns hot, but it's all show. The appearance of defiance, something you use when you're crumbling behind your mask. It's a fire that'll burn you from the inside out.

"Don't throw them away," I say. "You'll regret it."

"Why do you care what I regret and what I don't?"

In the old days, I would've said, "I don't give a shit what you regret." But today is today. So I say what's in my heart. "Because you don't deserve to regret anything."

She has one hell of a poker face. "Who are you to decide what I deserve?"

"You deserve more than what you've got."

"Doesn't everyone?"

"No."

From the expression on her face, I know she'd be folding her arms if she wasn't holding the box of photos in her hand. Her voice is calm. This doesn't feel like arguing. She's feeling me out. Testing me. "Who do you think you are, telling me what I deserve? Why should I listen to you?"

"Me? I'm no one. But I'm here. And it would be a shame if I let you throw your old photos away, knowing that you'd regret it."

"You talk like you can tell the future." Her voice is softer.

"I wish I could."

She's quiet for a moment, but not still—she fidgets, shifting her weight back and forth from foot to foot. "So what's your plan, Ghost? Other than to pay me money for the pleasure of cleaning out my garage?"

I shrug. "Stay out of trouble. Keep working until I have enough money for a place."

"A place of your own? So that you can party or what?" She's teasing me. Teasing—that I can work with.

"My brother is out in two months. I have only a few more weeks to save for a new apartment. He'll need a place to stay too. Somewhere he can stay out of trouble. I'm more worried about him than me."

Vanessa has nothing to say about that. She looks at me, frowning a little as if she's trying to figure me out. "I can't tell if you're lying to make yourself look like a good guy."

I laugh. "Not even lying would make me look like a good guy, Vanessa."

Her frown disappears, but she's still not smiling. Right then and there, I make it my mission to make this woman smile.

"Two months," she says. "Then out. Understand?"

"Two months. Yup. Got it."

She stares at me a little while longer. Up close, she's not exactly pretty. Big dark eyes, suspicious. A big nose, if we're being honest. And a big mouth with full lips. Her front teeth are slightly crooked, with a little gap in between. A thirst grabs me and I wonder what it would feel like to kiss her, to run the tip of my tongue over that space, back and forth.

Great. Something else to fucking fantasize about.

Invisible heat rolls over me like a wave. I stay still, trying not to show it.

"You're working tonight, right?" she asks.

I nod. "Every night."

"Don't forget to lock the gates when you leave."

"I won't."

She turns around and heads toward the back door with the box under her arm. A new understanding plants itself in my head. When people are nice to me, I'm immediately suspicious.

When people are mean to me, I think, "There, that's more like it." When people are half-cold and half-hot to me, like Vanessa is, I think, "I have to know more."

I watch her as she walks her fine ass back into the house.

🍾

THAT EVENING, I wake up with a pounding headache.

Yup.

I know what the problem is.

The windows of the house are dark. No one is home. I walk in through the back door and step into the bathroom. I lock the bathroom door behind me, run the shower, and strip. When the water is hot, I step inside the small blue-tiled stall. There's a bar of soap and a bottle of cheap shampoo. I'm the only one who uses this bathroom.

I wash my hair and rub the bar of soap over my face, neck, and arms. I lather up my torso and the suds get thick in my chest hair. My hands still haven't gotten used to this strange new body. There's so much more of me now—I've put on lots of muscle since prison. Abs, pecs, obliques. My workouts are paying off. Everything is hard and tight.

My hands slip downward. I rub soap on my balls. They ache. When I close my eyes and think about Vanessa, my dick twitches.

I put soap in my palm and give myself two slow, slippery strokes. My shaft thickens. Two more strokes and I'm hard as a baseball bat.

After five years in prison, you bet your ass I know how to touch myself. I'm not ashamed. I admit it.

I am good at jacking off.

Shit, I better be.

Closing my eyes, I take a deep breath of steamy air. In my

mind, I paint the blue sky, the avocado tree, the sunshine, the grass. When there's a lazy sketch of the backyard, it's time for the star of the show—Vanessa, standing there with the garden hose in her hand, her dark hair loose over her shoulders, a big smile on her face. This is definitely a fantasy because she's happy to be here. The real Vanessa would lose her shit if she knew I had deposited her in my spank bank.

Okay, concentrate.

Details, now.

Pearl necklace. Red lipstick. I like the black skirt, but let's make it three inches higher. The blouse is good, but how about we lose those top buttons? Yes. Better. I can see the lace bra through the fabric. Let's lose that too. But we can do even better than that, can't we?

Vanessa holds the hose to her chest and sprays cold water on herself. Goosebumps rise on her skin. Under the wet cotton, her dark nipples harden. With her free hand, she slowly undoes the remaining buttons on her blouse and peels the cotton away from her skin. Her big tits spring free, round and wet.

Excellent.

"I want you, Sal," she says.

No, no—we can do even better than that.

"I *need* you, Sal," she says.

Perfect.

I grip the head of my dick with my thumb, index finger, and middle finger. Quickly, I begin to jack the head, concentrating on the sensitive point where the head connects to the underside of my shaft.

Vanessa drops the hose, gets down on her knees on the wet grass, and takes my dick in her pretty hands.

"You're so big," she whispers.

I watch as her red lips take me in. She sucks enthusiastically on the head, keeping her dark eyes on me. Her tongue wiggles against my sweet spot.

"Yes," I murmur. "Now take it all."

I close my fist around my cock and jack myself off hard and slow.

There on her knees, Vanessa sucks me deep into her hot mouth. Her lips seal tightly over me. She leaves a red smear of lipstick on my shaft as she bobs her head back and forth. Her tongue slithers along the tendon at the base of my dick. Her cool hands cup my balls, massaging them tenderly while hot come swirls inside, ready to blow.

In the shower, I lean into the stream of water. With my right hand, I'm stroking my cock furiously. My left hand rubs my chest and swirls my nipples. The water, the heat, my own touch —I'm going to come soon. It's going to be good.

"Take it deeper," I whisper.

Vanessa puts her hands on my hips and impales herself. She begins fucking my dick with the back of her throat. Her mascara runs. I feel her soft, hot tits bouncing against my thighs. She looks up at me, seeking my approval.

"Yes, good girl." I run my hands through her hair and pull it gently. "Such a good girl."

In the shower, I close my left hand over my right, tightening my fist. I take a deep breath and stop stroking. With a grunt, I brace my hands against the tile wall of the shower and thrust my hips like I'm fucking the hell out of Vanessa's mouth.

What would she do if she knew I was thinking about her right now, like this?

Throw me out of her house, that's what.

When those red lips touch the base of my cock, I press on the back of her head and pin her there. She swallows, and her throat muscles clamp down on the swollen head of my dick.

"Fuck," I whisper. "Yes."

Hot come fills my hands, mixing with the water from the shower. I squeeze my eyes shut, swallow my grunts and climax in silence. I'm gasping, drowning, and twisting in my fantasy of Vanessa. In my mind, white come spills out of her mouth, wets her pearl necklace, and drips down between her breasts in a long, lazy trail.

God, I'm such a fucking pervert.

I shudder through the last of the spasms. Still high, I rinse myself and wipe down the shower stall. I turn off the taps and dry off. My tender dick, still hard, weeps at the tip. I glance at the clock on the wall. This whole operation from start to finish has taken five minutes.

Okay, wait up. Don't get the wrong idea.

When I'm with a woman, for the record, I take a hell of a lot longer than five minutes.

But this? This is maintenance. Batting practice before the game.

Refreshed by my climax, my body is less tense. My headache is gone. I get dressed, grab my backpack, and head out into the night.

AFTER A HARD NIGHT'S work and a long rest, I wake up and realize something—I've got an errand to run.

It's a lazy Sunday afternoon. Panaderia La Golondrina is on the same block where I grew up. I pass my family's old house on the way there and scope it out. It's been painted green. The old TV antenna on the roof is gone and all the long-broken parts of the house—the rain gutters, the busted screen door—have been replaced. The yard is kind of a mess, but there are toys every-where and there's a soccer ball on the roof. Someone new is growing up here, which is nice, but my mom's hanging flower-pots are all gone. She was so proud of those. Without them hanging on the porch, this looks like a different house completely—and I know, in my heart, not even the ghosts of my family live here now.

I walk the familiar sidewalk to the corner bakery. It looks exactly the same. The same OPEN sign in the door, the same painting of a *golondrina*—the bird from tattoos, a swallow—on the front window, the same faded Lady of Guadalupe mural on the side wall. Growing up, the smell of fresh bread was the smell of home. Twice a day. Once in the early morning, and once before noon. You could set your watch to it.

I open the door and walk in. There's one other person in the bakery, a middle-aged lady piling her tray high. I grab my own tray and tongs and head over to the glass case where I see the little brown sweet rolls shaped like pigs. There are two left. I grab them and bring them to the front to pay.

"Salvador, long time no see," says the old guy behind the counter. Everyone calls him Slim. He's about five feet tall and two hundred and fifty pounds. His family has owned and operated this bakery since Cesar Chavez Avenue was Brooklyn Avenue and the neighborhood was full of Jewish and Japanese families. Which is to say, a long, long time.

"Slim," I say, shaking his hand. "How's the family?"

He's like a big cartoon character. His eyebrows go up as he closes his eyes and frowns. There are four lines across his forehead. "Good, good. Carmen graduated last year."

His oldest daughter. "From high school? That's great."

"No, Sal. Culinary school. She's a chef now, downtown. High-class stuff."

As he bags up my bread, I think about what a little bitch time is. We all get the same amount and once it's up, it's up. Slim's daughter knew this and used her time well. Me? Well, you know how I spent my time.

I take out my wallet to pay when the other customer comes up behind me. I'm surprised when Slim waves her over ahead of me. "Señora Bustamante, let me ring you up right now."

The lady has two dozen pieces of bread. All kinds. *Conchas,* pink and white and brown buns covered in cracked sugar. They look like seashells. She's got thick slices of cake covered in butter and sugar. Big cookies covered in rainbow sprinkles. And the old-school stuff: more *puerquitos* like the ones I'm buying, some *elotitos,* small loaves of yellow bread shaped like corncobs. She asks for more—now she wants the sandwich bread behind the counter—but only if it's fresh, she says. How about elephant ears—does Slim have any *orejas* in the back? She wants some of those too. She and Slim have a long chat about her grandchildren and the weather and the carnival coming up at the church this weekend. I'm standing there with my two dollars in my hand feeling like an idiot as the lady grabs her big paper bag and slowly shuffles out the door.

Now there's no one else in the bakery. I look at Slim, confused. "What's up?"

Slim gives his head a slow shake and lowers his voice. "I got a big problem, Sal. I need your help."

I know that look. I don't like this. This is my old life. This is the shit I'm not supposed to do anymore. But I've known Slim forever, so I gotta listen. "Tell me."

"There's a new crew. Crossing the avenue. Young kids. The main one, he calls himself Creeper. They're demanding taxes for Las Palmas. I told them, 'You're crazy. Everyone knows this is *varrio* Hollenbeck.' They don't care. Disrespectful little shits. Threatened me and the wife. They scared her, Sal. Can you please talk to Ruben? Let him know? Tell him this is happening to me, to Perez, to *las viejas tambien.*"

Bad news. These new kids are shaking down Slim, plus the liquor store owner and the old women who run the dry cleaner's. This street forms the southern edge of Hollenbeck territory, but other gangs rarely step to us. Something has changed on the ground since I've been gone.

Slim is looking at me like I can protect him. Like I'm strong. After five years in prison and six months trying to be as invisible as I can be, the expression on his face makes me feel high.

Like I really am strong.

Like I really am the soldier I once was.

I feel myself getting dragged back, back to the life that was so easy, so clear to me. I knew the game back then. I knew the score.

I shake off the feeling as best as I can and take another look at Slim's worried face. All he wants me to do is pass on a message. I'm on parole. I'm not supposed to associate with known gang members. But I owe Slim this. I've known him since I was a little *mocoso* bothering him for free candy.

"All right," I say. "I'll go see him."

"Tell him to send some help. Please, Sal."

Ruben will do more than make sure homeboys are posted up on this block. If gangsters from Las Palmas are harassing people from our hood, this guy Creeper and his friends' days are numbered.

Blood.

I promised myself I'd never see blood on my hands again.

I'm just the messenger, I tell myself. *Just the messenger.*

"It's okay, Slim," I say. "I'll go see him."

Slim gives me the bread for free and throws in a half dozen rolls even though I tell him no. I'm torn by this. I used to get free stuff all the time when I was active in the gang. It made me feel powerful—who doesn't like special treatment?—but as I grew older, I learned the truth.

Nothing is ever free. Not a single goddamn thing.

You will pay for it. Maybe not today, but you will.

I shake Slim's chubby hand, put the bread in my backpack, and book it to the bus stop. The bus is about to leave when I flag the driver in the mirror. She stops and I hop on, panting. As I settle into my seat and slowly catch my breath, anxiety tightens like a screw in my gut. Slim has just put me on a path I've been trying to avoid for the past six months.

"Shit," I whisper.

Later that evening, Alan greets me like an old buddy when I walk into his place. Only a few people are sitting at the bar, chatting with the bartender. Alan grabs my hand and pulls me into a half hug. I know we're not really homies but Barry's hospital incident was a bonding experience for us, and I have to admit it's kind of nice to have a new friend.

I sound like a little kid sometimes, don't I? You don't understand. I never make new friends.

Alan hops behind the bar. "Do you have time for a quick drink with me?"

I check the clock on the wall. I've got two hours before my shift at Defiance starts. I have ten dollars left before I get paid tomorrow, so I think I can afford one beer. "Yeah. Sure. A quick one."

"You want something to eat?"

When I hesitate, he says, "On me?" He senses my reluctance and makes the choice for me. "I skipped lunch, so I'm hungry myself. We'll share a few things." He leans over to the bartender. "Hey, can you order up a couple slider plates. Brussels sprouts. Uh, and the flatbread. Thanks."

The bartender puts the order into the computer and I see a white kid in the kitchen window hop to action.

I watch as Alan takes two glasses from a refrigerator full of glasses. A refrigerator for just glasses. Damn, that is fancy. He pulls two pints of dark beer.

"Is that Feliz Navidad?" I ask.

"Yeah. See? The name works. You remembered." I watch as he turns the second glass perfectly so that an inch of perfect foam tops the pint. He puts a paper coaster down and places the beer in front of me. There's frost on the glass.

This is the life.

I open my backpack and take out the bag of bread Slim gave me. Alan grabs a small plate and I put down the *puerquitos*. Only one still has its raisin eye. That's the one I give to Alan.

"There it is," he says. He's beaming. He gets excited about shit. Here's something I've noticed—homies don't really allow themselves to be excited about things. You can be happy. You can be angry, you can be sad. But we don't really show it. Ever. You're told, "A real man doesn't show his emotions." "A real man doesn't get too excited about anything." Again, as I get older I realize, fuck this real-man shit. I think Alan is a real man. I mean, I don't necessarily want to get into any fistfights with him on my side, but he's cool and he gets excited about shit so maybe there's nothing wrong with that.

"*Salud,*" he says when he clinks my glass. We drink and he breaks his little pig in two. He takes a bite.

"Damn, you were right. That's exactly the same flavor."

"I told your ass. The same." I take a bite of mine and a drink of beer. The flavor fills my mouth. It's rich and sweet, but kind of spicy too. I never thought about the flavors of things before, but with Alan's excitement I feel like I'm tasting food for the first time.

Our dinner arrives—I've never had Brussels sprouts before, weird as fuck but tasty—and we chat about how he started his business and the problems he has day-to-day. During breaks in our conversation, I think about Slim, trying to run his business, afraid for himself and afraid for his wife. I'm worried about him, but also, I'm worried about myself when I go to see Ruben. Besides my welcome-back party, I haven't gone to see Ruben in

I hold out my hand and the girl shakes it, looking me in the eye. "Hello," I say. "What's your name?"

"Brianna," the girl says. She's wearing a Hello Kitty T-shirt, a pink skirt, and rainbow tights. There's a ketchup stain on her T-shirt. She's got a little bowl cut like my brothers had when they were kids. On her it looks cute. On my brothers? Well, they looked like a Mexican version of Moe from the Three Stooges. My hair was curly. I was Larry, I guess.

"In the house, what do we call you?" Vanessa says.

"Muñeca."

Little doll. "Muñeca," I say. "Nice to meet you."

The girl cracks a smile at last. Vanessa ruffles her hair and says, "Go upstairs and wash your hands. Change your T-shirt. You can play until dinnertime, okay?"

"Can I play with your phone?"

"No, *mi'ja*. How about the Tinkertoys? Are you going to make me the nail salon like you said?"

"The nail salon?"

"Yeah. I wanna see it."

Muñeca raises her eyebrows. "Okay." She turns and goes inside.

"We went to the nail salon on her birthday. She's obsessed with it," Vanessa says. She comes down the steps to my level and again, I'm surprised by how short she is. Even in heels, she barely comes up to my shoulder.

"So what have you got for me today?"

"See for yourself."

She looks at the boxes I've lined up on the driveway. There are five. I labeled them with some Post-it notes I found in a box of office supplies.

Looks expensive.
Looks important.
Looks useful.

Trash but I'm not sure.

I don't know what this is.

She reads the box labels. "I like your filing system."

"Thanks," I say. "I was just being honest."

Finally—I make her smile. Mission accomplished. But before I can get a good look at it, she covers her smile. Covers it—why?

I point to the stack behind the boxes. "There's an old dining table and four chairs. I found a high chair. And there's a wedding dress in a bag. I think you could sell those pretty fast if you wanted."

"There's a wedding dress?" she asks.

"It looks like a wedding dress. It's white."

"Where?"

I hold up the dusty garment bag for her and watch as she unzips it. When she pulls all the puffy white fabric out of the bag, the smile on her face brightens and I decide I've found my new life's work—to make this woman smile. As much as possible.

"It's my first-Communion dress." She holds it up. It's got big sleeves and a big skirt. It's covered with white roses and all these little pearls. I can't imagine this dress on a grown woman, much less a little girl.

She looks at my confused face and laughs. If I thought I wasn't a goner when I saw her smile, I'm definitely a goner now. Her eyes light up and her laughter is deep and real. It goes into me. It grabs me from the inside out and for a second I'm speechless.

"What?" she says.

"I didn't say nothing."

"Don't look at me like that. My mom chose it! She wanted me to be *fancy*."

I nod, even though I'm not thinking about the dress. "It's definitely . . . fancy."

"She was in love with Princess Diana. She wanted my dress to look like Diana's wedding dress." She touches the roses and a softness comes to her eyes. "I was eight. I wanted her to be happy, so I said yes to everything. We were at a dress shop in the garment district and the seamstress kept asking her questions. More roses? Yes. Bigger sleeves? Yes. A poufy skirt? Yes, yes, yes. She loved it."

"And you? Did you love it?"

Vanessa shrugs a little. "Yeah. I kinda did." Still smiling, she holds the dress to her shoulders and looks down. "During the class picture, I took up the whole back row. Like, this mountain of white. I did feel like Princess Diana, though."

Carefully, we put the dress back in the bag together. I don't remember ever meeting Vanessa's mom. I wonder a little bit about her, that woman in the old photograph with the sunken-in cheeks. She had that half-dead junkie look in her eye, a look I can recognize as an adult. But as a kid? Would I have trusted that woman? Would I have wanted her approval and love, just because she was the only mother I knew? What was that like for Vanessa?

I shake myself out of psychotherapy mode and walk Vanessa through the rest of the discoveries I made in the boxes. She listens and carefully creates her own piles, much more practical than mine: trash, sell, donate, keep. She has the final say, and she doesn't hesitate when she makes decisions. Things go or things stay, and that's that.

When we're done with the day's haul, I close up Ben's toolbox and carry the donation items to her car for her to drop off at Goodwill tomorrow. It's almost time for me to head out. "My bus leaves soon. I gotta clean up and find some food," I say, sorry to have to say goodbye.

She looks at me for a moment and I can see she's struggling with something. Finally—something she's got to think about. I wait.

At last she says, "When does your bus leave?"

"In an hour."

"If you want," she says, "you can have dinner with me and Muñeca."

I take another shower and change into fresh clothes. Feeling like a guest on his best behavior, I walk into the kitchen and take a seat at the table. The doorbell rings. When Muñeca says, "Pizza *again*?" I realize Chinita was right: the kitchen is not one of the many realms Vanessa has conquered. That's okay. Out of the corner of my eye, I watch Vanessa as she comes back from the front door holding a big box. She moves around the kitchen with purpose and energy. She's changed into a tight black T-shirt and sweatpants. She's taken off her lipstick but her hair is still tied up tight. I sneak a glance at her truly amazing cleavage as she pours Muñeca a glass of milk and makes her eat some carrot sticks.

"Vitamins too." She puts two gummy vitamins on the little girl's paper plate. Muñeca chomps them down, smiling at me. She's changed her Hello Kitty T-shirt into one with a zebra on it.

Vanessa takes a seat at last. We start on the pizza.

"I don't know what you do for work," I say. "Something to do with . . . accounting?"

"Right now, I'm a freelance bookkeeper," Vanessa says. "I keep the books for a few restaurants and restaurant suppliers downtown." She blots a slice of pepperoni and takes a bite. "But I'm studying for the CPA exam. I took two sections of it last March. I'm taking the last two sections in a couple months."

"CPA?"

"Certified public accountant."

"Mommy studies really hard," Muñeca pipes up.

"Mommy does," Vanessa says. She turns back to me. "How about you? Did you study when you were inside?"

"A little. I got my associate's degree."

She raises an eyebrow. "Really? What was that like?"

"The coursework was pretty easy," I shrug. "Way back when, I wasn't really bad in school. When I went."

As we chat, I put away two pieces of pepperoni. This feels nice. Relaxed.

Muñeca points to a tattoo on my hand. "What's that?"

"A ghost."

"Why do you have it?"

"It's my nickname."

"Ghost," Muñeca says, "are you a friendly ghost?"

I nod. "Yes. Not a scary one."

"Not the Halloween kind? The screaming kind?"

I shake my head. "Nope. Not that kind."

She points to the tattoos on my arms. "My daddy had some like those too. Did you know my daddy?"

Vanessa and I make quick eye contact. "Yeah, I knew your daddy. A little bit. He was my friend."

"A school friend?"

I pause. That's actually a good question. We were little troublemakers, constantly in and out of school, but were we ever in the same school at the same time? I frown. "I can't remember. More, I knew him from the neighborhood."

"All of my friends are school friends."

"Not all," says Vanessa. She crunches on a carrot stick. "You have soccer friends. Tell Ghost the name of your team."

This launches the little girl into a long, long explanation of how her peewee soccer team got the name Snickers when they wanted to be the M&M's and how it wasn't fair that even their second choice, Skittles, was already taken. Vanessa looks at me with a sideways smile. Muñeca goes on and on and when she's done, I stand up, tell her how sorry I am about how she has to be a Snickers instead of an M&M or a Skittle and that I have to go to work now.

"To be honest, I like Snickers a lot," I say.

"I do too," she says with a sigh, "but I like M&M's more."

I clear off the table. Muñeca goes upstairs to brush her teeth before bed. There are no dishes to wash, so I take out the trash for Vanessa as I head out the door.

"Thank you for the pizza," I say.

Still not finished with her day, the woman is folding a giant pile of laundry on her couch. She yawns but shakes it off. There are little T-shirts, miniature pants, dozens of tiny socks in a rainbow of colors, and a stack of yoga pants. I try and fail to look away from the flowery bras and thongs hanging on the armrest and my mind immediately goes where it shouldn't.

She sees what I'm trying hard not to look at and grins to herself. "Whenever you've got nowhere to go for dinner," she says quietly, "just come inside, okay?"

Goddamn.

"Okay," I say.

SEVEN

ON TUESDAY AFTERNOON, I walk up Ruben's street on the opposite side of the park. The houses here are smaller and newer, covered in stucco and shaded by big trees. It's quiet here. Everyone is still at work or at school.

Ruben is the perfect example of how a man can balance his gang responsibilities with a family. He takes care of business, goes to church, keeps his head down. He's always been the leader we needed, even during the hardest times.

At twenty-four, I'm already considered old. The youngsters look up to me, but I look up to Ruben. At forty-four, Ruben is an original gangster, an OG. An artifact. He's like an ancient turtle wandering around with a sign that says I'M TWO HUNDRED YEARS OLD.

His house is painted pink. The lawn is bright green and trimmed. The bushes are so square they look fake. The walkway and cement steps are paved with shiny red clay tiles. There are bars on the windows of the house and the front porch is caged with more bars and a heavy metal door. Calmly, I walk up the steps. I pause to swallow down my rising anxiety. Visiting Ruben, a convicted felon, is a violation of my parole. But a promise is a promise. Taking a deep breath, I press the intercom button.

"*¿Bueno?*" says Ruben's wife, Martha. "*¿Quién es?*"

"*Señora, soy Salvador Rosas. Estoy aquí para hablar con Ruben.*"

Silence.

I clear my throat and add, "Uh, I called earlier. He invited me to come at this time."

"*Ah, sí.* I'll be right there, *mi'jo. A ratito.*"

As I wait for Martha to come unlock the door, I look at the carefully swept driveway and sidewalk. There's a new heavy metal gate across the driveway, protecting Ruben's cars and shielding his backyard from view. Good—at least someone is making money in the neighborhood these days.

Ruben is now at the top of the structure for Hollenbeck, a shot-caller who oversees our entire operation. He's the liaison between the gangsters on the street and the Organization, the big homies on the inside. Corcoran. Pelican Bay. Folsom.

As I wait, I take a deep breath and let it out.

I try hard not to think of my dad and as usual, I fail.

Everyone knew him as Dreamer.

Ruben and Dreamer Rosas came up together. Best friends as little kids. Started on the streets as low-level soldiers and worked their way up to captains. Ruben was an example of how to do things the right way, whereas my dad was the example of how to do things the completely, spectacularly wrong way. Ruben—now he's the star at the top of the Christmas tree. The head honcho.

And my dad? Dreamer? Where is he?

Dead.

Worse than dead.

Gone and forgotten.

The metal door bangs open, shocking me out of my trance.

Ruben's wife is a pretty older woman dressed in black pants, a black T-shirt, and sandals. She has a big head of curly red hair and when she gives me a hug, it's warm and genuine. "*Mi'jo.* Long time no see. Come inside."

I follow her to the office where Ruben is sitting with his laptop. When Martha knocks on the door, he keeps his eyes on the monitor and shakes his head. "What's going on with this country, *mi amor*? I don't know. I just don't know. I want to stay current on what's happening in the world but every time I read the news, I just feel worse and worse."

"Ay, stop being so negative," Martha says in Spanish. "Life can't be all that bad. Look who's here."

Ruben stands up when he sees me and, just like Martha, immediately pulls me into a big hug. He's tall and lanky, with graying hair and a thick mustache—it's a good mustache, serious gangster *brochas*. He's dressed in a white muscle shirt and khaki shorts. In his bare feet, he would look like any old beach bum on a fishing boat—if it weren't for the faded prison tattoos up and down his wiry arms, the tiny bullet hole scar I can see under his collarbone, and the enormous scar on the back of his shoulder where the same bullet exited his body with a vengeance.

Martha asks me if I want a glass of iced tea and I say no thanks. Ruben stopped drinking ten years ago when he got out of prison on a five-year sentence. He lost a bunch of weight and started taking yoga. Clean living all the way.

Don't be fooled though.

Ruben is king for a reason.

I know the drill. I lift up my arms and he pats me down for wires as we talk a little bit about his kids, about my work, about my brother who's getting out in two months if all goes as planned. I ask him about his kids. They're all grown and moved out of the neighborhood, long gone. No interest in the family business, I guess.

"Should we take a walk?" he asks.

"Yeah, that would be good."

I watch as he puts on clean socks and a pair of new shell-toe Adidas. We make our way to the park and take a slow stroll around the lake. Kids from the local school are using the field for football practice. A couple of old homeless men sleep it off under the trees. A lone duck, big and ugly, slowly cruises the water, hoping for bread but not looking too optimistic.

Quietly, I tell Ruben about the crew from Las Palmas who are harassing Slim at the bakery and the other business owners on the southern border. I tell him everything that Slim told me, word for word. I have a good memory—when it comes to the gang, we never write shit down. Everything is said aloud.

I watch Ruben's face as I deliver the message. No emotions, just a slow nod like a professor listening to a student recite a poem. I can't tell if he thinks this is news or not. I'm used to his poker face. He's always been this way. Impossible to read.

When I'm finished, he stops and stands at the edge of the water. The duck comes to him but, realizing Ruben has nothing to give, swims away a little offended.

"I'll take care of it," Ruben says at last. He puts his hands in his pockets. "Spider's crew. Give them Demon for backup." He nods again. "That'll work."

I say nothing. Besides the message, I don't have anything to add to this conversation. Five years ago, I was one of Ruben's best soldiers, a steady earner. But now I'm nothing—a blank. For the last six months, I have hidden in a no-man's-land between gangster and dropout. I've done everything I can to stay clean and keep out of trouble—which means I've also been avoiding Ruben.

But I'd always known the clock never stops ticking. Soon the gang I pledged my life to would ask something of me again. Something I have to give, whether I want to or not.

Whether Ruben can feel my anxiety, I don't know. He looks me in the eye. "Do you need any money, *mi'jo?*"

As easy and as fucking wonderful as it would be to say yes, I say, "No. Thank you. I'm good."

For a long time, Ruben examines my face. He's reading me. I try to keep my features still, but I know it's no use. Ruben can see right through most people, including me. When he speaks at last, his voice is soft. "I know it's been hard for you, *mi'jo.* Learning about your dad. Being on your own. Keeping your nose clean. And I know it hasn't been easy for you to come see me."

It's the truth. I don't say anything.

Ruben continues, "When Trouble gets out, you have to make sure he understands the score. You know how that kid is. He's not like you. He's doesn't think things through. You have to convince him not to retaliate. We have to keep him safe. Keep him from losing his temper. Do you understand?"

I nod. He's right. My brother Eddie is unpredictable. That's how he got his name—Trouble.

"No retaliation from either of you. Is that clear?"

"Yes. I understand."

"You, me, Trouble—we have it the worst," Ruben says. "When I heard what happened to your father, I was in disbelief. I had a very dark moment, *mi'jo.* A crisis of faith, we call it. The higher-ups had green-lit my best friend. The one guy I grew up with. The godfather to my kids." Ruben shakes his head. "Was he a crazy motherfucker sometimes? Yes. Did he ignore my advice when I told him he'd get caught taking a cut? Yes. Did he act before thinking about the repercussions of his actions? Yes, all the time. But when push came to shove, Dreamer was loyal to the gang. There was never a more loyal homeboy than your father. A real man. Like you." He pauses. "If only I'd known sooner. If only I could've intervened—"

"There's nothing you could've done," I say. We both know it's true.

Ruben looks back at the lake. I'm about to reassure him when he says the words I've been dreading: "Things have changed since you left. We could use your help, Ghost."

There it is.

From the moment Slim looked at me over that counter, I knew my number was up.

When your gang calls on you, there is no such thing as *no*. There is no such thing as *I can't* or *I'm afraid*. To refuse is to invite a bullet to the back of the head, just like my father did.

So I say the only thing I can.

"Yeah. Whatever you need."

He nods. "Good."

Ruben sends me off without any instructions. For now, my only job is to wait. I know what he'll do. First, he'll send out informants to find out exactly what we're dealing with. Second, he'll come up with a plan. Third, I'll get a call from him telling me what to do next.

After our conversation, I go straight to work at the spa and lose myself in the only thing that makes me feel human: routine. My duties here are more demanding than they are at the gym. I drain the water out of the main Jacuzzi, clean the filters, and scrub down the tile. The disinfectants are strong and make my head hurt, but I work until I'm dog-tired and too fucking numb to feel anything.

No.

That's not true.

Nothing is strong enough to make me feel numb.

See, whenever I think about my father, anger and regret mix inside me until I'm not sure which is which. We barely ever saw eye to eye, but blood is blood.

When I finish my duties, I strip naked. The shower room at

the spa is glass tile the color of a swimming pool. I step in and wash off the dirt and sweat. I scrub hard at my skin but even here there's no getting clean from the truth.

I couldn't protect my father. I couldn't save him.

I hate my own uselessness.

I get dressed and erase all evidence that I've showered here. I stock the towels and toiletries and make sure everything is spotless. I do a final walk-through, lock up, and leave. By the time I get back on the train, my head is still full of scorpions, stinging me from the inside out.

When I arrive at the house, everything is quiet. I slip into the backyard and the garage. I lie down on the bed and even though I should be tired, sleep won't come.

Another truth: the gang needs me. I have to answer the call.

Back in the day, Ruben trusted me completely. It was a point of pride for me that when things needed to get done, I'd do them. I knew the score. I was respected. But now, I know the price for that kind of power. Years of my life, swallowed up by the monster and gone forever. Locked up, useless, as my father was killed and no one could do a goddamn thing about it.

This is no good.

I'm wallowing.

I'm getting anxious.

In the back of the garage, there's an old lawnmower. To distract myself, I reach inside the bag where I keep my stash in an old sock. Carefully, I take out the roll and count the bills. Twelve hundred and sixty-five dollars. Honest money, every cent. Back in the day, this was chump change. I'd walk around with four, five Gs in my pocket. If I spent it, there was always more to be made. My cut from the dealers on the street. My brother and I had our own side hustles, stealing and selling cars to chop shops for parts. Back then, money was easy. We spent it like water.

But now? This roll of bills has more value than anything I've ever earned. Twelve hundred and sixty-five dollars, plus the twenty-two dollars in my wallet. Seven hundred thirty-five more dollars and I've got enough for first and last month's rent plus a deposit on an apartment.

I peel a twenty off the roll and add it to the twenty-two in my wallet. Forty-two bucks for Spider's kids to enjoy an afternoon at the church carnival? Plus whatever Regina can scrape together? It's worth it, to me. That woman deserves a break too.

I put the money back in its hiding place and put my wallet in my backpack.

A dusty shaft of light cuts across the room. Carefully, I wash the small window inside and out with a rag and some water from the garden hose. Clean sunlight fills the garage. I'm still not sleepy, so I grab Ben's toolbox by the door and walk out into the backyard. The lonely half-assembled swing set is calling my name.

The task is hard enough that I can't just fall back into being a robot. There are nuts and bolts to this thing, and crosspieces and chains, and the instructions are ass-backward and make no sense. After two hours of work, I've got the frame put together. After another half hour, the three swings are up, all shiny, and I feel a little bit better about life.

Vanessa comes down the steps with a coffee cup in her hand. I'm surprised—it's Wednesday.

"I thought you were at work." I'm dressed in shorts and a T-shirt. I'm kind of sloppy and it bothers me to be in her company like this.

"Not today," she says. "I rearranged my schedule so that I could study." She's wearing a pair of yoga pants and another tight T-shirt. It's a Dodger baseball shirt, and she looks so goddamn good in it, I say a silent prayer of thanks to Fernando Valenzuela. "Why aren't you asleep?" she asks.

I wish I knew the answer to that question myself. "Just feeling wired, I guess."

She walks over and inspects the swing set. I glance at her bare feet on the grass. Her toenails are painted red. "Looks good."

Sure does. "Wanna test it out?"

She looks at me suspiciously. "I don't know. It's for kids. I might break it."

"Naw, you're crazy, girl," I say. "I tested it out already."

"How much do you weigh?"

"Two-ten and change. If these swings can handle me, they can handle you. Come on. Give it a try."

She puts her coffee cup down on the empty cardboard carton that the swing set came in. She looks at me with a skeptical half smile. "If the chain snaps, you're going to get it."

"If you fall because the chain snaps, I deserve to get it. I put this son of a bitch together." I hold the swing for her. "Come on. Get on already."

Vanessa sits down in the seat and the plastic strap cradles her sweet, round ass. Her hair is long and loose today instead of tied up. The sweet scent of strawberries and vanilla surrounds me—it's her shampoo. She smells so good I want to take a bite. She grabs on to the chains where my hands are and for a second, our fingers brush.

Okay, hold up.

Before we go on, you should know a little about my sex life.

The day of my welcome-back party, Ruben sent two—uh, let's call them *professionals*—to take care of me. God knows I needed their attention after five years of nothing but Mary Poppins and her four sisters. Those women almost broke my back that night. I came so hard and so often that when it was all over, I felt like I'd had five years of sex in twelve hours. I couldn't walk the next day. Ruben made fun of me for weeks.

Since that first marathon, I've been with a couple of other women from the neighborhood. Just a good time, a way to let off steam. But it's been about three months since I've enjoyed that kind of company, and at the contact between Vanessa's fingers and mine, I'm hard as a rock.

"Ready?" I ask.

"Not too hard."

I swallow down a groan. "All right, here we go." I pull back the chain and let go. When she swings back to me, I place my hands flat on her back and give her a gentle push. There's a beautiful curve to her spine. I can feel her backbone against my thumbs.

She doesn't strike me as the kind of woman who would yell, "Wheeee!" She doesn't. She simply smiles and looks at me over her shoulder. Her cheeks get rosy. She builds up a little momentum. Soon her dark hair is flying over her shoulders and she's pointing her toes as she goes forward, higher and higher. I can see the clean soles of her pretty feet. Every time she swings back toward me, I smell her shampoo. I feel her skin through her shirt. I feel everything and I realize for the first time that being around her has quieted my anxiety. Instead of feeling trapped inside my head, I'm free. Right now, I'm just a body, standing here in the open air, in the sunlight, pushing a pretty girl on a swing. I hear occasional cars passing on the street, the breeze through the branches of the avocado tree, the soft squeak of the chains.

"When you were a kid," she says, "swinging on the swings at the park, or at school, did you ever think you could go all the way around?"

"I always tried," I say. "I'd swing as high as I could and jump off at the highest point."

"What would that be? Five feet? Six feet off the ground?"

"Maybe."

"Kids are such daredevils." She's swinging on her own, so I stop pushing her. "I wonder," she says, "if in the history of playground swings, and the history of kids, anyone has ever gone all the way around."

"You'd be a legend." My eyes are on her ass now. Plump. The plastic presses into her flesh.

"A legend," she repeats. "I remember recess being the best time of the day—"

She's in the middle of a sentence when we both hear it—a loud snap.

EIGHT

THE BINDING HOLDING the chain in place comes loose and snaps off the frame. Before Vanessa falls I dive forward to catch her, losing my balance and slipping on the grass. I slide onto my back like I'm stealing second base. She lands in my lap, swing and all, laughing and cursing and screaming at me.

I am so mad at myself. I just assured her something wouldn't happen right before it did.

"Oh my God. Look. I told you. I told you my fat ass would break this swing! So embarrassing. Jesus."

Her cheeks are bright red, her hair is streaming all around me, and I'm so hurt and worried inside that I don't know what to do. Do I laugh, or do I say nothing? Do I make a joke, or do I apologize? It's like I've forgotten what a human being would do in this situation, and all I can do is lie here underneath her, paralyzed.

She turns to see if I'm okay and suddenly the laughter in her eyes is gone, replaced by concern. I don't want her pity. I try to slide away, out of her grip—this is too close, we're too close. But she puts her hand on my arm and pins me to the ground with that straightforward Vanessa Velasco stare.

She raises an eyebrow at me. "Until you were caught."

I smile. "Right. Until we were caught." What a fucking nightmare. I shake off the memory of the night my brother and I were brought in. "So my six months are up. Ruben's calling me back in."

"But what about you? What do you want to do? Stay clean or . . . get dirty again?"

"What I want has nothing to do with anything. It isn't my choice."

"Bullshit. You always have a choice."

I look at her. Maybe I was wrong about her. Maybe growing up in the neighborhood and being married to a homeboy doesn't mean jack. If someone wants to be sheltered, to close their eyes to the truth around them, they're gonna be sheltered no matter what. Choice? If I had a choice, does she really believe I would have chosen this?

"Listen." She leans forward and rubs my forearms, back and forth, bare skin against bare skin. "Grandpa Ben grew up on a cattle ranch. He told me about his cows. Big animals, hundreds of pounds each, a whole herd. One cow got out of line, started doing something it wasn't supposed to do, all he had to do was call his cattle dog to get the cow back. Those dogs weren't big. So you had this huge cow against one little dog."

"What does this have to do with—"

"If the cow was smart, if the cow could see past its history, it would know that all it had to do was trample the dog to death and run. But Grandpa Ben said this never, ever happened. The dog would get low to the ground, bare its teeth, bark, and growl. And all of a sudden, in the mind of the cow, this little dog was a wolf again. The cow would become so afraid, it would rejoin the herd. Anything to avoid the little dog."

"So are you trying to say that I'm a dumbass cow?"

"I'm not trying to say anything—"

"It's not as easy as you think it is, Vanessa," I say.

She narrows her eyes at me. "It's not as complicated as you want it to be, Sal."

I gather her hair off her neck and pull it back very gently. She lets me, tipping her chin up and exposing her neck. Her eyes never leave mine. Her lips part just a little. I can see the tip of her pink tongue in the shadow of her teeth.

"What do you mean by that?" I whisper. I can hear my own heartbeat, pounding blood through my body.

"I mean," she says quietly, "my whole life people have been trying to tell me what I am. A nerd. A good girl. An honor student. A slut. A whore. A failure. They were wrong each time. No one else is going to tell me who I am. Never again."

She's right. But her situation is not my situation. "That may be true for you. For me, it *is* complicated."

"The word *complicated* is nothing but an excuse to keep from thinking clearly and making a clean choice. It's a coward's word."

"A coward's word, huh?" Copying her earlier movement, I trace my fingertips over her cheek and down her beautiful neck. Her chest rises and falls. She takes a deep breath. "Tell me this, then," I say softly. "Why are you allowing this coward ex-con to live on your property? With your grandmother and daughter in the house?"

"The money," she says immediately.

"The money, huh?" I pull her hair a little bit. Her nipples harden through the cotton of her shirt. I'm so hard it's taking all of my willpower not to strip us naked and do what we both really want to do. "And why are you allowing him to touch you like this, out here in broad daylight?"

She reaches forward and runs her hands over my chest, resting them on my shoulders. "Because I like it," she says.

"What else do you like?"

She's looking at me through half-closed eyes, staring down her nose at me as I pull her head back. She runs her hands down my shoulders over my arms. "I like it rough."

Goddamn. Good girl Vanessa Velasco likes it rough. Of course she does. I lean forward until our faces are an inch apart. Her lips smell like fresh coffee. I imagine that they taste like sugar and cream. "And what makes you think I'd give it to you that way?"

"Because you like it rough too."

"How do you know that?"

"Because this is turning you on." She shifts her weight until my hard-on presses against her inner thigh. "I can feel it."

I bite back a groan. She feels so good. "You got an answer for everything?"

"Not everything. But the questions you ask are easy."

This is fun. Teasing each other, testing what the other is made of. A man would have to be out of his mind not to find Vanessa attractive on the outside. But that's nothing compared to what's on the inside. I'm fascinated by her and surprised by the fact that she appears to want to show me more.

"So how about this question?" I stroke her throat with the pad of my thumb. "Can I kiss you?"

Before she can answer, someone taps a car horn in the driveway. Both of us jump backward like teenagers caught making out. Vanessa scrambles to her feet and straightens her hair and clothes just as Chinita pokes her head into the backyard.

"Come on, lovebirds. Help me with these groceries."

"¡Abuelita!" Vanessa stomps toward the driveway without looking back at me. "Why do you say things like that? It's not nice."

Chinita's eyes scan me as I sit sprawled out on the grass. I lean forward to hide the bulge in my shorts, but not fast enough.

"Embarrassing, huh?" the old woman says, winking at me.

"Come on, Salvador. Stop frowning at me and help carry these bags. Let's put those big muscles to use."

After I help Vanessa and her grandmother put away all the groceries, Chinita makes us an early dinner. While she cooks, I sit with Vanessa and Muñeca at the kitchen table. When he finally gets tired of barking at me, Chancla the evil wiener dog settles down on his bed by the back door and chews on what looks like a human femur.

Vanessa and I help Muñeca with her homework. The coloring sheets are bilingual: *gato* and *cat, perro* and *dog*. The little girl is in a Spanish immersion school because Vanessa wants her daughter to know both languages inside and out. I think it's a good idea. Growing up, my friends and I spoke English outside the house and Spanish inside it, and to be honest we didn't know either language that good. English we learned to make our teachers happy. Spanish we learned for everything else—Spanish was the language our parents used to yell at us when we disappointed them, the language they used to talk to their relatives visiting from Mexico, the language reserved for conversations about the big, important things. Topics like, "What are you doing with your life?" Or, "Why are you getting bad grades? Are you trying to give me and your mother a heart attack?" Or, "Why can't you be more like your cousin? He's got a football scholarship. What do you have? No-good friends?"

Vanessa and I watch Muñeca as she colors and hums to herself.

"Did you speak Spanish or English in the house?" I ask Vanessa.

"Both, but English more," she says. "Chinita spoke English better than anyone I knew. Taught me proper grammar. How to be polite in the language."

"Did she learn English from Ben?" I ask.

"From Ben?" Chinita howls with laughter. She's carrying in a big pot of spaghetti to the table. "No way, José. I learned English in school. Back then, we weren't allowed to speak one word of Spanish. If the teacher heard you, you'd get it. Pow! With a paddle. I spoke better English than Vanessa's grandfather did. That Okie with his *y'alls*." She brings out plates and forks. Muñeca carefully puts her homework in a folder and puts the folder in her backpack. Vanessa moves the crayons out of the way while I set the table.

"How did you meet Ben?" I ask.

"He was working in a garage downtown," Chinita says. "He fell in love with me at a dance on the other side of the river."

"Tell Sal where you were working at the time." Vanessa flashes me that sideways smile.

"At a cracker factory. I guess I just got a taste for crackers!" Chinita's laughter soon collapses into coughing and phlegm and for a second she has to excuse herself to the bathroom.

"She always tells that joke," Vanessa says quietly, scooping some spaghetti into Muñeca's bowl. On the napkin, Vanessa puts two gummy vitamins, just like before. "Take your vitamins, *mi'ja*."

When everyone is seated, Chinita says a quick prayer and we eat. I have flashbacks to when I was a kid, a really little kid, when my mom and sister were alive and we used to eat at a table just like this one.

"Vanessa," Chinita says, looking at both of us over the rims of her rhinestone glasses, "tell Sal why you don't date."

"*¡Abuelita!*" Vanessa says. "I'm not having this conversation right now."

Chinita ignores that and turns to me. "She's tried to date. Men from the Internet. She finds them on her phone. I told her it was a bad idea. It didn't go well."

"*Abuelita,* stop."

"What was it, six, seven dates?" Chinita waves a ladle at me. "That's a lot with nothing to show for it, don't you think? Shaved her legs and everything."

Vanessa puts down her fork and rests her forehead on her hand. "You don't have to be so embarrassing."

"What's embarrassing about it? I'm just making conversation."

I can sense that Chinita's jokes are getting to Vanessa a bit more than they should, so I cut in. "I didn't know you could date using the phone."

"What?" Vanessa asks. She looks at me. "What do you mean?"

"I mean, I've been locked up for five years. Phones are a mystery to me. Everything they can do nowadays. It's like *Star Wars* or something." I smile and Vanessa's shoulders relax a little bit. "Why didn't the dates go well?" I ask. "What was wrong with the guys?"

Vanessa sighs and picks up her fork again. "It's not that they were all bad." She glances at Muñeca. The little girl is busy trying to twirl spaghetti onto her fork and not paying attention. "For the most part, they weren't crazy or weird or anything."

"Then what?" I ask.

"It was me."

"You?"

She nods. "I'm just not up for it, I think. I know I should get out there. But I'm so tired all the time. When I'm on a date, I don't know what to talk about except my job and my daughter. I guess there's nothing else in my life I'm excited about, and those topics aren't good for casual conversation."

"They're not?" I ask.

"No, Sal." She pushes the food around on her plate. "I'm so boring. I know it too. When I'm out, I try to be interesting. For example, lots of people like TV. Fine. I try to watch TV so I have something to talk about, but after the first five minutes, I'm asleep on the couch. I don't have time to spend on entertainment, but some people live for it. The next episode of a show. The next concert, the next movie. That's not a part of my life. So when a guy asks, 'Do you watch this show? Have you seen this movie?' I don't have anything to say."

"That doesn't make you boring," I say. "Not to me, anyway."

When dinner is over but before I leave for work, I play Tinkertoys in the living room with Muñeca. I overhear Vanessa talking to her grandmother in the kitchen. They're whispering, but neither one of them is good at whispering so I can hear everything they say.

"Vanessa, Muñeca's in school now. Why don't you go out and enjoy yourself a little bit? While you're still young?"

"Young? Who's young?"

"Stop it. You're only twenty-two. I think you should go out and enjoy yourself. And not with those *pendejos* you meet on the Internet."

"I can take care of myself, *Abuelita*."

"Listen, I know you can take care of yourself. That's not what I'm saying. Have a little fun. Get yourself a boy toy. You work and take care of your kid and that's it. That's all you know of life." Chinita pauses. "You need some gas in the tank."

"*¡Abuelita!*"

"What? It's true. Ever since your grandpa passed away, bless his soul, I run on batteries myself."

"*¡Abuelita!*"

"What? *Hijole,* you're closed up down there by now. That's not healthy."

"*Abuelita,* stop!"

"You know, Sal's not bad. He's built like a truck. What about him?"

My ears perk up like a dog's.

"No. Not Sal," Vanessa says.

In spite of myself, my heart drops a little bit.

"Don't you see the way he looks at you?" Chinita says. "Why not?"

"The Rosas family is pure trouble."

"Sal himself was never trouble. Not really."

Vanessa is quiet for a moment before she says, "That's true. But trouble follows him around." She's not wrong.

"Who cares? He's so handsome. Big too. I like 'em like that."

"*¡Abuelita!*"

"What? Loosen up, Vanessa. Imagine? Oh, a big handsome man for my granddaughter." Chinita switches to English. "He could get your motor revving at last. Grease you up good."

"*¡Abuelita!*"

"What?" Chinita's laughing dissolves into coughing. "It's the truth! I'm just telling the truth."

After I help Muñeca put away all her toys, I tap on the half-open door. Chinita's left the kitchen and Vanessa's sitting at the kitchen counter with a big textbook and a highlighter.

"Thank you again," I say, "for dinner. And the talk."

"You're welcome."

I don't want to go just yet. I clear my throat. "I need your advice."

"What's up?"

"This is just hypothetically speaking, okay? It's not real or anything."

She raises an eyebrow. "Okay."

"So, if a guy wanted to go out with a girl," I say slowly, "but he didn't think he had a chance in hell with her, should he still ask her out?"

Vanessa puts down her highlighter and stares at me. "Why is he so sure he doesn't have a chance with her?"

"I don't know. She's just so . . . different from him."

"In what way?"

"She's responsible. She has big dreams, big plans. He's just kind of"—I bob my head from side to side—"figuring things out."

"Is he a good guy?"

I grin. "More or less."

"Good guys are hard to find," she says. "I think he should give it a shot."

"But what if she says no? Won't he look like an idiot?"

She shrugs. "There are worse things in life than looking like an idiot."

"Like what?"

"Like not taking chances."

We lock eyes. Heat licks my spine, and her cheeks turn bright red. When she looks back down at her textbook, I notice her breath is quicker.

"Thanks," I say quietly. "That's good advice." When I open the back door, I realize I haven't told her something important. I turn around. "One more thing."

"What?" she asks.

"For the record, I don't think you're boring. Not at all."

She smiles, and I leave on that very high note.

NINE

ST. AMARO'S is our local church, the place where everyone is baptized, married, and sent off to the pearly gates—or those other gates, depending on who we're talking about. Hatched, matched, or dispatched, like the old-timers say. A one-stop shop. It's been in the neighborhood for over a hundred years. The building has seen better days, but the parish is strong and growing.

Every year, the church holds a carnival to raise money for its youth programs. There was never enough money for my brothers and me to go to Disneyland or Knott's Berry Farm or Six Flags, so the church carnival was our theme park, our wonderland.

Regina is right when she warns me the money won't last. Between cotton candy, darts, and rides for three kids, sixty bucks is nothing. But when I see Spider's kids running around the booths, playing with the Chinese finger traps and slap bracelets they got as consolation prizes, I see three happy faces, and the expense feels worth it. When the littlest one knocks out after a couple hours, I watch as Regina carries him home, the other two kids following close behind. Regina looks over her shoulder at me and gives me a sad smile. "Thanks, Ghost," she says. "This was a good idea."

I go back to the house. I've got a few hours before I have to catch my bus to work. It's a warm evening and as I walk up the driveway, I see Vanessa sitting on the front porch steps with a glass of lemonade. She's wearing office clothes—a black dress and heels.

"Hey," I say. "You had work today?"

"A couple meetings. Restaurant people don't really do weekends." She looks at me over the rim of her glass. "What trouble have you been up to?"

"Just the carnival." I sit next to her on the porch steps and tell her about Regina and the kids. "You want to take Muñeca up there?"

Vanessa shakes her head. "Maybe tomorrow. She'll get too excited before bedtime. Chinita's watching her now."

Sunset has turned her eyes a golden brown. She's wearing that string of pearls. If I touched it, it would be warm from her skin, and the thought makes me feel raw all over. "How about you? You want to go check it out with me?"

"What?"

"Yeah," I say. "Come with me. Let's walk around the carnival."

"Are you kidding?" she says. "I'm not going over there. Like some stupid teenager."

"What would you know about being a stupid teenager?"

"Enough."

"But we were never really stupid teenagers."

"Of course we were."

"When? When did that happen? You were in school all the time, chasing those As. I had to look after my brothers with my dad gone all the time. When did we have time to be stupid?"

She looks at me and cocks an eyebrow.

I laugh. "I mean, stupid in the way normal people are stupid when they're young." I stand up and take her hand. "Come on." She puts the empty glass down on the step. I can't remember the last time I held hands with anyone, but this feels comfortable and strange at the same time. Her hand is soft and small, cold from holding her drink, and when she stands up I catch that strawberry and vanilla scent of her hair.

We stroll the two short blocks to the church and walk in through the gate. Even though I was just here, the sun's gone down and now the rides are all lit up, a hundred colors. The littlest kids are gone and now it's adults—well, adults pretending to be stupid teenagers, anyway.

We're surrounded by people from the neighborhood, but Vanessa doesn't take her hand out of mine. She's not afraid of me, and just as important, she's not afraid to be seen with me. Damn. Part of me wants to take out a bullhorn and announce, "Everyone. Look. Vanessa Velasco is holding my hand. You thought I was a just a lowlife. You were right, I am, but now this beautiful woman is holding my hand so it doesn't really matter what you think."

Goofy and a little light-headed, I lead her through the crowd. Without asking her, I buy her a churro. I let go of her hand to pay the vendor. I put the churro in her right hand and immediately take her left one again. "Eat it," I say.

"It's full of sugar. I'm on a diet."

"Fuck your diet. Eat the goddamn churro," I growl. I watch her as she takes a bite through her laughter. "How is it?"

"Hot. It's good."

"Let me try some."

She's short, so she holds the churro up high. "You're so big," she says. "You're like this giant bear walking around a carnival." Before I can take a bite, she shoves it in my face. I laugh. Sugar flies down my shirt and now we're both giggling, hands still locked together. I wipe the sugar off with my arm and look down at her. Those rosy cheeks, those beautiful dark eyes, that deep honest laughter of hers. I want to kiss her so bad I hurt—like, physically, I hurt. Everything seems to disappear around us, blurring out while Vanessa comes into sharper focus.

We exchange a look. "You okay?" she asks.

"Kind of."

"Easy, Ghost." She pats my arm and turns toward the games. "Hey, win me something."

She's trying to distract me, and I let her. Because honestly, what man doesn't like proving his masculinity with carnival games? I haven't met one yet that doesn't go completely stupid about these when it comes to impressing a girl. I reach into my wallet—that billfold's getting very light—and put some money down for the attendant. He puts two softballs in front of me and gets out of the way. I pick up one of the balls.

Vanessa finishes off the churro and, because she's a mean old thug on the inside, says, "I thought you were a catcher."

"Just that one time," I say. "It wasn't so bad. I got six packages of ramen for it."

"What flavor?"

"Spicy chicken."

She snorts.

Salvador Rosas's Book of Life Lessons, Volume One, Lesson One: Get yourself a girl who can joke about prison sex.

I wind up and throw the ball hard, hard enough that it makes a loud crack against the back wall. The milk bottles go flying off their little stand. Vanessa cheers. The bored-looking carny reaches up and pulls down the nearest stuffed toy, a stoned penguin with sleepy eyes, a red, yellow, and green beret, and long woolly dreads.

"But I don't want the stoned penguin," Vanessa says.

"Why not?" I ask. "It's kind of funny."

"I don't want to explain weed to my kid just yet, okay?" she says.

The carny raises his eyebrows. "Which one, then?"

She points to the Hello Kitty in the far corner of the booth. The carny looks like he's not going to do it but when I mad-dog him, he reaches for the metal hook behind the counter. With some effort, he gets Vanessa her Hello Kitty. She gives it a big hug before she takes my hand again. She's so cute right now, twenty-two going on twelve.

"Did any of your Internet dates throw a softball hard enough to win you a Hello Kitty?"

She shakes her head. "No."

I've got a few ride tickets left in my pocket so I lead her toward the Ferris wheel. We get on.

"We're too big. It's going to break," she whispers, just like she did before getting on the swing set. "This thing is for little kids."

When I sit down, something squeaks. I look at her worried face. To put her at ease, I swing the carriage back and forth. It creaks like an old pirate ship, but nothing bad happens. "See? We'll be fine."

The carny looks at me with a frown. "Sir, could you please stop that?"

I nod and settle down. "Oh, sorry, sorry."

Vanessa shakes her head at me and sits down. The carny places the safety bar across our laps. Vanessa secures the Hello Kitty against the side of the carriage. I'm squished into my corner. I pull my arm free, lay it across Vanessa's shoulders, and pull her in close. Now we're comfortable. She cuddles against me, and now I know why the Ferris wheel is such a beloved ride.

The ride starts with a burst of music like a jack-in-the-box. We glide backward and over a couple of times. The Ferris wheel stops to let other passengers on. At the very top, our carriage swings back and forth before it goes still.

Now I can see my neighborhood from a different viewpoint, high above. The lights of the carnival are bright and beautiful. The smells of tacos, hot dogs, and popcorn fill my nose. People pack the church parking lot. Cars line the street, and in the surrounding houses, lights in the windows show where families are talking or watching TV or having dinner.

"How are you doing?" I ask.

"I'm all right."

She's looking at the same things I am. I wonder if she is seeing the same details. I stroke her hair and take another risk. "So what do you think?"

"About what?"

"Starting something with me?"

She takes a deep breath but doesn't say anything.

"What are your doubts?" I say.

"Are you kidding?" She snorts. "You're seriously asking me that?"

I laugh a little. "Okay, well. Besides the obvious."

"You have your own life. I have mine. You're trying to rebuild from the ground up. I'm trying to secure my daughter's future. We're heading in different directions."

She isn't wrong. Life has disappointed her in such deep and cruel ways, I don't blame her for protecting herself. But even as she tells me this—the truth about how we're not right for each other—I feel how right it is to talk to her, to hold her hand, to show her who I am. "I have an idea," I say. "Probation."

"What?"

"I'm only around for two months, right?"

"Right."

"Spend those two months with me." I look into her eyes. "I want to be with you, Vanessa."

"Sal—"

"I'll be gone before I have a chance to disappoint you." When the words leave my mouth, I try to ignore how pathetic they sound. "We're adults, not dumb kids. We won't lose our heads." I run my fingers through her silky hair. "I swear to God, every time I look at you, I feel . . ." I reach for the most honest word I can find. "Thirsty."

Vanessa says nothing but shivers under my touch.

I hear a distant car alarm, a barking dog, and kids laughing. Dull orange streetlights shine on the trees in the park. I can see the inky black lake through their branches. Next to me, Vanessa is warm and alive. She's letting me hold her and I can feel her breathing. I take a deep breath and think, *This is home*. For better or worse, this is my home, it is me and I am it.

"It's nice up here, ain't it?" I whisper.

She nods. "Yeah."

"What are you thinking?"

"I'm thinking you're crazy."

"That's because I am."

Those dark eyes burn into me, full of challenge. "Tell me something."

"Anything."

"Are you sleeping around? Am I just another ride in your carnival? Ferris wheel, bumper cars, carousel?"

I smile. "Say yes to this, and you'll be the only one I'll ride."

She snorts. "Jackass."

"What else do you want to know?"

"Prisons are filthy. Have you been tested?"

She's right to ask. "Once when I got out. Once last May."

"Last May? Why?"

"The last woman I slept with had some kind of scare and asked me to get tested a week after we were together, so I did.

All clear. I haven't touched anyone since." Not true—I touch myself, but I leave that part out.

"You haven't had sex in three months? Why not?" She looks at me skeptically.

I shrug. "No time. Extra shifts, more work. I need that money." I brush my thumb against her jaw. "You?"

Her smile fades a little. "It's embarrassing."

Vanessa Velasco, embarrassed? In front of me? "The things I've done versus the things you've done?" I say. "You have nothing to be embarrassed about."

She rests her cheek against my shoulder and closes her eyes. "I'm ashamed to say it out loud."

"Say it, and see how you feel afterward."

She takes a deep breath. "Five years."

I blink. What? How could a fine-ass woman in the prime of her life, who looks like a walking wet dream only hotter, live celibate as a nun for five years? I'm speechless. Then I realize— it's Sleepy. She's been faithful to her husband. A sudden ache in my heart surprises me, and I say the first word that pops into my mind: "Fuck."

"I've had lots of opportunities," she says softly, "but none of them felt right."

I can understand that. "How about me? Do I feel right?"

When she looks up at me, the lights of the Ferris wheel sparkle in her dark eyes like stars. Her voice is so soft the wind almost takes it away. "Two months?"

I reach forward and cup her cheek in my hand. Her skin is soft. I trace the tip of my thumb across her cheekbone, back and forth. "Two months." Her skin is delicate, smooth and brown— even darker than mine.

"My kid can't know there's anything going on between us."

"Okay."

"Don't play with me. Don't lie to me. When it's done it's done."

"Okay."

She takes my hand. "Two months."

We're quiet for a long time. The lights flash pink and green.

"I'm going to make my move now," I whisper.

"Now?"

"Now."

I close my eyes and hold my breath. When we kiss at last, I'm surprised that what we share is quiet, shy, and polite. Vanessa's mouth is small but her lips are full and firm. She tastes like cinnamon and sugar. I can feel the grit of a grain of sugar on the corner of her lips and quickly, I lick it away with the tip of my tongue.

When I do this, a sound like a sigh comes from her throat. I put my hand on the back of her neck and pin her gently against me. I'm hot—hot all over. She's trembling. I can feel her hands rise up and rest on my chest. She's rubbing me through the cotton of my T-shirt. I flex a little into her palms, gratified when I hear her make that same sound again. She likes touching me. Good.

When Vanessa opens her mouth just a tiny crack, I swear invisible sunlight washes over me, bathing me with her heat. I'm under her spell. The kiss is so good, we don't stop. We keep going even when the Ferris wheel begins spinning again. The ride picks up speed and a cool wind blows over us. The metal carriages creak and groan, the tin-can jack-in-the-box song repeats itself. My eyes are still closed, so I seem to feel, hear, and taste everything at a higher level. Whether I'm dizzy because of the ride or because of Vanessa, I don't know. I don't care.

All of a sudden the carnival is a wonderland again, and I'm lost in it, lost in its pleasures.

That first kiss is followed by another, and another. Vanessa lets me kiss her when we get off the Ferris wheel. We stroll along the crowded walkway next to the line of carnival rides. We hold hands and don't care who sees us, which is strange to me, because everyone here knows us. I think back to what she said about being told who she is—a nerd, a whore, a failure—and I see the truth. She really doesn't care what people call her or think of her. I wonder if I'll ever be in that position and what it will take to get me there.

Until then, I hold her hand like a balloon I don't want to lose.

If there ever was a moment for happiness, almost pure happiness, I'm thinking this is it. I was locked up at nineteen and didn't breathe fresh air until twenty-four. It's like I died and came back to life, and here at the gates of the cemetery is this angel I couldn't even dream up, she's that perfect.

My angel is walking around in black high heels.

"Don't your feet hurt?" I ask.

She shrugs. "I'm used to it."

"I didn't ask if you're used to it, I asked if they hurt."

"I guess so. But I'm used to it, like I said."

She's wearing a black dress with no sleeves and that pearl necklace. "Ain't you cold?" I wish I had a jacket to put on her.

"I'm not cold. It's summer. I'm fine."

"Are you sure?"

"Will you stop?"

"Stop what?"

"Fussing over me?"

"Am I fussing?" I guess I am. "I just want you to be comfortable."

We take another lap around the parking lot and it feels too small. I want it to be big, big like a football field, big like the whole world, so that I can keep walking with Vanessa.

She says, "Hey, I want another."

"Another what? Churro? Hello Kitty? Name it."

"A kiss."

"Coming right up."

I lean down and give her a sweet one. I nip at her bottom lip and she grips me tighter.

"I want more of you," I whisper in her ear.

"Oh yeah?"

"Take me upstairs with you. The bedroom."

"My bedroom? Ha, no."

I'm not going to ask her to meet me in the garage. Even I have my limits. But when? And where? My brain races. Trying to impress a lady when you have no money in your pocket is difficult at best. Then I get an idea.

"Okay." I look at my phone for the time. "What are you doing tomorrow night?"

"What I do every night." She rolls her eyes. "I study, do housework, and watch my kid."

"Does Chinita have anything tomorrow night? Cards, bingo?"

"Sunday night? No."

"Ask her to watch Muñeca. I want to take you with me."

"Where?"

"Don't worry about it."

She frowns at me. "Where are you taking me?"

"It's a surprise."

"Ah, no. Forget surprises. I don't like surprises."

"You'll like this one, baby. I promise."

I kiss her again, right on her frown, and turn her back toward the wall so that I can reach down and sneak a feel of her ass. Through the thin fabric of her skirt, I can feel the skinny straps of her thong. She steps closer to me, pressing her body against my hard-on and pinning it between us.

"Easy," she whispers. "You're going to get us both arrested."

I laugh against her lips. "Not me. Just you. Arrested for looking so damn fine."

Lights from the rides around us wash over her face—pink, blue, green, gold. "You are so cheesy," she says.

I'm about to lean down and kiss her again when I feel a sudden tap on my shoulder. I jump backward, angry at myself that I let someone get the drop on me. It's an old habit, keeping my head on a swivel, and here I am, not paying attention. This is deep in ESHB territory but still. Still.

Behind me is not a gangster but a small skinny man in dark green coveralls. I recognize him—Miguel, the church groundskeeper. He's worked at the church forever. He's in his forties but he looks much older, and he has a facial tic that causes him to blink a lot, like he's got something in his eyes or someone is shining a bright light in his face.

"Salvador," he says in a small voice, "I'm sorry to bother you, you and your, your lady here. Hello, miss."

Reluctantly, I let go of Vanessa, reach over, and shake his hand. It's like a bundle of sticks. "How are you doing, Miguel?"

"Okay, okay," he says. "I saw you here earlier and I wanted to give you something, but you left before I had the chance." He's wearing a utility belt and attached is a big ring of keys. He reaches down and detaches it. "Your father—I was so sorry to hear about your father. I hope they find him. I hope he turns up."

I nod. Even here in Wonderland, I can't escape the truth. To be polite, I say, "Yeah, thank you. I hope so too."

Miguel's hands have a slight tremor. "Before I went into rehab, your father became one of my good friends. We spent some time together, and I have a lot of respect for him. A lot, Salvador. He's a nice guy."

Rehab? So Miguel and Dreamer used to shoot up together. "Yup. Sure."

The keys jangle like bells as Miguel's skinny, shaky hands pull a smaller key ring free. "I've been keeping this with me, just as a reminder of him. He forgot his keys at my place a few days before he disappeared. I didn't want to get rid of them, but I didn't know who to give them to until I saw you today. They might be important."

He hands over the smaller ring. There are three keys there, two ordinary-looking house keys and one smaller key, maybe to a padlock. Vanessa and I look at the keys and at each other. She knows I can see his ghost in them, my father's ghost, in these everyday objects he probably touched a thousand times and carried in his pocket like coins.

"Anyhow, that's all I wanted to tell you." Miguel tips the brim of his baseball cap and nods to himself. "I hope they find him, Salvador. I hope he's okay."

I shake Miguel's hand again and the groundskeeper walks away, a nervous bouncy walk that jangles the remaining keys on his belt. I slip the small key ring into my pocket.

"That was weird," I say to Vanessa. She's cradling and petting the Hello Kitty in her arms like it's a real cat. Her own nervous energy is coming out as she studies my face. "How are you doing?"

I shrug. The conversation leaves me with a weird, unsettled feeling in my stomach. "All right, I guess."

We head back to the house. "Was your dad always on drugs?" Vanessa asks.

I'm not surprised by her direct question. That's her style. "Not always. Just after my mom and sister died. On and off. I guess it got really bad when Eddie and me got our asses locked up."

"I don't recall a time when my mom was clean," she says quietly. "Sleepy struggled with it even before we got together. It got him, eventually. Me, I won't get near it. No needle, no pipe, no pills. Weed was as far as I'd go."

"Same," I say.

"ESHB was always here," she says. "*Abuelita* told me the gang helped the community a lot back in the day. When people couldn't trust the cops. When businesses needed protection from other gangs. When there was no one else to go to, *varrio* Hollenbeck had our backs." She pauses. "But then the drugs came. And the guns." She squeezes my hand, and I feel her pain. "I wish they hadn't."

I'm quiet. The cars Eddie and I stole for the gang—those were a drop in the bucket. Drug sales are ESHB's lifeblood. The gang taps money from the streets and sends it up to the Organization. Our operation is lucrative, in the millions. But the price? Violence and an uneasy peace with our product. Ruben once said to me, "If not us, then who? Don't fool yourself, *mi'jo*. Our neighborhood is safer when we have control of it."

"Do you ever think of moving out? Leaving Hollenbeck?" I ask Vanessa.

"I thought a lot about it when my daughter was born. We could've sold the house and left."

"Why didn't you?"

She squeezes my hand again. "Because this is my home," she says. "A lot of good people live and work here. Generations and generations have raised their families here. We're a part of this neighborhood as much as any gang."

I walk Vanessa up to the front porch. The empty lemonade glass is still on the front step. I pick it up and hand it to her. She pulls me in for one more kiss. Her hands are full so I take the opportunity to touch her face and her throat, to stroke the back of her neck underneath her dark hair, to run my fingertips over the warm, smooth pearls of her necklace. Her skin is hot. I slip her a little tongue and she does the same to me, and we stroke each other with the tips of our tongues, learning each other's flavor. I'm so turned on I'm half crazy, a heartbeat away from grabbing her and carrying her off into the shadows, when I hear the little paws and storm of barks behind her.

Chancla charges and mashes his evil face against the screen door. Muñeca follows behind him and comes outside, blocking the dog from escaping and mauling me.

"Mommy!" Muñeca holds her arms out. She's wearing her pajamas.

Vanessa hugs her. "Hello, *mi'ja*. Ready for your bedtime story?"

The girl's eyes are on me as she nods.

"Did you see what Sal got for you?" Vanessa holds up the Hello Kitty. "It's not your birthday or Christmas. It's a special surprise gift."

Muñeca grabs the stuffed cat and squishes it just like Vanessa did when I won it for her. Vanessa leans down and kisses the top of Muñeca's head.

The moment feels like it should be private, and yet it's not. Vanessa is including me in it, and I feel welcome. I feel right.

Time is passing even though I don't want it to. "I'd better get going if I'm gonna make my bus," I say quietly.

"What do you say to Sal?" Vanessa whispers to the little girl.

"Thank you!" Muñeca says, kissing Hello Kitty's yellow nose.

"Thank you," Vanessa echoes. "That's right. Thank you, Sal."

I walk down the porch steps and look up at Vanessa. "See you tomorrow night?"

Muñeca holds on to Vanessa's skirt and gives me the same direct stare as her mother's.

"Tomorrow night," Vanessa says. "Okay."

TEN

I PASS the next twenty-four hours in a haze.

Work, exercise, sleep, food. I run through my routine.

But all I can think about is her.

When it's time to go, Vanessa drives. Because the bus and the train rides take so long, I forget how close Santa Monica really is to East L.A.—my two worlds are just a few miles apart.

In the dark car, I reach over and rest my hand on her knee. Tension is like a thick chain pulled tight between us. We don't move. We don't talk. Minutes pass. If she reaches over to touch me back, I think I might burst into flames.

Vanessa exits the freeway and I direct her to a parking space in an alley. After we park the car, she follows me to an unmarked door. She's wearing a hoodie, a Dodgers baseball cap, and workout pants that show off her amazing ass. I still haven't told her what we're doing.

I unlock the heavy metal door and lead her into the dark. I flip some switches and light fills the empty hallway. The keypad for the alarm is beeping, so I punch in the code to disarm it. I lock the door behind us.

"Where are we?" Her eyes are wide. She's nervous.

"You'll see." I walk down the long hallway past the office and storage rooms. I hang my backpack up on a hook. At last she spots an old sandwich board propped up against the wall, showing the logo of the business, Serenity Day Spa.

"You brought me to your work?" she asks.

"Yup. Come on."

I open the frosted glass door to the main spa and turn on all the lights. It's an enormous, cave-like room, with high ceilings and walls tiled in blues and greens. I flip another switch and start the waterfall that drops from the ceiling to the pool below. Vanessa follows me from room to room as I turn on all the Jacuzzis and the steam room. I watch her as she follows me, impressed but jumpy, afraid we're about to get caught. Afraid we don't belong.

"How did you find this place?" she asks.

"The owner of the gym where I work. He referred me."

"How long have you been working here?"

"Just a little over six months."

"You clean this whole place by yourself?"

"There's a daytime crew. But I do the big stuff at night."

"We're going to get in trouble, Sal," she says. "I don't want you to lose your job."

"This place is mine just like anyone else's."

"But—"

"The owners wouldn't care that I brought you here. I do good work. I'm cheap. They love me."

"I don't know—"

"Vanessa, will you just relax? We'll be fine. Here." I lead her to the reception desk, where I turn on the sound system. It's programmed to a kind of meditation music that puts me to sleep, which I guess is the point. I flip through the stations and find one just for us.

"Look. Lowrider oldies."

She slowly shakes her head at me. "You're crazy."

"What? You're all high-strung. This music—it'll relax you. You'll see."

"Forever Mine" by the O'Jays starts playing and I turn it up. Vanessa still looks skeptical so I take her in my arms. As we slow-dance, I rest my head on the top of her baseball cap, the cloth button right under my chin. Absentmindedly, I wonder if Vanessa and I, like the people in the song, could be made for each other.

When the song ends, I kiss her. "Give me two hours," I whisper against her lips. "Enjoy yourself. Showers, steam room, Jacuzzis, sauna, hot and cold pools. There are robes and towels in the locker room. Shampoo, lotion—whatever you want. There are magazines and a TV in the lounge. Read. Take a nap. Relax."

She glances down at the information brochures on the receptionist's desk. The prices are listed there. "I could never afford to visit this place," she says.

"Not 'never.' Just 'not yet.'" Wow, where did that come from? I almost sound optimistic.

Her dark eyes search my face. "You're full of surprises. Secrets."

"Not secrets. Secrets are bad," I say. "I just have things I don't tell everyone. Only people who deserve to know. That's not keeping secrets. That's just me being me."

"Ghost." She touches my lips. "Now I know why they call you that."

She doesn't know the truth about how I got my name. A dark feeling touches my heart but I drive it away—no, not now. Not here. That feeling doesn't belong anywhere near us tonight.

"Are you sure this is okay?" she asks.

"Yes. I'm sure."

Wealthy women use this place as a sanctuary, a place

where they can forget the outside world and the things that worry them. Vanessa has plenty to worry about. I am fully aware of my limitations—I can't solve her problems for her. But I can help lift the weight of them for a little while. I can help her get strong enough to handle her problems on her own.

I kiss her again. "Go play, baby."

With a smile, she disappears into the locker room.

Just like the night Barry busted his head open on a chair, I do eight hours of work in two. I work like a goddamn machine, not thinking, not stopping, just go, go, go.

I skim all the pools. I scrub and hose down the showers. I clean the bathrooms. I mop up all the floors. I restock the toiletries and pile the shelves with clean towels. I change a light-bulb that's gone all blinky. I dust the lounge, straighten the magazines, and water all the potted plants.

As if she can predict what I'm going to do next, Vanessa moves one step ahead of me, teasing me with her presence in the maze of rooms. As soon as I go into the shower room, she moves into the steam room. When it's time for me to go to the steam room, she moves to the sauna. Always one step ahead.

I'm vacuuming when she passes me in the hallway. She slaps my ass and winks at me. Her hair is tied up in a towel and her little body is wrapped up in one of those big robes. I see the soles of her bare feet as she walks away from me. I would follow those feet anywhere because those are the feet that led her to me. I thank them silently. *Thank you, feet, for bringing Vanessa to me.*

And just like that, I'm dazed again.

I shake it off.

Concentrate, Sal.

I finish up by spraying the whole spa with the expensive room freshener the owner had custom made. Panting and sweating like I've just run a marathon, I put away the cleaning supplies and take out all the trash.

When I'm finally done, I can't see Vanessa anywhere. Shaking with anticipation, I strip and hop into one of the showers. I run the water as hot as it will go and scrub everything away. As the water swirls down the drain, three things hit me, all at once.

First, I'm about to make love to a woman I want like my next breath.

Next, we have this place to ourselves.

Third, no one will find us here.

I dry off, brush my teeth, and shave. I put on a robe, reach into my backpack, and slip a few important accessories into my pocket. Then I take one last look in the mirror.

Not bad, I guess. I run my hand through my hair. Water makes it even curlier and darker, almost blue-black. Without any stubble, my face is lean, sharp—I'm in good shape right now. But I have no illusions. As far as looks go, I'm way down on the Rosas family totem pole. My father was a legendary player. My younger brother is the handsome one, followed by my youngest brother, who's growing up to be a pretty boy. Me? I look a little like a brick, all hard edges and right angles. Luckily for me, some women like bricks.

Make this good for her, fucker.

I walk down the hall to the big Jacuzzi. The room is filled with the sound of falling water. Steamy heat rises up and fogs the tiles on the walls. Vanessa is here, sitting at the far end of the pool. She's resting her head on a folded-up towel and the water bubbles up to her neck. Her eyes are closed and her face is relaxed and I realize I've never seen her sleep. There's something intimate about it, like someone letting down their guard completely in front of someone else. An expression of trust.

I take off the robe and step down into the hot water. When I hiss from the heat, she opens her eyes. Her face is still, but her eyes follow me as I move toward her.

Men love to look at women.

Is the opposite true?

I splash my chest with hot water. She stares, taking in my muscles, my tats. Her eyes linger on the rose tattoo over my heart—my brother and I got them to match our father's. Up and down my arms and torso are dozens of tattoos. Names of long-buried friends. Ghosts, spiderwebs, skulls—the marks of death in life, to show I'm not afraid. And across my chest, a big *placa* —EASTSIDE. Where I'm from. Who I am.

Close to her now, I rub my hands over my abs, the abs I worked so hard to get. The water comes up to my waist, so she can't see how hard I am, but when her lips curve into a small smile, I know she knows. Of course she knows. I'm so keyed up I think I could make this water boil with my body heat alone.

I'm standing right in front of her. At last she lifts her head and sits up. Her smooth shoulders rise out of the water. Lights on the bottom of the pool illuminate her beautiful brown skin. I still can't see her breasts, but if I squint I can see the suggestions of her nipples through the bubbles on the surface of the water.

I can't help myself. I reach down into the water and wrap my hand around my cock. I give it a single pump, then rub my aching balls. She keeps her eyes locked on mine, but I see a muscle in her throat tighten as she swallows.

Over the sound of falling water, I say, "Only if you want this, Vanessa. We can still turn back."

She doesn't say a thing. Instead, she stands up. Water runs off her skin and for the first time, I see her naked body. Her softly muscled arms. Her sharp collarbones. Her full, round breasts with dark nipples that shrink and tighten as soon as they hit the cool air. I watch, hypnotized, as she fills her cupped hands with water and drizzles the water over her chest.

Droplets race down her breasts and drip off the tips of her nipples.

My mind goes completely blank.

When I grab her and pull her close, her skin sizzles against my chest. I cover her hot lips with mine and kiss her like I'll die if I don't. I swallow her surprised gasp, then use my lips to slowly explore that smooth, firm flesh of hers. We kiss and kiss and kiss. Her fingers dig into my biceps and when she opens her mouth, I press the tip of my tongue against hers. When she moves her sweet little tongue against mine, my knees almost buckle under the water.

I wrap one arm around her waist and press my hand flat between her shoulder blades. When I hold her tighter, her moan vibrates through my whole body. Her eyes close and her head rolls back. I kiss her chin, her jaw, her throat. I drop kisses along the side of her neck and when I find her pulse, I lick it, meeting the quick little flicker with the tip of my tongue.

"Sal," she gasps. "Oh God."

Finding my balance, I bend my knees and lift her a little higher. Her smooth inner thighs rest across the tops of my quads. If I shifted my weight just a little, I could slide her right onto my throbbing dick. Just the thought makes my dick throb even harder—but I catch myself. I tell myself to take it slower—to make it good for her.

"Are you okay?" I whisper.

She rests her hands lightly on my shoulders. Her eyes are glassy and her cheeks are red. Water clings to her eyelashes and she's panting. She's breathing so hard, I'm convinced that if I just reached down and touched her, I could make her come in a heartbeat.

But no—slower.

Slower, I remind myself. Make it good.

I tip her back, just until her gorgeous tits are level with my face. I want to squeeze them, but my hands are full holding her. So I do the next best thing. I kiss them. Against my lips, her skin breaks out into goosebumps. When I reach her left nipple, I suck it into my mouth and circle the tender tip with my tongue. She closes her eyes tighter. Her legs clamp around me, and her nails dig softly into my shoulders. That beautiful nipple turns hard between my lips. I release it with a loud, filthy smack and do the same to her right nipple. I alternate, one and then the other, back and forth, until they're so stiff, the pink tips could cut glass.

I drop her down low and kiss her lips again. She drags her hands through my hair, and I shiver at the sensation of her nails against my scalp. We've just started, and from the way she touches me, the way she holds me, I know the truth.

This is going to be a mind-blowing night.

I whisper in her ear, "You want me to tell you what to do, baby?"

Fire blazes in her eyes. We both know she's a tough woman. What I want to tell her—what I hope she knows—is nothing turns me on more than a tough woman who submits to me in bed. A woman who rules her own world, but lets me rule her in bed? Fuck, there is nothing hotter than that.

She cups my face in her hands and kisses me, deep and hungry. She rubs her body against mine in a slow rhythm, squeezing her thighs and rubbing her breasts against my chest. Then she breaks the kiss, looks me in the eyes, and says, "Yes."

Quietly but firmly, I tell her to get out of the pool, dry off, and put on the bathrobe I just took off. I watch her climb the steps out of the Jacuzzi, my eyes feasting on her. I watch the water tumble off her, first her back, then her waist, then her breathtaking ass. It's round and tight and I can't help it—my hand goes down to my dick again and I begin to jack myself off slowly under water.

She dries herself off, then turns around to face me. Now I see all of her, all at once: gorgeous tits, little waist, big luscious hips. There's a neat patch of dark hair between her legs. Before I can really get an eyeful, she reaches down, slips the bathrobe over her shoulders, and ties the belt.

I squeeze the shaft of my cock and run the tip of my thumb over the head.

"Sit on the edge. Put your feet in the water."

She hikes up the robe and does what I say. I move through the water to her. My dick is still in my hand. I let go, reach down, and run my thumbs along the arches of her pretty feet. She smiles. I run my hands up her calves and rest my palms on her hot, smooth inner thighs. She's staring at me, eyes half-closed, as I pull her thighs apart. The robe gapes open, but I can't see past the shadow of the cloth.

"How long?" I ask. "How long since you let a man touch you?"

"Five years." Her voice is deep and ragged.

"Why now? Why me?"

"Because you feel right."

Music to my ears. "Why me?" I ask again, wanting her to say it again. Instead, she says something even better.

"Because I trust you."

I lower myself into the pool and hot water washes over my back. I spread her legs wider.

"Lean back," I say.

She's breathing hard. She leans back on the tiles, resting on her elbows and looking down at me between her legs.

"Perfect," I tell her. My heart is beating itself to death against my rib cage as I open the robe, exposing her at last.

I'm no stranger to pussy. When you're a gangster, it flies at you from all directions. But when I look down at Vanessa's pussy, my dick falls in love at first sight. Framed by her short, neatly trimmed hair, her lips are plump and perfect, the color of sweet, dark plums. Hands shaking, I run the tips of my thumbs up and down her lips, grazing her tender flesh as I watch her face. She inhales sharply, as if I've burned her, but lets out a shaky breath when I repeat the movement, this time slower.

"It's beautiful," I say. "You're beautiful."

A minute passes, then two. I keep stroking her with the lightest touch I can. Up close, I watch her pussy transform. The lips swell and grow slick. The folds shift and soon I can see the tiny tip of her pretty clitoris, hardening. My mouth waters for it but still I hold back. More strokes, as light as a feather. Her pussy opens for me, flaring out like a flower, and soon I can see her beautiful pink opening. I've barely touched her. I haven't done anything except pet her lips, and already she's trembling for me, hot and wet.

I slide my hands under her round ass and pull her closer to the edge of the Jacuzzi. Now her pussy is level with my mouth. Again I run my thumbs up and down the slippery lips. When I spread her open at last, she moans. She's so wet, I watch her pretty pink pussy drool onto the tiles.

At last, I lean forward and kiss her. She tastes like heaven—sweet and salty—and I lap at her, drinking her in. When I push the tip of my tongue into her, she jerks forward. Her eyes are shut tight. For the first time, I realize she's opened the robe completely. Her hands wander lazily over her tits, rubbing them, playing with her nipples. She's high on sex, doped up. I watch her face when my tongue finally finds her clit. She gasps and thrusts her hips forward, pushing herself greedily against my face.

That's it, I tell myself. Now slowly, take her home.

I lick her hard little clit from the root to the tip, my tongue slipping through her folds. She's dripping onto my chin so it's not hard for me to reach up, stroke her opening with the tip of my finger, and slide it in up to the first joint. Her walls are slick and tight—tighter than any pussy I've ever seen. As I lick her clit up and down and she bears down on my finger, I realize I've got to be careful with this girl—she hasn't done this in five years, and she's tight as a fist.

Gently, I press my finger deeper and deeper until it's inside her all the way. The surface of her skin is feverish, but inside, she's like an oven. Under the water, my dick twitches, impatient. I pull my finger out halfway, then thrust it back in. She flinches, but I soothe the ache by sucking gently on her lips.

I close my eyes. Her flavor and scent fill me. Her clit swells and sweetens like a hard candy against my tongue. This is the finest pussy I've ever tasted. I feast on her, holding back and surging forward, teasing her orgasm. Slowly, secretly, I slide in a second finger alongside the first. Her muscles squeeze me, cracking my knuckles. I'm drowning in her wetness.

She's breathing hard. When her thighs clench and she pinches her nipples hard, I begin to fuck her with my fingers, dragging them out before pressing them deeper and deeper. I zero in on the tenderest spot of her clit and tongue her with a steady, savage rhythm. She's trembling. Her climax is playing with her, coming to the surface before diving back down.

At last, Vanessa takes one deep breath and holds it. She squeezes her eyes shut and her mouth freezes open. Her pussy seizes my fingers. I grind my tongue against her angry little clit and she comes so hard, I can feel the vibrations down my arm. I keep licking. I don't stop. A long, rolling orgasm seizes her, and in my mouth I taste her release, sweeter than any candy.

ELEVEN

"NICE GUYS FINISH LAST."

Have you heard that one?

It's true.

When Vanessa recovers, she takes my hand and leads me to the showers with a funny, dazed expression on her face. She hangs the robe on a hook, turns on the water, and pulls me into the steam.

We wash the chlorine off, then get slippery with body wash and shampoo. Vanessa lets me wash her hair before she takes her sweet time with me. I stand still, light-headed and half-crazy as this gorgeous woman runs her hands all over my body. She lingers on my chest and drags her fingertips over my abs. She scrubs the muscles of my back and squeezes my ass. With an evil little smile, she reaches down and soaps up my aching boner. She gives my balls a thorough lather, rinses me off, and turns off the taps.

For the first time in my sad and sorry life, my stars and planets finally get their shit together and align or do whatever it is that stars and planets do.

I know this, because at that exact moment, Vanessa Velasco gets down on her knees in front of me.

She takes me in her hand and gives my shaft a squeeze. Her touch is pure electricity. My nerve endings crackle.

"I'm out of practice. It's been a long time."

I try not to smile and fail. She's staring at my dick like it might suck her back. I stroke her hair, brushing the wet strands away from her forehead and cheeks. "Maybe it's like riding a bike," I say. "Maybe you never forget."

"Like riding a bike, huh?" She raises her eyebrow at me. "What if I fall down?"

"I'll catch you, baby."

Carefully, she grips the base in her wet fist. I watch as she lifts me toward her lips, closes her eyes, and kisses the tip like she's taking a pull off a beer bottle. When she sucks gently on the head, I hiss. When she slides her lips down my shaft, a strange low groan rises from my chest. And when she takes me deep at last, every muscle in my body goes rigid.

The sweet, wet sound of her going down on me is pure music. I feel every part of her—the hard ridges on the roof of her mouth, the smooth insides of her cheeks, her wicked little tongue. The muscles of her throat close around me, tight and hot. When she reaches up to massage my balls, pleasure scorches me from the inside out. A breath away from coming, I take her wrists and push her gently away. My dick slides out of her mouth, slick and heavy.

Without saying anything, I pull her to her feet, get down on my knees, and spread her legs apart. She's dripping wet. I swirl my tongue against her clit, then French-kiss her pretty pink pussy. I feast on her, holding nothing back. I press two thick fingers deep inside her.

She gasps and grabs my shoulders. Her legs are trembling. Her eyes are open. "Sal," she whispers.

The walls of her pussy are slick and strong. I curve my fingers at the first joint and rub her G-spot. When she tries to wiggle out of my grasp, I hold her tighter and suck on her hard little clit. Her muscles flutter and contract. She's fighting off another climax. Good. I drag her as close as I can to the edge. Then I pull out my fingers, slide them into my mouth, and drink her honey.

Panting, she watches me as I reach into the pocket of the robe and pull out the condom. With shaking hands, I tear it open and roll it on. The rubber strains around me. My whole body is hot and tingling like a sunburn.

Without speaking, I grab her, lift her off her feet, and pin her back against the tiled wall. Panting, she stares at me through narrowed eyes. I tease her slit with the swollen head of my cock. She pushes her hands flat against my chest and braces herself between my body and the tiles. I lower her onto my dick and when those pretty lips stretch around my head, she whimpers.

At the soft sound, I go still. My willpower is almost gone. I'm shaking. But I don't go further—I don't want to hurt her. "Are you okay?" I whisper.

She opens her eyes. Without a word, she reaches down between us and wraps her tiny hand around my shaft. Blinking through the pain, she takes a deep breath and slides me inside her tight cunt.

Holy.

Fuck.

I fight off my climax with the rage of a junkyard dog. It's not easy. I'm not used to feeling good. I work like an ox. When I lift, I hit the iron until every muscle howls in pain. I eat just to make it through the day. I hardly drink. I don't smoke. I don't do drugs. I jack off as fast as I can. I have sex only when the need for release overpowers my ability to sleep or think.

The truth is, I'm not good at feeling good.

So I am not prepared for what happens next.

Hot, slick, perfect—Vanessa's pussy grips my dick and pulls me deep. She kisses my mouth as I adjust my stance on the tile floor. I find my balance. When I thrust at last, my nervous system almost shuts down, unable to handle the pleasure.

Slowly, I thrust and pull back, again and again, learning how we fit together, memorizing the feel of her around me and all the ways she responds to my touch. Her legs are wrapped around my hips and she embraces my shoulders. The scent of her sweet pussy rises and mixes with the smell of the latex condom heating up between us.

When she kisses my neck, I close my eyes and try to catch up with the moment. More than anything, I want time to slow down. I want the camera to pan back so that I can watch myself as I make love to this beautiful woman.

"You feel so good." Her warm whisper feels amazing. I want to tattoo the words on my skin.

You feel so good.

No one has ever said that to me. I don't spread goodness. Only pain. Only regret.

I bow my head and stare deep into her dark brown eyes. We are fucking so hard that steam rises from our skin. Her lips are parted, and when I give her an extra hard thrust, her beautiful tits jiggle and she moans, deep and long.

I kiss her one more time. "Are you ready?"

"Yes." She locks her fingers behind my neck, hanging on tight. "Oh God, Sal."

I shove her body against the wall. When her pussy flutters around me, I realize she's about to come again. Her abs contract and her nipples harden. When a third orgasm ripples through her body, I grab her hips and bury myself even deeper, kissing her and swallowing the gasp of pain that escapes her lips.

I throw my head back, close my eyes, and the darkness grips

me. I pound my aching dick into her. One minute passes, then two. I'm moaning loudly. She says my name, again and again. In this moment, there is nothing in the world but Vanessa, her taste, her scent, her touch, her body.

Being with her is everything I hoped it would be, only better.

When I come at last, a carnival of lights explodes behind my closed eyelids.

WE WASH UP, put on clean robes, and stumble into the lounge. I sit on the sofa and Vanessa climbs into my lap, stretching her legs on the cushions and resting her head against my shoulder. For once, all the tension I've bottled up has drained out of me. I wrap my arms around her and she sighs softly. I'm warm and every joint in my body hangs loose.

"So." I kiss her temple. "Worth the wait?"

"I guess." She shrugs.

"You guess?" I say. "Damn. Stone cold."

We both laugh softly.

We talk about everything and nothing. Her words flow over me. I'm trying hard to listen to her, but I'm distracted by the smooth skin of her legs and the feeling of her plump round ass in my lap. I can still taste her on my tongue. Jesus. I'm getting hard again. I shift my weight beneath her, taking some of the pressure off my dick. She keeps talking. I could listen to her all night.

After a while, her voice gets drowsy. She slips from English to Spanglish to Spanish and back again. "I miss him sometimes," she says.

And just like that, another ghost walks silently through the room. "How did it all go down?" I ask. "With Sleepy?"

She speaks entirely in Spanish. "I knew him from the neighborhood, but we didn't get together until my cousin's *quinceañera.* He asked me to dance in front of everyone." She smiles to herself and I find myself in the weird position of being slightly jealous of a dead guy. She continues, "He was my first kiss. I was so embarrassed. Seventeen years old and I'd never been kissed. It happened right behind the church hall while they were serving the cake. I could hear my grandmother calling for me. 'Where is Vanessa? Have you seen my granddaughter? She loves cake!'"

"Apparently she loves something more," I say.

Vanessa laughs. "Afterward, we started texting. Soon I was sneaking out to see him. We'd drive around in cars—always a different car. I didn't know whose cars they were. Never asked. We'd listen to music. Talk. Smoke out."

I sit up and gasp. "Vanessa Velasco, I'm shocked."

"Things happened. We were careless. Three months after my first kiss I missed my period. So I told him. We told my grandmother. She cried. The next day, Sleepy and I went to city hall and got married." She sighs and shakes her head. "Did you know I got into all the colleges I applied to? Every single one offered me a huge financial aid package. But the baby was due in October. Sleepy was convinced he could get a job and make it all work. So I told all the fancy universities no. I committed to Cal State L.A. and made appointments for prenatal care."

She grew up fast, just like I did. I stroke her hair, her cheeks, her neck.

"Sleepy and I were happy for three, maybe four months. Then we started fighting. He wasn't looking for work. He was spending so much time with the homeboys. He started to spend nights away from the house. First one, then two, then whole weeks." She shrugs. "I lost him, Sal. I lost him before I lost him, if you know what I mean."

I understand her. Homeboy was out of reach, probably even to himself. "I'm sorry, baby."

"He died in August. Brianna was born in October. She never met him." Vanessa slides her fingers through mine. "Can I tell you a secret?"

I nod.

Her voice drops to a whisper. "When I'm sad, I like to imagine them passing each other in heaven. Him, going up. Her, coming down. He'd give her a big hug and tell her he loves her. Because he would have. In his own way."

We're quiet for a long time. From the way she shrinks into a small ball in my arms, I can tell she hasn't told anyone this. "You must miss him a lot," I say.

"Sleepy? Sleepy was . . . hard to live with. He kept so many secrets, and he never let me in." She pauses. "But I miss Brian."

Homeboy's real name. Brian. I hold her close and kiss the top of her head. I can feel her secret sadness wash over me. She wipes away a tear with the sleeve of her bathrobe and slips back into English. "I overshare. Sorry." She sniffles and shakes her head again. "Oh man. So awkward."

"Not awkward," I say. "Just honest. Real."

"When I went on all those dates, that was my problem. I didn't want to chitchat about TV shows or sports or movies. I hate small talk. So I would jump right into big talk—expectations, relationship stuff, regrets—and guys would listen and be polite, but they would never call me again. I was ghosted again and again and again. I think they were scared."

I want to tell her it's not that they were scared. It's that they were pieces of shit who only wanted sex without having to pretend they weren't pieces of shit.

"Men are so frustrating," she continues. Her shoulders tighten up a little. "You're all hiding something."

"I'm not hiding anything," I say. "Everyone knows I'm a lowlife. That's no secret."

She laughs a little. Her warm breath brushes my throat. "Maybe that's why this arrangement suits me so well."

"What do you mean?"

"We can be ourselves. The expectations are clear, and there's a two-month expiration date. We don't have to pretend to be anything we're not."

I nod again, but the truth is, I'm pretending right now— pretending that I'm not fucking falling for her with every passing second. "You're cruising for a bruising," my father used to say, usually to warn my brothers and me we were about to get a beatdown. We used to laugh at him and his weird old-fashioned sayings, but I think of that saying now. I'm cruising for a bruising. I'm going to find a way to let her down. I'm going to disappoint her—of course I will. I'm a piece of shit.

To distract myself, I slip my hand under her robe and slide it up her thigh. I kiss her little earlobe and whisper, "So if we're not pretending, what are we doing?"

She closes her eyes and smiles. "Playing."

I kiss her again before moving down to her neck. Her skin is smooth against my lips. She's so soft, it's unreal. "Playing?" I whisper. Another kiss. "Do you like to play?"

She leans back slightly and spreads her legs a little, inviting me in. When my fingers graze her pussy, she whimpers. I stroke her, lazily, until she's slick again and her little clit is stiff. I circle it with the very tip of my index finger, sliding around in her silky wetness. She buries her face against my neck. Her little gasps grow faster. I push my fingers into her again and she grabs the front of my robe, squeezing the fabric tight in her fist.

"Do you like it when I play with you?" I ask quietly.

"Yes."

"Is this what you want?"

"Yes."

The only sounds in the room are her soft breaths, the quiet rustle of fabric, and the wet click of my fingers sliding in and out of her pussy. I stroke her clit with the side of my thumb, back and forth, back and forth.

"Sal," she whispers. "This is crazy. I've never come . . . so many . . . times."

When she says this, satisfaction rolls over me like a wave, and I realize my mission for the next two months has changed—I'm going to become the best lover this woman has ever had. When we're done and she goes on with her life, I want her to look back on our time and remember the low-life thug who gave her so many orgasms she literally couldn't believe it.

"*Hermosa,*" I whisper, "you are made to come."

To prove my point, I make her come twice more—once on the end of my fingers, and once on the end of my tongue. Soon we're sprawled out, half on the couch and half on the floor, the bathrobes long gone. Her whole body is flushed. Her cheeks are bright pink. Her skin is slick with perspiration. Her pretty nipples are puffy and tender from my relentless sucking and licking. I've left hickeys on her neck and up and down her inner thighs because the caveman inside me likes seeing my marks on her.

I pile the sofa cushions on the floor and lay her on top of them. Just for the hell of it, I go down on her some more, sucking on her lips and tonguing them while they're inside my mouth. When I tease the rim of her pussy opening with little licks, she tightens up and more hot liquid slides out of her, shiny and sweet.

I watch as she reaches down between her legs and begins to stroke herself, rubbing her pink clit with two fingers of one hand while sliding the middle and ring fingers of her other hand in and out of her opening.

I've lost count of how many times she's come tonight.

But that doesn't matter.

She's still horny.

I can understand. After five years without sex, I was an animal. Nothing was too much. The two hookers that Ruben hired for me understood my situation and tag-teamed me the whole night after I got out. By morning my balls were like mashed plums but I still couldn't stop. I couldn't stop.

Vanessa can't stop.

Her lips are parted and her pupils are dilated like she's hypnotized by the sight of me tearing open another condom. Her hands work her pussy in perfect rhythm and I realize, for the past five years, this is how she's taken care of herself.

"Is that how you like to touch yourself?" I ask quietly.

She nods.

"That's hot."

I reach down. I take the end of my cock in my fist and jack it lightly, just halfway down the shaft and back up, twisting my wrist on the upstroke. I do it again.

"Is that how you like to touch yourself?" she asks.

"One of the ways."

"We're good at touching ourselves, aren't we?"

I smile. "There are worse things to be good at, baby."

Her eyes widen as I move her hands out of the way. Just because I can, I cover her pussy with my mouth and lick all the fresh, sweet liquid off her lips. I slide over her and cast a big shadow over her body. She wraps her arms around my torso and raises her hips. I position my cock at her opening and without pausing, thrust into her so deep that we both groan. She's so tight, the wet crush of her pussy would be painful if it wasn't so goddamn amazing. I freeze and take a deep breath. Every nerve ending in my body is raw. Unlike my first orgasm, this one was a long, slow build. It's going to be a monster.

Vanessa runs her fingernails lightly over my back and looks deep into my eyes. "Are you okay?" she whispers.

All of my muscles are pulled tight and trembling like the string of a bow. Am I? Am I okay? Playing with this woman is like dancing on the edge of an abandoned well. Sooner or later I'm going to fall.

Heart pounding in my ears, I lean down and kiss her again. "Yeah, I'm okay," I lie.

She blinks as she searches my eyes. I have nowhere to hide from her. Without saying another word, she flexes her internal muscles and squeezes my dick. The pleasure is so sharp, I howl like a wolf and collapse down on her, laughing a little as I try not to crush her with my weight.

"Fuck," I say. "You're ruthless."

Smiling, she runs her fingers through my hair and kisses my chin. "Don't you forget it."

I raise myself up again and look down at her. On her back, she looks a little younger, and in my shadow, her dark eyes almost glow. I give her one quick thrust. She inhales sharply and bites her lip.

"Okay?" I ask softly.

She nods.

I rest my hands on either side of her head. I pin her hips with mine and when I thrust again, there's a bounce to the cushions that intensifies the friction between us. She spreads her legs wider. I pull out almost to the rim of my cock head, pause, and swing my hips forward hard. This feels so good I almost want to cry. The inside of her pussy is tight and slick. The muscles at her opening grip the base of my cock like a fist. At the very tip of my cock, she's scorching hot. I have a big dick—I'm not bragging, it's big, that's what I have to work with—so I can feel the way every inch of her cunt grips me. It's a secret she's shared with me. A secret no one else alive knows.

I thrust again and again and again. I shut my eyes tight—I can't look at her or I'll come immediately. I lean back and give her a deep, hard fucking. A dozen thrusts. Two dozen. Three. I hammer her sweet little pussy until my body is one raw, exposed nerve. Still, I hold back. Pressure swirls in my balls until the desire to come is so powerful I can't breathe. Air is trapped in my lungs and I can't inhale or exhale. I can only thrust. I can only fuck.

"Open your eyes." Her voice is clear.

I do it. I look into her face.

She can see me—all of me.

I can't hide.

The orgasm thunders out of me. Every muscle, every nerve ending ignites with pure pleasure. Seconds pass, but time slows down. I'm still coming, locked tight in the grip of the moment. I grab her arms like a drowning man.

"Yes, Sal," she says, "just like that. Let go."

TWELVE

AFTER I DO one last walk-through of the spa, I lock up all the doors. We drive home. The early-morning fog disappears by the time we reach downtown. Sunrise hits the skyscrapers and the cranes that mark all the new construction sites between the buildings. Everything turns golden. Morning commuter traffic picks up before the East L.A. interchange and we get caught in a little gridlock not far from home.

"This is not so bad," Vanessa says.

Hundreds of brake lights flash in front of us. "It's not?"

"No. It's Labor Day. Muñeca has the day off school. I don't have any meetings. Do you have to work tonight?"

"Yeah, at the gym." I'm stroking her hair as she drives. I'm exhausted—wrung out—but I don't want to stop touching her. My thoughts are fuzzy. I have to do something else today, but I can't remember what. And then there's my problem with Barry. "I have to talk to my boss tonight," I say. "I'm not looking forward to it."

"What's the matter?"

I explain to Vanessa how Barry wants to take me on as a personal trainer.

"You get a raise, right?" she asks.

When I tell her how much I make now and how much the new job would pay, even I can't believe the difference. What kind of idiot turns down money like that? "I don't want the job, but I don't want to tell him no."

"Why not?"

"It's a lot of money, number one."

"Money's important, but it's not everything."

"Working out is me time." I sigh. "Jesus, that sounds so cheesy. Like I have a bubble bath and listen to smooth jazz."

"Maybe it's cheesy, but it's honest. You work out alone and it's important to you. Any other reasons you don't want to do it?"

I think back and remember something Barry said that didn't sit well with me. "I asked my boss if clients would be turned off by my appearance."

She looks sideways at me. "Which part? The brownness, the terrifying muscles, the angry face, or the prison tattoos?"

"All of it? Together?" I smile and squeeze her knee. "He said that his clients would kill to look like me. It made me feel . . . I don't know. Wrong."

"How so?"

I struggle for the words. "Rich people—they will pay thousands of dollars for tattoos in shops. They'll wear baggy clothes, listen to gangster music, wear *chola* makeup. They copy the fashion and listen to the music. They daydream about what this life is like without understanding what it really is. What it really means." I'm frustrated by my clumsy explanation. I don't know how to say it. My body—it's not a product to sell. "It's complicated," I say at last.

She slowly merges across three lanes and takes the off-ramp to our neighborhood. ESHB graffiti marks the freeway walls, the street signs, even the curbs.

"It doesn't sound complicated to me," she says.

"But he stuck his neck out to hire me. He's sticking his neck out again to offer me this job."

"No offense to you, Sal, but that's utter bullshit. Be realistic. You don't owe him anything. He hired you because you're cheap. He's hiring you as a trainer because he's in a bind and you'd be his new gimmick to hipsters. He'll probably want to put you on the website too. On the posters and brochures." She puts on an old-fashioned announcer's voice, goofy and loud. "'Look at my new trainer. He's hard. He's been in prison. He's from the streets. Work out with a real-life gangster!'" She passes the park and turns onto her street. "If it feels wrong, just say no."

"What should I tell him?"

"Don't tell him anything if you don't want to. Just say, 'Hey, thanks for the offer, but this is not the right time.' Or, 'This job is just not for me.' You don't owe him an explanation. He runs a business. He'll change course and find another solution." She parks in the driveway and turns off the engine. When she turns to me, my heart skips a beat. I still can't believe how beautiful she is.

"We don't have to say yes to every single thing that comes along," she says. "We don't always have to be . . . pathetically grateful for what people toss our way. We have a choice, and sometimes the correct answer is no."

The lights in the house are still off. I reach forward and run my fingers through her hair. Everything she's just said makes sense to me. I kiss her softly. "I'm glad you didn't say no to me."

She smiles against my lips. "Sometimes the correct answer is yes."

I follow her out of the car and take her in my arms in the shadow of the avocado tree. I can't get enough of her. I wish we could continue this for the rest of the day. I want to make love to

Vanessa in a bed. I want to fall asleep with her naked in my arms.

"Will you have dinner with us tonight?" she whispers.

The fuzziness in my head clears and suddenly I remember what I have to do tonight. "No, I can't. I'm meeting my friend Alan later this afternoon. He owns a bar in Santa Monica."

I see the little flash of hurt in her eyes before she blinks it away. "Oh."

"I'd rather stay here with you. But I promised I'd come see him. He's a nice guy." I kiss her again.

Her face relaxes. "So when can we . . ." When I kiss her neck, her voice trails off.

"I'll be back early tomorrow morning, baby."

"Okay."

We kiss one more time on the back porch and separate as soon as we hear the dog barking inside. A split second later, Chinita opens the door with a yawn and Chancla bolts out past us to do his business in the tall grass.

"Good morning, lovebirds." Chinita reaches into the pocket of her bathrobe and takes out a pack of cigarettes and a hot-pink lighter. "You both look very relaxed. Congratulations on finally consummating the relationship."

"*Abuelita,* I'm too tired to be angry at you." Vanessa walks past her grandmother into the kitchen.

"Oh, then you must be very, very, very tired." The old lady winks at me as she lights up. "Good work, Sal."

I collapse on the narrow bed in the garage and sleep like a dead man. No dreams, just darkness, deep and quiet.

Hours later, I wake up slowly. My eyes sweep the garage. I realize I've done a lot of work in here. No boxes or stacks of newspaper remain. The floor has been swept. Vanessa has sold most of Ben's old tools. I arranged the remaining tools on a pegboard where she can find them. Only the truck remains. I still have to sort through its bed full of junk.

I close my eyes and stretch. My arms and legs feel heavy and light at the same time. I take my time remembering my night with Vanessa. I wonder if this is really my life or one I made up to cope with my usual shitshow of a life.

Either way, I'll take it.

Whistling, I get dressed, pack my bag, and walk into the kitchen to wash up. Muñeca, Chinita, and Vanessa are playing Candy Land at the kitchen table. Muñeca pops up and runs to me, throws her arms around my legs, and says, "Sal, you're the blue gingerbread man."

"The blue gingerbread man?"

"The game piece," Chinita says. "She wants you to play."

"Oh. I see." I get down on my knee. "Thank you. I can't right now, but we can play later."

She puts the plastic piece in my hand. "Mommy's the green one. Chinita's the yellow one. I'm the red one. You're the blue one."

"*Mi'ja,* Sal can't play right now," Vanessa says. "We'll save it for him when he gets back. Come finish the game with me and Chinita."

I pick up the little girl and raise her high. She squeals. I put her in the chair and carefully put the blue piece back in the box. "For later, okay?"

"Okay."

My eyes meet Vanessa's. "Have a good night." My voice is calm, but just being close to her sends heat racing through my body. "I'll see you all tomorrow."

I make the trip out to Santa Monica in the daylight, bright sun shining in through the windows of the train. Warm wind whips my face when I exit the station and walk the few blocks to Bay City Brews. Ocean air fills my nose. It's just past five o'clock when I walk through the door. The hostess leads me to the back of the bar where I follow the hallway to Alan's crazy beer laboratory.

Alan is waiting for me, a big smile on his face. "Hey, I'm glad you made it!" He's wearing a T-shirt that says PUNCH IT, CHEWIE.

Full of energy, Alan walks me through the process. First, he shows me sacks of grain and specialty malts that he uses for his beer. He shows me his different tanks, each with a funny name —a mash tun, a lauter tun, a brew kettle, a whirlpool. There are fermenting tanks and storage tanks. There are stacks of kegs. He shows me his bottle filler.

Next, Alan shows me two books: first, an old textbook about brewing, and second, his brewer's notebook with all the ingredients, amounts, and times he's used to brew his different beers. On each page, he's taken careful notes about how to fix problems and which mistakes not to repeat. "Beer is four ingredients: water, barley, hops, and yeast," he says. "All I do is experiment with that formula." The book represents thousands of hours of work. I think about the weight-lifting book in my backpack—it's the same thing.

Today we're making his Dogtown IPA, which I remember was the bitterest, most refreshing of the beers in the flight. My mouth waters when I remember it.

"IPA stands for India Pale Ale." He shows me the recipe, neatly written. "These are the grains I use. Here are the hops. I use this kind of yeast. This is how long we have to wait before bottling—IPAs need a long fermentation." He closes the notebook and hands me a hairnet. I put it on. I wonder if Alan knows hairnets are straight old-school gangster accessories, to be worn with a big handful of Tres Flores pomade. I smile to myself. Alan continues his lesson. "India used to be a colony of England. Pre-refrigeration, barrels of beer brewed in England

didn't survive the long ocean journey to India until brewers
learned they could load the beer with hops to help preserve its
quality. Thus, IPAs were born."

I give up trying to hide my ignorance and ask him what the
hell a hop is. In between all of the very long words, I figure out a
hop is a little green pinecone-type thing that grows on a vine. It
preserves beer and gives it a bitter taste. Alan shows me some of
the hops he uses. I inhale. They smell fresh and spicy, a little
like a Christmas tree.

Alan is cheerful as he walks me through the process. I watch
the liquid boiling in one of the kettles. "We add hops in the
beginning of the boil for bitterness," he says. "We add hops later
in the boil for aroma." I watch as Alan carefully adds yeast to
the cooled beer. He tells me it will hang out in tanks for a few
weeks until it's ready.

After we clean up, Alan takes me out front to the bar. He
pulls a cold pint of Dogtown IPA—a batch he made last month
—and without a word, puts the glass and a big steak salad in
front of me.

I start to refuse but he cuts in. "Just eat, Sal. I'm a nerd who
likes talking about what I do. There aren't a lot of people who
listen as well as you do."

Between bites, I wonder why Alan's taken a shine to me. I'm
pretty sure he's gay. As a straight man, I can flatter myself into
thinking he's coming on to me, but I'm also pretty sure that's not
what's happening here.

"So how did you first start making beer?" I ask.

Alan looks over his brewmaster notebook, checks the old
textbook, and makes one more note. "I had just moved here from
Alabama to teach. I'd never been away from home." He looks up
at me and for the first time, his smile fades a little bit. "As much
as I love it here, it can be a lonely place. It may not seem like it,
but teaching is isolating. Most of my adult colleagues were

older. They had families so they didn't go out and socialize very much. I lived in a studio apartment by myself and went to work and came home and that was it."

"How long ago was that?"

"Almost fifteen years." Alan closes both books carefully and tucks the pencil behind his ear. "I was taking a walk in my neighborhood when I came across a home-brewing store. Out of curiosity I went inside. I struck up a conversation with the owner. I'm from a rural area, so back home, every family had a still. Moonshine's in my blood, so we had a lot to talk about. He sold me my first home-brewing kit and I got hooked. I learned there was a community of home brewers in this city. They welcomed me in. That's how I made my first friends in California."

He pulls up a barstool next to mine. From this spot, we can see the whole bar, the back door to the front door and all the customers and staff in between. "It's a process, Sal. Just like brewing beer."

"What is?"

"Making . . . making a man. Making yourself." He pauses. "You know, you remind me a little of myself back then."

I put down my fork. What do I have in common with this skinny white dude? "What the hell are you smoking?"

He laughs. "I'm serious. Back home, I was angry. Alone. I lashed out. I did things I regret. My town was small and everyone had made up their minds about me a long time ago. When I turned eighteen, I enrolled in the nearest college and got my degree. I opened up a little bit. Then I moved here. I opened up a little bit more. Eventually I made friends and soon I realized I had allies. People who weren't going to judge me. People who weren't going to write me off." He nods to himself. "But all of that—it's a process. It takes time."

"What about mistakes?" I ask.

"I made lots of those."

I gesture to his notebook. "Did you write down your mistakes so you wouldn't make them again?"

"I should have."

Alan and I chat a little more. I finish my dinner and swallow down the last of my beer. Hops. Their aroma swirls in my nose, in my brain. Grapefruit peels. Fresh-cut grass. Christmas trees. Because of Alan's teaching, I can taste each flavor in a way I couldn't before. Like being able to hear the different instruments playing in a song.

The words come out on their own. "Will you teach me more about brewing?"

Alan nods as if he knew that question was coming. "Sure." He slides the old textbook across the table. "Read that. Come back on Thursday. I'll show you how I make my *Weissbier*."

WHEN I TELL Barry that I can't accept his job offer, he leans back in his swivel chair and looks at me like I'm a ball of hair in a shower drain, backing everything up. "Are you being serious right now?"

I nod. "Yup."

"Why not?"

I remember what Vanessa told me to say. "It's just not the right time for me. I appreciate the offer, though."

Instead of being the happy-go-lucky flexible business owner she predicted he'd be, Barry goes for one more hard sell. He lists all the reasons this job would be perfect for me. The flexible hours. The skills I'd be picking up as a trainer. The travel—Barry and his staff attend conferences all over the country promoting the gym. He tries to sell me on the free shit—companies regularly dropped off sample products for gym clients to try, everything from new equipment to nutritional supplements to workout clothes to shampoo.

And the last thing.

"Are you really saying no to this truckload of money? Sal, are you kidding me?"

When Barry laughs in disbelief, I realize Vanessa was right about one thing. He's already imagined me on the website. He's already imagined me on his brochures. He wanted me to be part of his brand. After all, what says "defiance" more than a real-life lawbreaking thug?

"Seriously, Barry. Thank you for the chance, but it's not for me." I stand up and hold out my hand. "I hope you find the right trainer for the job."

Barry shakes my hand with his eyebrows raised. "All right, bro. Suit yourself."

When the last trainer and client leave for the night, I turn up the music in the gym and stare at the water pouring from the tap as I fill the mop bucket. I take stock of my situation and realize a few things.

First of all, this is not glamorous work.

This is the work of the invisible, the ones who don't want to see or be seen, the work of ghosts like me. Underpaid, often exploited, ignored, dismissed.

This is not easy work. In fact, it's a bitch.

I turn off the water and wheel the bucket into the men's restroom. As I swab the deck, I have another realization.

This work may be a bitch. But it's my bitch.

Tonight, I turned a corner. I'm not the young kid I used to be. The one who said yes to everything. The one who was so hungry for approval, he'd do anything that was asked of him, no matter how wrong it felt. Beat people up. Scare people. Sell drugs. Steal cars.

Granted, working as a trainer for Barry is none of those

things. But it would've felt wrong. And this time, the money, the approval, the happiness I would've brought my boss—none of it —was enough to convince me to say yes.

Alone with my thoughts, I clean three toilets and restock the stalls. I polish the mirrors and scrub down the sinks. I restock the towels. I do the same in the women's restroom. I wipe down all the weights and workout equipment and mop the gym floor. Outside the big glass windows, the night darkens, then lightens again. The sky turns pale.

I turn off the music, take out my weight-lifting notebook, and begin my workout. The iron feels good this morning. I watch my muscles move in the mirror. Each repetition makes me a little bit stronger, body and mind. I write each exercise down faithfully—no shortcuts. I blaze through my cardio, running full tilt on a treadmill until I'm pouring sweat. I wipe down the machine and hit the shower.

On the train ride home, my mind is quiet, calm in the knowledge that for once in my sad, sorry life I've done the right thing. I get off at my stop. On the corner by the park, there's a woman in an apron selling hot *atole* and tamales out of a shopping cart. She's ready for the crowds of kids on their way to school and adults on their way to factories downtown. I buy a cup of *atole* and enjoy it as I slowly walk home. The hot corn porridge is thick and sweet, the perfect breakfast. The orange streetlights turn off just as the sunrise takes over.

I feel strong.

Alive.

I unlock the door to the garage and shut it quietly. When I turn around, I am only half-surprised to see Vanessa lying in my bed.

THIRTEEN

WITHOUT SAYING ANYTHING, I put my backpack and the Styrofoam cup on the workbench. I stand by the door with my arms crossed.

Her cheeks are red. With a smile, she sits up. The sheets slide down. She's wearing a lacy pink bra. Her brown skin glows in the sunlight from the windows. Her dark hair is loose and wavy, tossed over her shoulders. My fingers twitch, aching to touch her.

Her eyes scan my face then slide down my chest. I flex my arms. The sleeves of my T-shirt are snug against my biceps. When she swallows, I see the muscles flex in her throat. Through the lace her dark nipples get hard. My cock does the same.

"You're late," she says.

"I had a little breakfast."

"Was it good?"

"Not as good as this is going to be." She watches as I remove my shirt. My muscles are swollen and twitching from my workout. "What have you been doing while you wait for me, baby?"

Eyes on mine, she throws off the bedsheets. Her panties fall on the floor—a lacy thong. She spreads her legs for me to see. Her hands slide slowly down her torso.

"Have you been playing with yourself?" I ask.

"And thinking of you."

Fuck. I'm on fire. It's only been a day but I need her like I need water, food, sleep. I'm starving for her. I take off the rest of my clothes, but I don't go to her. Instead, I take my dick in my hand and begin to stroke myself, slow and gentle, because the sight of her has already put me on the edge.

"Show me," I whisper.

She opens her legs wider. I can see the faint bruises and hickeys I left on her thighs. A sunbeam from the window falls right on her slick pussy and I think maybe we got it wrong about the image of the gates guarded by Saint Peter. These are the real pearly gates. This is the way to heaven.

Her nails are short, no polish. I watch as their neat tips slide between the soft folds and spread the dark lips apart gently. She shows off her pink opening to me. The image burns itself into my brain.

I take a deep breath. I can smell her strawberry shampoo. I can smell the fabric softener on the pink T-shirt and shorts that are crumpled on the floor by the bed—her getaway outfit, what she'll put on after she's had her morning fuck. I can smell the faint sweet scent of her pussy. My cock throbs in my fist. With my other hand, I rub my abs and palm my balls and notice her eyes are locked on my dick. She licks her lips.

"Show me how you touch yourself, baby."

At first, she puts on a show, gasping and moaning like a porn star. It's hot, but I know she's doing it for me, not herself. I let her keep going. She fingers herself, running the tip of her middle finger around and around her clit but never over it. After a while, she's so turned on, she finally forgets about entertaining me. Her legs fall wide apart and her head falls back and her mouth falls open and now she's just jacking off in silence, breathing deep and fast.

This is much hotter.

Her eyes are closed, so she flinches in surprise when I take a step forward and pull down the cups of her bra. Her beautiful brown breasts spill free. I lick one nipple while stroking the other with my fingers. She's panting now. The garage heats up. A little sweat breaks out on her chest and forehead. I suckle her harder. The tips of her nipples harden like dark pearls. My kink shows itself—I imagine the taste of her milk on my tongue.

"We have to . . . we have to hurry," she whispers. "I have to go back inside before they wake up."

I stand up and dump my backpack on the workbench. Out of the mess, I dig out a condom, rip the package open, and roll it on. I grab her arms and pull her up. I give her one long, hungry kiss. I take one of her hands and slide her fingertips into my mouth. I take her other hand and put it to her lips.

"Taste yourself," I whisper.

She opens her eyes and runs her tongue over the tip of her middle finger.

"What do you taste like?" I ask.

"Sweet," she says.

Quickly, I turn her around and bend her over the narrow bed. She rests her hands on the thin mattress and arches her back. Between two perfectly smooth butt cheeks, I see the plump wet lips of her pussy and the tiny star of her ass.

I run my thumb lightly down her crack. "You know I'm a little kinky, right?"

She laughs, deep and rough. "I had a feeling."

"You ever had it here?" I touch her asshole.

Her voice is soft. "No."

"Want to try it?"

She looks at me over her shoulder. "Is it good?"

"It can be. If you do it right." I stroke her a little bit. The slick hole tightens. "Later. We have lots of time to explore." I put my hands on her hips and position the pulsing head of my cock between those beautiful wet lips. I take a breath. In one movement, I yank her backward at the same time I thrust forward into her. My dick goes deep. Her pussy grips me.

We moan. I ride her slowly, watching her ass jiggle every time I thrust into her. I grab the thick muscle of her ass cheek, pinch, let it go, and give it a hard spank with my open hand. She moans again and squeezes me hard. I gasp.

"Yes. God, yes." She grips the pink bedsheets in her fists.

"Two months," I say. "You're going to get two months of hard fucking, Vanessa. Is that what you want?"

"Please."

"I'm going to make you come until you don't know which way the ground is. Which way the sky is." I get my balance on the concrete floor, bend my knees, and change my angle. Now I'm pounding the front wall of her pussy with the head of my dick. Vanessa groans and arches harder, wiggling her ass against my abs. "You want that?"

"Yes."

"I'm going to show you what this beautiful body can do." I spank her again and she clenches tight. I almost shoot off but I shut my eyes and fight off the orgasm. When I have a little control again at last, I reach forward and run my fingertips over her mouth. She parts her soft lips and I slide my index and middle fingers inside. Her hot tongue brushes my skin. "This mouth was made to be fucked," I say. When my fingers are slick, I reach down between her legs and finally give her hard little clit the attention it deserves. When I rub her hard, she bucks—bucks like a bronco—and I wrap my arm around her waist to hold her still while I thrust into her.

"This pussy was made to be fucked, wasn't it?"

"Yes."

"This pussy was made to come."

"S-Sal." Her voice is broken.

"Come for me, *hermosa*."

With a grunt, she pushes herself against my hand and explodes. As soon as I feel the tremors, I shove my dick as high inside her as it will go. Her muscles ripple up and down the length of my shaft, squeezing me until I can't hold back anymore. In the middle of her orgasm, I catch mine. I shut my eyes and let it wash over me, hot, wet, perfect.

When I can breathe again, I reach over the workbench, grab a few tissues, clean up, and toss the condom in the trash. Vanessa gets dressed and when I turn around, she's wearing little flannel boxer shorts with hearts on them and a pink T-shirt that says WORLD'S BEST MOMMY.

Again, I'm kind of kinky so I find this pretty hot.

Honestly, though.

Who am I kidding?

Every damn thing she does is hot.

She looks at my chest and laughs.

"What?" I look down.

Stuck to my right pectoral is one of the Post-it notes I used to sort the junk in the garage. It says, *Looks useful*. I pick it off and put it with the rest of the labels on the workbench.

"Do you find that funny, Vanessa Velasco? Have I been useful to you this morning?"

She sits back down on the bed and giggles. "Very useful."

I like to see her laugh. I pick another one off the bench and stick it on me. "How about this label?" *Looks important*.

"Definitely important," she says. "A very important person. VIP."

Her cheeks are rosy. In the sunlight from the window, her

dark eyes turn the color of honey. I switch labels again. "This one is better." *Trash but I'm not sure.*

She shakes her head. "No. Not true."

"Hmm." I take off the label and put on one more. "This one seems right." *I don't know what this is.*

She laughs again, but when she looks up into my eyes, her smile fades a little. She holds out her arms. "Come here."

I sit next to her on the bed. She climbs into my lap. The cheap bedframe snaps and screams but holds. She wraps her arms around me and kisses my mouth. I hold her hips and fall into her kiss. She's unbelievably beautiful. Looking at her right now—relaxed and happy and freshly fucked—is like looking straight into the sun. I have to close my eyes.

A rattle by the bed makes us both jump. We break apart, afraid to get caught. We're still for a second, and the workbench buzzes. I let out a breath. It's my phone. We look at each other.

"Get it," she says quietly. The expression on her face has changed. Suspicious.

"It can wait."

"No, here." She pulls away from me, stands up, picks up the phone and hands it to me. I notice she glances at the screen to see who it is, but it's an unknown number.

Looking at her, I open up the cheap phone and take the call. "Hello?"

"Ghost."

It's Ruben. Shit. Vanessa pretends to straighten up the bedsheets, but she's listening. "Hey," I say. "What's up?"

"*Oye,* Spider's going to come see you."

"Spider?"

"Yeah."

"When?"

"I'm not sure. Soon."

I'm almost certain this has to do with the Las Palmas kids

shaking up Slim, but we never talk details over the phone. I nod before I realize Ruben can't see me.

"Are you there?" he asks.

"I'm here."

"That's it. That's all I wanted to tell you." A TV is playing in the background, some kind of game show. I hear Ruben's wife laugh. "You doing all right?" he asks. "You need anything?"

"No, no, man. I'm good."

"All right. Take it easy, then."

"I will."

Ruben hangs up. I snap the phone closed and put it in my backpack. I pull on a pair of shorts and sit back down on the bed that Vanessa has just made for me. But the happy, relaxed expression on her face is gone. Now she's like a shut door.

To my surprise, she doesn't ask me any questions about the phone call. Instead she says, "Two months is nothing, you know."

"What do you mean?"

"Life is long. Years and years. Two months goes like that." She snaps her fingers.

I blink at her, confused.

She stands by the bed, reaches down, and touches my face. My stubble scrapes against her skin. Her small hand is cold. "You can stay out of trouble for two months."

Guilt hits me like a dump truck. To distract her, I take her hand and kiss it. I pull her close and wrap my arms around her. "Don't worry about me, baby."

I hold her and kiss her softly until finally—finally—she relaxes again.

"You okay?" I whisper.

She nods.

When she leaves, she pushes the door shut hard until the latch clicks. I lie on my side and listen to the muffled sounds of the neighborhood waking up: cars passing on the street, doors opening and shutting, Muñeca chattering and skipping down the driveway on her way to school. On the floor next to my bed is that last wrinkled Post-it note.

I stare at it for a long time until I fall asleep.

I don't know what this is.

I'M WAITING at the bus stop when the skin prickles on the back of my neck. I know that feeling—trouble's coming.

I look up from the brewing textbook Alan lent me. Cars pass on the street. An ancient cowboy pulls a Radio Flyer across to the other side of the street. It's full of cactus paddles—*nopales* —probably cut from his backyard. Except for me and the old man, the sidewalks are empty.

I close the book and stash it in my backpack. I put up my hoodie and shove my hands in the pockets.

Trouble's coming. Someone's coming.

Thirty seconds later, they turn the corner and head for me in a slow shuffle. Three homeboys in white T-shirts and khakis. They're Hollenbeck. I don't recognize the two younger ones. But the third one I know well.

Demon was coming up around the time I was sentenced. He's a full-fledged member now, Ruben's fixer. He's short but barrel-chested, pure muscle. His ears stick out a little—a characteristic that made him a target for bullies when we were little. These days he's a true *pelón,* with a clean-shaved head and facial tattoos. He walks ahead of the other two like the lead dog. They follow his every move. As he comes closer, I catch the bump on his waistband. He's strapped.

His temper gave him his name. I once watched Demon give a kid a concussion for buying him the wrong cigarettes. Before any of us could stop him, Demon grabbed the kid and slammed his head against the stucco wall of the liquor store. The kid wasn't even in a rival gang. He was one of us. Demon took the full force of Ruben's anger, but in the process he seemed to earn Ruben's respect. Ruben is a calm, logical person. He started to use Demon like a weapon.

Demon and his two minions circle me slowly, lazily. I nod at them. They nod back.

The younger ones look to Demon for their cues. He puffs out his chest a little bit and fixes his crazy eyes on me. "Ghost," he says.

He holds out his hand. Fist bump, chest bump. The other two copy him. Demon introduces them. "These *mensos*. Lil Man, Ray Ray." They look me up and down. Neither of them looks older than seventeen. They don't smile. I recognize their hard faces—I used to wear that mask.

"You two, pay attention. This here's a soldier. A real *soldado*." I can't tell if Demon's being funny or not, so I don't say anything. "Watch this guy. Five years inside. Always down for HB."

Like the old-timers we are, Demon and I do a quick roll call of all the homeboys we know, a list of who's who and what's what. Some are locked up. Some left the neighborhood. Some are dead. The two youngsters just stand there waiting, bored but patient.

"So, you ready?" Demon switches topics. His smile sharpens. "Ready for what comes next?"

The only thing I know is that Spider is coming to see me. "Yeah."

"I hear you're working. Ruben says you got two jobs."

I nod.

"I hear you're a really good janitor. On your knees. Scrubbing the floor."

He's annoying me on purpose. I have to cut him down a little. "You must hear a lot with those ears."

Demon doesn't miss a beat. "Sure do. I even hear you're staying at Chinita's."

There it is.

Straight to the heart of what I'm afraid of.

"For now." My voice is calm, but inside my anger bubbles up hot and fast. I'm not surprised that Demon knows where I'm staying. He keeps tabs on everyone for Ruben. But I don't want to hear the truth aloud. More than that, I don't want to get Chinita or Vanessa or, God forbid, Muñeca involved. They have nothing to do with this. Every protective muscle in my body flexes, and Demon knows it.

"How's what's her name? Vanessa?" His eyes widen and he sucks air between his teeth. "Goddamn, that bitch is fine. You tapping that?"

Before I can make the decision to rip his face off, my bus pulls up to the curb and the door opens. The bus driver, an older black lady, knows me. She makes eye contact with me, but she looks concerned. Standing together in a group, the tatted-up homeboys and me would scare even people familiar with this neighborhood. I nod at her.

"This is me." I step past Demon and grip the straps of my backpack to keep from taking a swing at him.

He smiles. "See you around, Ghost."

I climb on and the driver shuts the doors behind me. I exhale.

"Good evening," the bus driver says. "You okay?"

Those are my homeboys. This is my hood. I *should* be okay. I even say, "Yeah, I'm okay. Thanks."

My hand shakes as I tap my transit card on the reader. When I take my seat in the back of the bus, I silently pinch my arm until the tendon screams with pain, until the old bruise comes back like a dark shadow rising out of my skin.

One day passes, then two, then three. I work myself hard at both my jobs. I exercise until my body has no energy left to feed my anxiety. In the mirror at Defiance, the man staring back at me with the furious eyes is bigger and leaner than anyone who's ever mad-dogged me before. Sweat drips off my skin. My lungs burn. I let the pain wash over me. "Pain is weakness leaving the body," as the saying goes. My physical body is strong.

But my heart? My mind?

How do I strengthen those two things?

I don't know.

All three mornings, Vanessa sneaks into the garage to meet me. We go at it fast and hot before she has to leave for work. I sleep with her scent on my skin.

On the fourth morning, Vanessa meets me on the driveway.

I glance at the house to make sure no one is watching. I scoop her up in my arms and spin her around.

"I've been thinking about you all night," I whisper. "Get in there."

"No." She smiles.

"No?"

"Get some sleep. It's Saturday. I have to study."

"Study?" I kiss her again. In my mind, she's wearing a little Catholic schoolgirl outfit. Short plaid skirt, little blouse, knee-highs—

"When you wake up," she says, "come into the house and give me a study break."

My dick presses against her. It wants its morning quickie. "How am I supposed to sleep when you say shit like that?"

"How are you supposed to sleep?" She reaches down and squeezes me. I growl. "By closing your eyes and counting sheep until you run out of them. One, two, three, four. Like that."

I put her sassy ass down and obediently go into my cave. I set my alarm for exactly six hours. At one o'clock, I stomp into the kitchen, take a shower, and come out wearing a T-shirt and shorts. Chinita and Muñeca aren't home. Only Chancla the evil wiener dog stands guard by the front window, cussing at anyone with the *cojones* to walk by.

"Vanessa?" I call. "You here?"

"Come upstairs."

Hell yeah. I take the steps two at a time.

FOURTEEN

I'M hard by the time I reach the top of the stairs.

At the end of the hall is a bedroom. Its door is half-open. I step inside.

A big picture window overlooks the street and the park. The glass is old and distorts the light like a lens. On the far side of the room, another window is open. A breeze passes over my face as I close the door and lock it behind me.

The room is not messy, but it's full of things. Against one wall is a chest of drawers with a couple of perfume bottles and framed photos on top. The closet door is open. Dresses and clothes in dry cleaning bags hang inside. In the middle of the room is a bed with a huge wooden frame—dark wood. A big dark red quilt covers the bed. Underneath my bare feet is a thick oriental carpet.

Vanessa's bedroom. I didn't think I'd ever find myself here.

By the open window is a small desk piled with books. Vanessa shuts her laptop, turns off her desk lamp, and stands up from her work. She yawns and stretches. She's wearing a pair of jean shorts and a gray tank top that lifts a little to show off her belly. When her yawn fades, she smiles at me.

"Hey," she says.

"Hey, schoolgirl," I say. "Is it time for that study break?"

She runs across the room and jumps into my arms.

There are so few times in my life that anyone has ever been this happy to see me. My body doesn't know how to take it. My chest grows hot. I'm jumpy and giddy. When Vanessa kisses me, I have to stop myself from enjoying this too much.

For the hundredth time, I tell myself to disconnect.

Some people have angels and devils sitting on their shoulders. I have two Sals. Stupid Sal sits down with Less Stupid Sal inside my head.

Less Stupid Sal says, "Listen, asshole."

Stupid Sal replies, "What?"

"Remember, she's using you for sex. Just enjoy it. Stop catching feelings for her."

"But she looks like she likes me."

Less Stupid Sal stands up and slaps Stupid Sal. "She doesn't like you, *pendejo*. She likes gangsters. She likes the D."

Vanessa pulls off my T-shirt and slides down my shorts. I take off her clothes and unclip her lacy purple bra. When I lay her down in the bed, her boobs jiggle a little and my whole body tightens up.

"We can be loud," she whispers as I slip off her panties. "Muñeca's at her best friend's house. Chinita's with the *chismosas*. Nobody will be home for hours."

"The window's open," I say. "Don't you care about that?"

She shrugs. "No."

I kiss her neck and massage her warm, sweet tits in my hands. "You don't care what the neighbors will think?"

"What will the neighbors think?"

"That Vanessa Velasco likes to talk to God." I lick her nipple until it hardens.

She gasps. "Oh, yeah? What else?"

"That Vanessa Velasco likes Salvador Rosas's dick a lot."

"Or she pretends to."

I smack the inside of her thigh as she giggles. "Little thug."

Her giggling fades away as soon as my lips find her pussy. I'd eat her out in a snowstorm but lying in this big bed, with the breeze and the quiet afternoon outside, I think I could die here. Her flavor fills my senses. Minutes pass. Time slows down. Her gasps turn to little moans and her little moans turn to long silences. She's holding her breath.

When she reaches down to spread herself open for me, I lean back to look at her. Dark lips, soft as sweet dreams. At her center, a dark pink rose, glistening and alive. She tightens her muscles and I watch her bloom and unbloom.

"What are you showing me here?" I ask quietly. I run my fingertip around the rim of her opening.

She flexes again. "My pussy."

"Say the other word for it. The dirty one."

Her eyes are dark as night, all pupil, no iris, like a bird's. Her voice drops to a whisper. "My cunt."

I push my finger into her. "Whose cunt?"

"Mine."

"*Whose* cunt, *hermosa*?" I brush her clit with my thumb.

She grunts and shuts her eyes. Her whole body trembles as she fights back the orgasm. "Yours."

Music to my ears.

The mattress is high off the floor. She's on her back. I withdraw my hand, climb out of the bed, and drag her across the covers until her head is hanging off the edge of the bed.

"Let's see what that pretty mouth can do."

I take my steel-hard dick in my hand and slip it between her open lips. At this filthy angle, I can see my cock sliding in and out of her tight throat, the outline of my shaft clearly marked on her neck. I thrust slowly, giving her a chance to control her gag reflex. When we have a good rhythm, I reach forward and swirl her clit with my fingertips. When she moans, I feel the vibration in my balls.

"There you go. Good girl."

She takes all of me. I shut my eyes. I slide my middle and ring fingers into her tight pussy and apply gentle pressure to her clit with the pad of muscle at the base of my thumb. She grows wetter. She whimpers.

"Play with your tits."

The sight of my dick rammed down her throat, plus her beautiful hands playing with her big breasts, plus her hot pussy wrapped around my fingers. It's too much.

I flex and freeze and hold my breath. Using all of my willpower, I pull out of her mouth. My dick is rigid and dark purple. I'm ready to bust. She climbs back onto the bed and puts her head on the pillow. She's looking at me as I reach down into the pocket of my shorts for the condoms I brought upstairs.

"I have a surprise for you," she says.

"What?"

She leans forward and whispers in my ear. "No more condoms. I went to the clinic. I'm on the pill."

That catches me by surprise. "Are you serious?"

"I'm serious."

I hold up the condom. "So you don't want me to put this on?"

"No."

"You trust me?"

"I told you I do. Do you trust me?"

"Yes." A weird feeling bubbles up inside me. I can't figure out what it is—a mixture of nervousness and vulnerability. "So . . . you can't get pregnant on the pill?"

"No, Sal. I counted the days. It's effective now." She pauses. "Well, there's a zero-point-something chance."

"They probably have to put that on the package for macho-ass supersperm like mine."

She rolls her eyes at me. "Don't make jokes. You want this or not?"

When I was younger and more reckless, I had a couple of close calls. I don't take those chances anymore. "I haven't gone bareback in a long, long time."

She takes the packet out of my hand and puts it on the nightstand. "How about you try it with me?"

This girl is driving me crazy. Making love to Vanessa, skin to skin? My already-throbbing dick twitches. "Yeah. Okay."

She holds out her arms. "Come here."

I climb onto the bed. Vanessa runs her hands through my hair and down my back. I kiss her. We close our eyes. Her flavor intoxicates me, sweeter than sugar, stronger than liquor. I'm high when she reaches down and guides my cock into her. I break the kiss, look into her eyes, lift myself up on my arms and thrust gently. She's warm and wet and slippery. I drag out my dick slowly and her pussy sucks at me. I thrust it back in and she grunts. Without a condom, I feel everything times ten.

We don't talk. There, in her big bed, I make love to Vanessa slow and deep. This is an afternoon fuck between two thirsty adults. No music is playing. The only thing I can hear are the birds outside and the sound of her breaths, getting quicker and slowing down, matching the way I bring her to the edge and pull her back down.

When my heart feels like it's going to burst from holding back, I tuck my arms behind her knees and spread her wide. I ride her harder and harder. The springs in the bed are squeaking. The wood frame creaks. When she looks down to watch me fucking her, I know I can't fight the orgasm much longer.

"You close?" I whisper.

She looks into my eyes, reaches down between us, and rubs

her pretty clit with her fingers. At once, her mouth opens around a scream and her pussy erupts around me. The contractions are so strong, I can't breathe. She squirts—the hell? I've never been with a squirter before. I thought that was some made-up porn stuff. But she squirts all over the bedsheets, and before I can make some smart-ass remark, my balls give out and I come.

I come *hard.*

No, that's not it.

I explode.

I couldn't hold back if I wanted to. High as hell, I fuck her through the orgasm. Each thrust is a shot of pure pleasure pounding through my body. I feel it from my head to my feet. I fill her with hot come. She's still coming, so the contractions in her pussy milk the last drops from me and I think for the first time there has to be a God. There has to be a God who planned out something that feels so good.

When we're breathing again at last, I kiss her forehead. When we look into each other's eyes, we automatically start laughing. It seems like the appropriate thing to do.

"Fuck," I whisper.

"That was so good."

We both watch as I pull out of her. It's messy and sweet and good. Like the pervert I am, I spread her swollen lips open with my fingers. Come drips out of her pink pussy onto the bedsheets. I stare, hypnotized. This is the most beautiful thing I've ever seen.

Vanessa kisses me and pulls me down next to her on the bed. She rubs my back and arms and face until I'm high as a kite. When I close my eyes, I'm not sure if I'm falling asleep or waking up from a dream. It has to be a dream. Nothing this good ever happens to me.

Her fingers slide down my biceps, down my forearm. Then she stops.

"What's this?"

I open my eyes. Her hand is frozen on the bruise I gave myself after my run-in with Demon. It's gotten darker. Blue and purple.

"I hit myself at work," I lie. "On one of the weight machines. I wasn't paying attention."

"Jesus."

"It'll be all right. It doesn't hurt. Just ugly." I don't like how that lie came out. Easy. I didn't have to think about it.

To keep her from asking more questions, I grab her and pull her close. I line up our bodies until I'm spooning her. It's warm in the room but the breeze cools our skin. I take a deep breath and let it out. I stroke the curve of her hipbone and try to understand why we feel so good together, how our bodies click together like two puzzle pieces.

We lie like that for a long time. Just breathing. In and out.

From our spot on the bed, I can see the five photos lined up on her dresser.

There's one of Chinita and Ben at the beach. Vanessa is six or seven, riding on her grandfather's shoulders.

There's two of Muñeca. In one, she's just a baby in her baptism gown. In the other, she's on a pony at Griffith Park, laughing.

There's a photo of Sleepy, looking hard in his white T and khakis, posing on the sidewalk. He's nineteen. We thought we were men back then, but when I look at him now I think, *That's a boy. That's a child.*

There's one more photo on the dresser. A mother and a baby. At first I think it's Vanessa holding Muñeca, but when I look closer, I see that the mother's eyes are bright green, like Ben's.

"Is that you and your mom?" I ask quietly, pointing.

Vanessa nods.

I remember the hollow-eyed fortune-teller in the Halloween photo from the garage. "What happened to her?"

"Not sure. She was in and out of my life when I was little, but I haven't seen her since my grandpa's funeral." Vanessa sighs and settles against me. "She first ran away when she was sixteen. Lived in Las Vegas, met some guy and got pregnant. She came back with me a year later."

"Do you know your dad?"

"Peter Velasco. Truck driver. I know his name and he knows mine. He's never tried to reach out to me. I don't want to know him. Not now, not ever."

I'm quiet for a second. I think about the ways our parents let us down, about the ways Vanessa and I have had to build ourselves from scratch, without their help.

"When I was a little kid, I hated and loved her at the same time," Vanessa says. "I hated that she left me. I hated that she didn't care how much she hurt me. But most of all I hated how happy she made me whenever she came to visit. She'd stay for a day or two. We'd have so much fun together. I could pretend I had the best mom in the world. Then she'd sneak away in the night and disappear for years at a time. She broke my heart a dozen times. And I let her. I always let her."

"You were just a child. Of course you did."

"When I got older, I realized that all of my hatred had turned to anger," Vanessa says. "I was angry at her. I still am."

In silence, I wonder if having a terrible mom is better than having no mom at all.

As if she can read my thoughts, Vanessa says, "I remember going to your mom and sister's funeral, but my grandmother never told me the details."

The ancient ache inside me comes back to life. "A car

accident."

"What happened?"

"It's . . . a long story."

"I don't mind."

I kiss the back of Vanessa's shoulder and hold her tighter. This is an old story but I still have to brace myself before I tell it. "When my grandpa was shot, my dad took his place in the gang. He told me my grandmother died of a broken heart."

"How old was he?"

"Sixteen."

"Young."

"It all happens when we're young, doesn't it?" I kiss her shoulder again. "He was a daydreamer, a kid with big plans, always thinking up the next new scheme. That's how he got his name—Dreamer. He met my mom when he was twenty. Her family were all farmworkers from Salinas. She met him while she was visiting family here in L.A. He called out to her in the street. She was with her mom. Can you believe the balls on my dad?"

I laugh, thinking about the anger on my old-school Mexican grandmother's face.

"He found out where she was staying. Visited her. Courted her, the old-fashioned way. He was such a charmer that her parents and grandparents gave him their blessing when he proposed. This kid—a tatted-up gangster with no family and holes in his shoes. They said yes. On one condition."

"What?"

"My dad had to go straight. So he did. Charmed the bosses to let him go."

"What?"

"Yeah. Hollenbeck cut him loose. They even let him stay in the neighborhood. He got work at the slaughterhouse. A good job, at night. My mom and dad bought the house. Had me right away, then my brothers. Last, a girl. She was a surprise. We loved her more than anything."

"How many years apart were you all?"

"Let's see. Eddie's a year younger than me. Angel's five years younger. Esperanza was four years after Angel."

Vanessa does the math in her head. "You were ten years older than her?"

"Yeah. She was three when she died." I remember standing at the gravesite. I didn't know they made coffins so tiny. Next to my mom's it was like a toy. I blink away the memory to keep from getting dragged down.

"God. What happened?"

"The slaughterhouse shut down. My dad lost his job. It was a good one—a union job with good wages. He was a skilled worker, but there was nothing available like that, especially for that money. He got on unemployment, kept looking, got discouraged. The bills piled up. Four kids and a mortgage payment. My mom cleaned houses and babysat but the money was running out fast.

"My dad started talking to Ruben again. Started hanging out with his old homies, the ones who were still around. I think he was desperate. My mom would yell at him about it. She'd scream the house down. The fights would get so bad, I remember taking my brothers and sister into the laundry room and running the washer and dryer so they couldn't hear the things my mom and dad would say to each other."

I take a deep breath. "One night the fighting was so bad, my mom packed a suitcase. My dad was screaming, shaking with anger. She ignored him. Then—I think to really hurt my dad—she took my little sister out of bed and put her in the car seat. My sister was crying. She was wearing her Little Mermaid nightgown. Her hair was messy. My brothers and I stood on the porch. We didn't know what to do. We told them to stop fighting. We begged my mom to come back in the house. But that night she had made up her mind. She was driving to her family in Salinas. It was a two-lane highway. A drunk driver going in the opposite direction collided with her head-on. She and my sister were killed instantly." I pause, the pain running through me like lava, hot and slow. "And that's pretty much when my life went to hell."

Vanessa says nothing, but I can hear her sniffles and feel the tears that land on my arm. I'm raw from the story, as if telling it has torn open old wounds.

I never talk about that night. In group therapy in prison, I mentioned that my mother and sister passed away, but I never said how.

My dad never talked about it. My brothers and I never speak about it. We share this great shame—the inability to save our mother and sister. The inability to go back in time and find a way—drag them back inside, take the car keys, slash the tires, anything—to undo the damage. To get back everything that's been lost.

Vanessa turns around in my arms and faces me. Her dark eyes are wet and I regret making her feel bad.

"I'm sorry," I say. "I didn't want to upset you."

"No." She touches my cheek. "You didn't have to tell me. But you did. Thank you."

I pull her against my chest and stroke her hair. The breeze washes over us. I take another breath and let the pain run its course. I can feel Vanessa breathing in my arms. She makes my anxiety melt away.

How does she do this? What is it about her? About us together?

After a long time, I whisper, "I better get dressed and go downstairs. Chinita might come home."

Vanessa opens her sleepy eyes and looks up at me. "Listen,

Sal."

"What?"

"If you want," she says slowly, "you can sleep up here. For the rest of the two months. I mean, if you want."

If I want? An invitation to sleep in the world's most comfortable bed in the arms of the world's most beautiful woman? "Are you sure?" I ask.

"I'm sure."

I hesitate to tell her the next thing, but she needs to know. "I'm on parole, baby. That means cops can come by at any time and search the house. You understand that, right?"

"Who cares? We have nothing to hide."

I pause. "What about Muñeca? What are you going to tell her?"

"I've thought about that." She touches my face. "We'll just tell her . . . you're 'Mommy's Special Friend.'"

"'Mommy's Special Friend'?" I laugh.

"Yes. 'Mommy's Special Friend.' Who's having a two-month sleepover."

I kiss her again and again and again until we're both ready for round two. We make love slowly, almost lazily, and I pull another orgasm from her sweet, beautiful body. We take a quick shower in her bathroom, get dressed, and head downstairs together. Vanessa hops in the car to go pick up Muñeca. I sit on the porch and watch her pull away.

Just as the afterglow fades away, some fresh anxiety takes its place. It takes a seat on my shoulders, heavy and hot.

Vanessa's opening her life to me, taking down her barriers one by one. She trusts me.

I'm afraid of her trust.

Ruben owns me. The gang owns me.

I'm falling in love with Vanessa, but I can't tell her the whole truth about who I am without hurting her.

FIFTEEN

ONE WEEK BECOMES TWO. Two become three. A month passes before I realize it.

Vanessa and I find our rhythm.

Every morning, just as the sun comes up, I walk in through the front door of the house instead of slinking around the back. Chinita and Muñeca are still asleep. I tiptoe upstairs and lock Vanessa's bedroom door behind me.

Sometimes Vanessa is at her desk, studying. Sometimes she's curled up under the covers, reading a book. Sometimes she's sitting up on the bed, dressed in something sexy, touching herself and getting her pretty pussy ready for me.

I watch her transform, bit by bit. She gets a haircut and paints her nails bright red. She buys new lingerie and orders things from the Internet that leave me speechless and horny as hell.

"Do you like it when I wear this?" she asks. "Will you try this on me? Do you think this will feel good?"

My answer for her is always yes.

Yes to the corset and thigh-high stockings that make her look like Bettie Page. Yes to the black Velcro bindings we use to tie her wrists and ankles to the four wooden posts of her bed. Yes to the new vibrator that makes her come so hard she cries with pleasure. Yes to the jeweled plug we're both still too giddy and nervous to try, even though the idea of putting it in her makes me so fucking hard I can't breathe.

Yes, baby.

Yes.

She's stockpiled five years of orgasms. I'm more than happy to help her catch up.

It's a strange sleeping arrangement. We're hot-bunking that bed—she takes it at night, I take it during the day. We make love in the mornings before she leaves for work. We spend dinner-time with the family before I leave.

But I wonder. What would it be like to sleep—just sleep—with Vanessa? I lie alone in her bed and imagine it. Does she snore? Does she talk in her sleep? Is she the kind of sleeper who kicks and rolls around?

I want to add this knowledge to the list of a hundred things I've already learned about her.

For example, she's got a pale scar across her eyebrow where she fell off the bed as a little girl. She covers it up with makeup during the day but in the morning it's there, a little secret just for me.

That crazy energy she uses to tackle everyday tasks? She uses it in bed too. I'm fitter than I've been in my entire life and I can barely keep up with her. As soon as one orgasm passes, she takes a deep breath and starts sprinting toward the next one.

I know she misses Sleepy. She talks about him sometimes when we're alone. Having the chick you're sleeping with tell you about her late husband might make some *vatos* uncomfortable, but it doesn't bother me that much. I figure, I got my dead too. Not everyone knows how to talk about death. When you find someone who speaks that language—the language of grief—

it's a big relief. You don't feel so alone, I suppose. So she talks about Sleepy, and I listen.

"Do you know what I liked best about him?" she says.

"What?"

"That he was always *trying*. He was always *trying* to do better, to be better. No one *tried* harder than that *pendejo*." She smiles to herself. "He was like this goofy puppy who just wanted to be loved. He'd do anything for it. He had so much heart." Her smile fades. "Maybe too much heart. When the discouragements piled up, he just couldn't cope. He took everything to heart. It's a difficult balance, isn't it?"

"What is?"

"The human heart. It needs to be soft enough to feel things but hard enough to survive them."

Vanessa lets me see her deepest thoughts, but she also lets me watch her day-to-day life. Sometimes I watch her iron her clothes for work. She's detail oriented. Sharp creases, starch. Her shoes aren't new, but she polishes them up and makes sure there are no scuff marks. I lie in bed and watch her as she sits at her dressing table. Her routine is exact, even though it's a mystery to me. Creams and lotions and powders. Makeup and perfume and hairspray. Lipstick—first a pencil, then a brush. So much work. But when she's done—*¡híjole!* What a knockout. A work of art.

Her accountant exam is coming up. I watch her study. I see her notecards and notebooks. The schoolgirl inside her is ferocious. She is chasing that better life for herself and her daughter. I have no doubts she'll catch it.

She likes her coffee with lots of cream but no sugar. She doesn't like mayonnaise because Chinita used to use it as hair conditioner and the smell makes her nauseous. She doesn't believe in karma because bad stuff happens to everyone regardless of whether they deserve it or not. When she's stuck in traffic, she likes to think up insults for herself and comebacks to match them—"That way I'm always prepared."

I like her details, her quirks, the thousand things that make Vanessa who she is. I'm fascinated by her in a way I've never been fascinated by anyone else.

Together, Vanessa and I clean out the rest of the garage. There's just a little bit left to do. We lay out all the junk from the bed of Ben's truck. There's an old moonshine still and tubing. I remember that both Alan and Ben are from the boondocks where people make their own liquor. There's a box of *Playboy* and *Penthouse* magazines from the '70s stashed in the cab of the truck. We get a kick out of those—the out-of-focus photography, obsession with tan lines, all that pubic hair, growing wild and free. Vanessa's a little grossed out to find her *abuelito*'s spank bank, but she sets them aside to sell on eBay.

Tucked under the junk in the bed of the truck is a little bicycle. It's pink with training wheels. The wheels are flat and the frame is dotted with rust. Dusty streamers hang from the handlebars. I pick it up and rest it on the driveway.

"Hey, look at that. That's cool," I say. "Yours?"

Vanessa looks at it but she doesn't seem nostalgic about it at all. "I think it's too beat-up to sell. Just toss it in the trash."

There's a basket, warped. The seat looks new, just dirty. Under the grime, it's not a bad little bike. "I could fix this up. It wouldn't be hard. For Muñeca."

Vanessa makes a face. "Nah, I'll just get her a new one. She won't want that."

Something is strange about the way she says that. "What's wrong with this one?"

"Nothing's wrong with it. Besides it being disgusting and rusted out, I mean."

"Really?" I have a feeling I know what's wrong with this bike. "Did Ben teach you to ride? Did he get you this?"

"No, it was just . . ." She runs her hand over the seat and rubs her hands together to get the dust off. "It was just one of my mom's dumb ideas. She came to see me after one of her vanishing acts. Four days after my birthday because she forgot what day it was. She brought this bike, brand-new. We went to the park. She played with me all afternoon, from lunchtime until dark. It was perfect. But then she left again. I didn't touch the bike because I didn't want to ride it without her. I waited and waited. Two years passed before she came back. By then, I was too big for the bike." Vanessa sighs. "Yeah, just get rid of it."

I call up my old buddy Yoda, a little dude from the neighborhood who's a genius mechanic with—how do I say this?—a talent for moving vehicles of dubious origin. Back in the day, Yoda resold or chopped all the cars my brother and I lifted for Hollenbeck. Today he shows up at Vanessa's with his flatbed tow truck. I slip the bicycle into the truck bed when Vanessa isn't looking.

Yoda's in his navy blue coveralls. While his assistant gets the pickup onto the truck bed, I introduce Vanessa to Yoda, who shakes her hand with his greasy one and immediately makes heart-eyes at her.

"*Mucho gusto,*" he says. "*Encantado, señorita.*"

I clap him hard on the back, shaking him out of his trance. "So how does this work?"

He shrugs. "*Pues,* same way. You give me the car. I give you the *feria.*"

"We never did this in broad daylight."

He shrugs. "You never sold me a car that wasn't stolen."

"True."

He hands me an envelope full of cash. I hand the cash to Vanessa. Yoda drives away with an old Chevy truck. Everyone wins.

Later that afternoon, I watch Vanessa sitting on the back

porch with Muñeca. She paints her daughter's nails. Their dark heads bend toward each other like a heart. When she finishes, Vanessa caps the bottle and asks, "Okay, what song this time?"

"Mary Poppins!"

"Again?"

"Again, Mommy!"

Vanessa takes her daughter's hands and whistles the spoonful-of-sugar song on them. Muñeca sings a mixed-up version of the lyrics. When the whistling is done, Vanessa kisses her daughter's forehead. "Are they dry now?"

"I think so."

"Can you put your Tinkertoys away in the big box? I'll come help you in a few minutes."

"Okay." The little girl stands up, carefully opens the screen door, and skips inside.

"Why do you do that?" I ask. "The whistling?"

"You blow on the nails to help them dry. I thought it was boring so I started whistling. Same thing. It's air with added music." Vanessa laughs. "Once we tried to do the song from *The Addams Family* but Muñeca snapped her fingers and messed up the nail polish."

Right then and there, I realize three important things.

First, Vanessa became the kind of mother she needed when she was little.

Second, one month with Vanessa has already passed. I only have one more month with her.

Third, I wish I could control time—stop it, slow it down, rewind it. I would rewind this month and play it again and again.

On the other side of town, Alan continues my crash course in beer. So far, I've helped him brew a *Weissbier,* three different kinds of IPAs, a lager, and a stout. I brewed a batch of Dogtown

IPA by myself while he watched. We'll know in a few weeks if I screwed it up.

I try not to question his misplaced trust in me, but I have to admit, it's fun to cook in his crazy lab. He teaches, I taste. He brings out dishes of spices from the kitchen and has me smell them to see if I can detect the aromas in the beers. He says we're "developing my palate."

All I know is, if high school had been this fun, I wouldn't have dropped out.

I have dinner at the restaurant once a week. Alan comps me every meal, but I tip the servers in cash. Sometimes his brewing buddies come by and I join them at their table. To my surprise, I can understand what they're saying about sixty percent of the time.

Once, Alan even introduces me to the guy he's seeing, an eye doctor from Marina del Rey. The dude comes by to pick up a growler, a glass jug of Feliz Navidad. After he leaves, I elbow Alan in the ribs.

"Am I supposed to tell you he's cute?" I ask.

Alan laughs. "Only if you think he is."

I flash him a thumbs-up.

I'm studying the differences between ale yeast and lager yeast in Alan's notebook when he taps me on the shoulder. "Come here. I have to show you something."

I follow Alan into his office, basically a walk-in closet off the main kitchen. Inside, there's a bulletin board, a desk, a phone, a computer, and a printer. There's barely room for Alan. I stand in the open doorway. From a tall stack of papers on the desk, he digs out a large envelope and hands it to me.

"Do you have your high school diploma?" he asks.

"Yeah." I open the envelope. "I have an associate's degree."

"Even better."

"What is this?" I take out a catalog from Greenbriar University, a technical and vocational school near Glendale. I open it. "Brewing science certificate."

"Greenbriar offers a hands-on program in beer." Alan can't contain his excitement. "There's a working brewpub on campus. They offer courses in the history and science of beer, including all-grain brewing." He takes the envelope from me and pulls out an application form. "I requested an application for you. I want to write you a recommendation."

I look at him. I always suspected he was crazy. "What? A recommendation?"

"You are killer at this, Sal. You have an amazing instinct for flavor. You have mechanical and technical aptitude. You're exacting. I've seen it. You'd be perfect for this program."

I flip through the pages of the catalog. There's pictures of a brewery and a restaurant, along with happy smiling students in goggles doing lab work and examining samples of beer from big silver tanks. "I don't know, Alan. I can't afford this."

"This is a special application. For their scholarship program." He holds the paper in front of my eyes. "One scholarship a year. Open to anyone. All books, tuition, and supplies paid."

I take the paper. "Have you seen my record? Why would these fools give me money? They'd have to be drinking too much of their own beer before they let my delinquent ass in." I close the catalog. I make a joke because it hurts less to joke than to admit I'm actually interested in a program that would never accept me.

"Sal," Alan says, "listen to me. You've just started, but you are *good* at this. I know you enjoy it. Apply. It's easy. Fill out this form plus an essay—"

"An essay? Fuck that—"

"—A *short* essay. Add my recommendation. Then drop off the package at the admissions office. I know the director of the hospitality management program. I've sent him many students over the years. He'll like you."

"I don't know—"

"Sal." Alan folds his arms. "You don't have to know. You just have to apply. Will you do that? Just try?"

I put everything back in the envelope. "Maybe."

"Promise me you'll apply. For me." Alan looks at me over the frames of his glasses. He's wearing a backward Bay City Brews cap and a T-shirt that says THERE ARE TWO KINDS OF PEOPLE IN THE WORLD: THOSE WHO CAN EXTRAPOLATE FROM INCOMPLETE DATA . . .

I LOOK him in his kind, geeky face and say, "Fine. I promise."

It's a blazing hot afternoon. In L.A., summers last until October. In the backyard, I've repaired the bindings on the swings and tested them again and again. Muñeca swings lazily back and forth. Chancla the dog rides in her lap. His long ears drape over Muñeca's arm.

The rest of us are sitting on the back porch. No breeze. Everything is still. Sunshine bakes the garden. Different smells mix and rise up into the air: *epazote, hoja santa,* cilantro, *yerba buena,* rose petals, and fresh-cut grass.

I borrow the Ensenada bottle opener on Chinita's keychain. The cap pops off and my nose fills with the scent of Bay City Brews' Ocean Avenue Wheat, a *Hefeweizen* I made with Alan's supervision.

I pour the ice-cold liquid out into glasses for Vanessa and Chinita. It's a cloudy, light golden beer with a fluffy white head like a marshmallow. I pour a glass for me.

"*Salud,*" we say together, and clink glasses.

I take a drink. The familiar flavors roll around in my mouth. Cloves, a spice Alan taught me about. Vanilla. It's refreshing.

"Hoo-ey!" Chinita exclaims. "That is some good *cerveza,* Sal. You made this?"

"With help, yeah." I take another drink and look over at Vanessa. "What do you think?"

She smiles and my stupid heart sparkles like the Fourth of July. "It's delicious."

Together, Chinita and Vanessa help me fill out the application Alan gave me. We sketch out an essay about why I'd be good for the program. Vanessa wants me to talk about my fucked-up childhood and my time in prison, but I hesitate. I don't want the admissions officers to feel sorry for me.

"It's not about pity," Vanessa says, "it's about truth. This is your truth. What is so wrong with being real about who you are?"

"There's nothing wrong with it." I go quiet, lost in my thoughts. I'm having trouble explaining what I'm feeling. "It's just . . . I don't know."

After a minute, Chinita says, "He just doesn't want that to be all they see. Is that it, *mi'jo?*"

I nod.

We open a second bottle and I get some essay ideas sketched out in the back of my notebook. The application is due in a few weeks so I don't have much time to lose.

At the bottom of the form, there's one more space. *Optional: Please add any relevant experiences or circumstances not included elsewhere in your application.*

I take a deep breath. By the porch, the *hoja santa* is growing dark and wild. Its name means "holy leaf." The smell is strong and unforgettable, a little like root beer. I take a drink of the *Hefeweizen* and close my eyes.

In my nose, the aromas of the beer blend with the aroma of

the plant. The balance between sweet and herbal strikes me like lightning.

That's it.

Beer brewed on the Westside with ingredients from the Eastside.

A brand-new recipe.

I stand up and pick a huge handful of *hoja santa*.

"What are you doing?" Vanessa asks.

"I have an idea." I look at her and smile.

"What?"

"A surprise."

"You know I don't like surprises."

"You sure about that?" I say with a wink.

Early the next morning, Vanessa and I are just coming down from our orgasms when the dog starts barking ferociously downstairs. The doorbell rings.

"Who is that?" she murmurs. "It's seven a.m."

Vanessa blinks and yawns. She pulls on a T-shirt and shorts. I put on a pair of sweatpants and run a hand through my hair. Now that it's grown out, it requires more attention. Gel and messing around in front of a mirror. Kind of a pain. It looks like hell right now.

I follow Vanessa downstairs.

"*¿Quién es?*" Chinita pops her head out of her bedroom. She's wearing a bathrobe and slippers. Her hair is in curlers again, covered by a rainbow-colored scarf.

Just as Vanessa opens the door, I see the police cars outside.

Fuck.

Officers surround the house, front and back. The three standing on the front porch are identical—old Mexican dudes with shaved heads and big mustaches, in plain clothes with jackets that say LAPD. Their hands rest not-so-casually on their guns.

"Good morning, ma'am. We're here for a parole compliance check," says the first one. "Is Salvador Rosas home?"

"It's okay, baby," I whisper. "Just a routine checkup, like we talked about. Do everything they ask, okay?"

She looks up at me, a little fear in her eyes. "Okay."

"Good girl." I squeeze Vanessa's shoulder and step out in front of her. "Hello, officers. That's me. I'm Salvador."

With that unsmiling professionalism I've come to expect from my many run-ins with law enforcement, the officers cuff me and sit me down on the curb in front of the house for the whole neighborhood to see. The *chismosas* come over to talk to Chinita, who's holding a nervous-looking Muñeca in her arms. Adults come out with coffee mugs, ready for another show before work. Kids come out in their pajamas, staring.

Today, I'm the show.

Shirtless, tatted-up, no-good Sal. In cuffs.

Everybody.

Look at me.

Vanessa lets the officers search the living room, the kitchen, and the bedroom where we sleep. She unlocks the garage. I panic for a second, thinking they'll find my stash of money in the lawnmower. But why be afraid? That's legit money, the first I've ever made. I've got the stubs and receipts to prove it. In the end, they don't find it anyway.

Vanessa gives them my backpack. They check my papers, including my pay stubs and my parolee information with the name of my parole officer and the number to his office downtown.

Everything checks out. Since there are no guns, drugs, stacks of cash, stolen cars, random car parts, or severed heads on the property, the cops uncuff me and leave, no doubt to go brighten somebody else's day.

Chinita gets the little girl dressed and takes her to school.

Vanessa calls in to work and reschedules her morning appointments to the afternoon.

We sit in the sunny kitchen together over cups of hot coffee. I've put a T-shirt on but Vanessa is still in the clothes she slept in. For someone who spends lots of time on her appearance, she is surprisingly calm about facing strangers in her pajamas and bed head. She was calm throughout the whole ordeal, as if letting a herd of cops stomp through her house was no big deal.

"So what was your sentence?" she asks.

"Five years for carjacking and three counts of grand theft auto. Three years on parole. My brother got the same sentence, but he was an asshole in prison so he's had to stay inside longer."

"When did you start stealing cars?"

"I don't remember. Young. The older *vatos* showed us how. Homeboys would drop us off in nice neighborhoods, we'd lift the cars, drive them back here to Yoda's shop, and take our cut. The rest would go to Hollenbeck. That was that." I take a drink of coffee, remembering how valuable we were to Ruben back then. Low drama, high profits. "We liked it because we could keep our hands clean—slinging drugs and banging are messy. Dangerous. Junkies are in your face all the time. Homies are always beefing over turf. But stealing cars from strangers—we could pretend we were Robin Hoods instead of straight-up villains. We were good at it too."

"How did you get caught?"

"The Organization raised our taxes. Ruben got more aggressive with operations and upped everyone's quota. My brother and I were working double time to make those dues. One night, we got careless. Out in Pico Rivera, we were grabbing a Honda Accord. Nothing fancy, just an easy car to steal and chop.

"We were tired, not sleeping much. We weren't paying attention. I was about to start the car when we heard shots. No freeze, no warning, no call-out, just bullets.

"My brother got out of the car. The owner came charging out of the house, shooting at everything. Eddie got shot once, twice. When he went down, I lost my shit. Without thinking, I ran over to the owner and tried to grab the shotgun out of his hands. The guy—he had a gun, but he was just a regular dude. He looked scared as hell. I could tell he'd never been in a fight before. But he wouldn't let go of the gun. So I twisted it and smacked him in the face with the stock. That's when he finally let go. I threw the gun over the neighbor's fence."

"Weren't you afraid?"

"I should've been. But I wasn't thinking." I put down my mug. "The owner ran away. I tried to pick my brother up and do the same thing. That's when I saw the blood. A fucking river of blood, running down into the gutter like a goddamn nightmare."

The hideous memory rises up. Eddie's face, pale and plastic-looking. His eyes are closed, like he's sleeping.

"He'd already passed out," I say. "Later on I learned his axillary artery had been shot to hell. That's the name of it—axillary artery." I point to my underarm. "Get cut there, and you bleed out fast."

"What did you do?" Vanessa asks.

"The only thing I could. I stayed with my brother."

SIXTEEN

FUCK.

I don't like talking about this.

I rub my hands through my hair and look up at Vanessa.

On her face, I don't see the fascination and excitement some people have when I tell them my background, like they're watching some true crime drama on TV. But I also don't see any embarrassment. Lots of people, even people who think of themselves as do-gooders, are embarrassed by the truth of my reality. They don't want me to talk about it, and when I do, they get the weird look of mice caught in a trap—like they'd rather chew off their own foot to escape the room, to escape from me. These people are worse than the ones who've come to eat popcorn at the freak show. These people don't want to see the real me. They want to see their own goodness reflected in me and my struggle to be a better man. They don't want to be reminded of my failures. They don't want to be reminded of any failures, including their own.

But in Vanessa, I see none of this nonsense. I see a woman, sitting across the table, listening to me without judgment.

"I just sat next to him in the street," I say. "I pushed on the

open wound with both hands—I held on, as tight as I could—
and waited until the cops and paramedics showed up. Eddie
went to the emergency room. I went straight to jail." I smile.
Dark humor keeps me from hurting too much. "In my mug shot,
I'm covered in my brother's blood. I look like a fucking chain
saw murderer."

Vanessa doesn't laugh. Instead, she stands up and wraps her
arms around my shoulders. She kisses my cheek and neck.

"You saved your brother's life."

"No. I made bad decisions," I say. "Even when I made them,
I knew they'd catch up with me. With us."

"Yeah, but all that's behind you now. You're moving
forward, right?"

I nod. "Right."

I follow her upstairs, carrying the weight of the things I can't
tell her. My promise to Ruben. My agreement to go after Las
Palmas. I'm repeating history again, and I don't know how to
stop myself.

We lie down in the bed where we just made love. Vanessa
holds me, stroking my face until I'm halfway between awake
and asleep.

"Do you regret the things you've done?" I ask.

Time unwinds behind my question. One minute. Another.
Vanessa's hands are like a warm breeze sliding over my skin. "I
regret a lot of things," she whispers. "Falling in love with Sleepy
was stupid. I lost everything I had worked so hard to build. I
broke my grandmother's heart. I regret all of that. But Sleepy—
he gave me my daughter." Vanessa's voice is as soft as her touch.
"She is the love of my life, Sal. I wouldn't trade anything in the
world for her."

I wonder if there's room in this woman's enormous heart for
me. Will I be just another decision she regrets? Right before I
close my eyes, I touch her hand. "I'm sorry for this morning."

"DON'T WORRY ABOUT THAT." I feel her kiss on my fore-head. "Sleep now."

Three days pass. Summer blazes on, endless. I work out scenarios where I call up Ruben and tell him the truth. I practice my lines: I can't do it, I'm out, I'm no good, I've lost my stomach for it, I'd be a liability to you.

But when it comes time for me to dial his number on my phone, I remember my dad. I remember what Hollenbeck did to him, and I put the phone back in my pocket.

Now it's evening. Chinita is sitting on the porch with her cigarette. The rhinestones on her glasses twinkle in the light from the setting sun.

"Tell me, *mi'jo*. Be honest. Have you ever seen a foxier sixty-eight-year-old than me? I mean, let's be honest here."

It's her birthday. She's been day-drinking with the *chismosas*. She's wearing a party hat covered in rainbow glitter. The glitter has rained down on her cheeks like freckles. She takes another drag and exhales. "Maybe with a push-up bra and a *faja,* I could have the body of, I don't know, a forty-year-old? The face could be a little better, but some mascara, a little lipstick . . . I could pass for fifty, *que no*? I could get me a younger man. What do you think?"

"I think you look good, señora." I bend down and kiss her cheek. "Vanessa's sending me to get your cake."

She's grinning at me. I can smell the cloud of gin around her. "Only if you promise to pop out of it and do a little dance for me, okay?"

I walk three blocks to La Golondrina Bakery. There's a kid behind the counter, a new employee I've never seen before. He looks like he's just moved here from Mexico. He doesn't speak English so I ask him for a *tres leches* cake with strawberries.

"Y *por favor escriba en el pastel, 'Feliz Cumpleaños Chinita,'*" I say.

The worker takes the cake from the case and brings it to the back room to write the message on top. As he goes out, Slim walks in. His shoulders are slumped and his face looks swollen. He has a black eye. When he sees me, he comes out from behind the counter and puts his hands on my shoulders.

"Ghost." His voice is quiet. "You said you would talk to Ruben. I don't know what to do."

"I did talk to Ruben. He hasn't contacted you?"

"No. He hasn't. Things have gotten worse." Slim looks behind my shoulder out the window and his voice drops even more. "They got me. Closing up shop last week. I wouldn't pay them—I couldn't pay them—and they beat me up. Me, an old man. Why? Why would they do this? Where is Hollenbeck? Las Palmas would never pull bullshit like this back in the day."

"I don't know, Slim." I take a deep breath and wonder why Ruben hasn't taken action. Slim is right—something like this should have been shut down immediately.

Slim's face creases with worry. "My wife—she doesn't come to work with me anymore. I don't want her here. I told her to stay home and I hired an assistant to help me out. But this doesn't make sense. This is our family business. Our bread and butter. I've been doing this all my life only to get beaten up in the parking lot of my own shop." He pauses. "I had to buy a gun."

"What? Where is it?"

"Under the cash register."

Slim stops talking when the assistant comes out of the back room with the pink box. The assistant lifts the lid and shows me the message on the cake, neatly written in red gel. I pay the kid and pick up the cake.

Slim walks me to the door, out of the earshot of his assistant.

"Ghost, *por favor*. I'm begging you. Talk to him again. Tell him to do something. We're hurting out here."

I'm caught in the spiderweb. Invisible threads wrap around me one after the other until I can't break free. I look into the man's worried face and I feel his fear.

"Okay. I'll see what I can do."

On the walk home, I take out my phone. With one hand, I hold the cake. With the other, I dial Ruben's phone number.

He doesn't answer. I leave a message, just the basics. "Hey, it's me, Ghost. Call me when you can."

He doesn't return the call. After dinner, before I go to work, I try again. "Ruben, call me. It's Ghost."

No response.

On the train to Santa Monica, I sit looking out the window, wondering what Ruben is thinking.

The next morning, despite her birthday hangover, Chinita puts on her sunglasses and walks Muñeca to school before going to the salon to get her hair dyed. Vanessa says it'll take hours. She's taken the day off to do some last-minute cramming for the last two sections of her CPA exam tomorrow. She's nervous and jumpy, as if she hasn't studied at all, which is ridiculous—she's been studying like a maniac ever since I moved in.

When I wake up at noon, she's sitting at her desk, whispering to herself and twirling the ends of her hair around a pen. Anxiety rises off her like steam.

I sit up. I know what relaxes her. "Baby."

She looks up at me and blinks. "What?"

"Come take a hot shower with me."

"But I don't have time—"

"You have a little time for this."

When I stand up, she puts down her pen and takes my hand. I lead her to the bathroom. There's a huge old-fashioned bathtub in there, probably as old as the house. I strip us naked, pick her up and put her in the tub. I turn the taps and climb in. As hot water rains down on us, Vanessa stands there, staring up at me as I scrub down her pretty body. I wash her hair and massage her temples and rub her neck. But it isn't until I kiss her that I feel her tension drain away, bit by bit. My hands slide down her back and I cup her lush ass cheeks. I pull her close and nudge her belly with my hard-on.

"All clean?" I ask her.

"No," she says with a wicked smile. "Much dirtier."

Vanessa reaches behind me and turns off the water. She giggles as I pick her up and carry her, dripping wet, back to the bed. When I drop her on the mattress, her tits jiggle. I climb on top of her and kiss her, hungry and deep, while my fingers swirl and pinch her hard brown nipples. I do this for a long time. Soon she begins to squirm, trying to rub herself on me like an animal in heat.

She breaks the kiss. "Sal. Please."

I smile. "Please what?"

"Touch me. Please." She reaches down to stroke herself but I pull her hands away.

"I thought you were too busy."

"Please." Her pretty fingers move down between her legs but I push them away again.

"You're going to get something good," I say, "but you have to be patient."

I tour her body again, kissing all of her sweet spots—her lips, her neck, the insides of her wrists. I take her big tits in my hands and suck gently on her already-tender nipples. I put my hands on the insides of her thighs and spread them apart, nice and wide. I kiss her inner thighs and watch as her pussy lips swell and glisten. To tease her, I blow across her clit. When it stiffens, she shivers and goosebumps break out all over her body.

"Sal."

I lift her feet off the bed, take her hands and place them on her shins. The position of her arms spreads her thighs even farther apart.

"Keep your hands there. Understand?"

"Yes."

She's showing me everything. Clear liquid drips like a tear from her pussy down over her tight little asshole. My hard-on pulses, aching to plunge in.

"Are you gonna let me play with you, baby?"

"Yes."

My eyes linger on the tiny virgin opening. "All of you?"

She bites her lip. "Yes."

Our stash is in the top drawer of her dresser hidden underneath a few folded T-shirts. I take it all out: the vibrator, the plug, the lube.

I go down on her and watch her face transform as I lick and suck and tease her. She shuts her eyes and drops her head back. Her lips part. I watch her chest rise and fall with each gasp. When I tongue her clit, her nipples stand straight up and a hot red blush covers her chest and cheeks.

She's so wet, the sheets are already soaked. But I want more. I lean back and flip open the cap on the bottle of lube. I squeeze the clear, cool liquid on her ass and she flinches.

"Cold?" I ask.

She nods.

"I'll warm it up for you. Don't worry."

I lower my mouth and suck on her pussy lips again, her honey sliding down my throat. I swirl my tongue around and around her clit, just like I saw her jack off the first time we had sex in the garage. When I do this, she clenches and moans. I do it again, this time putting a little pressure on her asshole with the tip of my middle finger.

"Oh, God," she whispers.

"Relax." I can't help it. I laugh a little to myself.

"What?" she says, looking down at me. "Why are you laughing?"

"I'm not laughing at you, baby." I stroke the inside of her thigh. "I was just thinking that 'Relax' is a pretty fucking cocky thing to say when you're not the one about to get something shoved up your butt."

She smiles and shakes her head at me. "I can't believe I'm letting you do this to me."

I press her ass again and the first joint of my finger pops in. She gasps and bears down on me.

"See what happens when you let a gangster live in your garage?" I say. "Before you know it, he's in your bed with his finger up your ass."

We're both laughing now. She sits up and kisses me on the lips. "Nothing about you is what I expected, you know that?"

I look into her eyes. "You're better than what I expected. You're real."

She lies back down. With gentle strokes, I lick her and kiss her while I slowly work my finger deeper into her tightness. Her pussy is small but her ass is even smaller. I can't get my mind to work out the mechanics of getting my dick in there, so I decide today is all about playing.

I keep going down on her, taking her to the edge of her orgasm and back. The room heats up. When she's taken my entire finger, I slide it in and out, getting her used to the friction. Every time she flinches, I suck on her clit. Every time she whimpers, I slide my tongue into her pussy and comfort her. Mixing pleasure and pain, we move two steps forward, one step back.

"Have you done this before?" she asks quietly. She's out of breath from the effort of holding back her climax.

"Couple times. But not with a virgin." I withdraw my hand, uncap the lube, and spread more on her ass. She jumps when the cold liquid hits her. I take the brand-new plug and coat it until it's dripping. It's a small steel plug with a red jeweled heart on the end. My dick hardens when I imagine Vanessa buying it online and thinking of me.

"Ready?" I ask.

She grips her shins again like a good girl. "Okay."

"Breathe."

I go down on her, holding nothing back. Her sweet flavor intoxicates me. The girl is wet and hot and ready to come, but we are on a mission. I lap at her clit and push the pointed end of the plug gently into her. When she whimpers, I lick her harder and push again. Her tight muscles resist and relax around the smooth metal. It's an insanely sexy thing to see. Vanessa's eyes squeeze shut and she's panting.

"Don't fight it, baby."

"It hurts," she hisses.

"You want me to stop?"

She shakes her head. "No. All the way."

Slowly, I turn and twist the plug, pressing it forward. Her ass stretches around the widest part. I push quickly and the rest of the plug slides in automatically. The little red heart covers her hole like a button. It's sexy as hell.

"There it is," I whisper. "How does it feel?"

She opens her eyes. "Weird. But okay."

"Good."

I sit up and spread cold lube over my hot, hard dick. I jack off and the wet, nasty sound makes me even harder. I look down at Vanessa, flushed and spread wide open with a plug up her ass. She looks like a fucking goddess. In my heart of hearts I would never allow myself to imagine a picture so beautiful.

I lean down and kiss her. Our tongues swirl together.

"You taste yourself?"

"Yes," she whispers.

"You let anyone else do this to you? Play with your ass?"

"No, Sal. You're the first. The only."

"You told me once you like it rough. Were you lying to me, baby?"

"No. That's how I like it."

I grip my cock in my fist and speed up my strokes. "How about right now? You want me to treat you rough?"

"Yes."

I should be more gentle. I shouldn't do this. But I can't help myself when she begs. I slide the head of my dick up and down her puffy, wet lips.

"What do you need, baby?"

"I need you."

I look into her eyes and slam my cock into her to the root. She screams. I thrust twice and she comes all over me, squirting and spasming, eyes wild. She doesn't let go of her legs. I can see her nails digging into her own flesh. The orgasm is long and hard. It slams her like a truck then backs over her body again and again.

"Fuck," she whispers, "fuckfuckfuckfuckfuck."

But we're not done. I pull out of her, stand up, and drag her until her ass is flush with the edge of the bed. I put my hands on the backs of her knees and push her legs high and wide. I bend down and suck that nectar out of her pussy again—she's always sweeter after she comes.

"I need you," she says. "Come in me, Sal."

I'm going to explode out of my skin. I adjust my stance and get my balance. I grab the vibrator next to her head and switch it on. I put its tip right on her clit just as I plunge into her pussy again. From this angle, I can feel the cold, heavy metal of the plug in her ass. I go deep and fast, slapping my balls against her like some kind of animal. I turn up the intensity on the vibrator. Vanessa's eyes roll back and her jaw drops.

"Oh, my God."

"You're giving me everything now," I say. "Do you feel me, *hermosa*? That's me. Fucking your ass and your pussy at the same time." I rub the vibrator back and forth against her poor pink clit. Her nipples are hard as steel. She grabs on to my forearms. She's shaking.

"Sal, you're going to make me . . . I'm going to . . ."

I shove the vibrator against her. Her back arches and she explodes again, less than a minute after her first orgasm. My cock drowns in her hot liquid. When her pussy begins to milk me, I can't hold back. Blood pounds through my veins. My heart is beating so hard, it rattles my rib cage. My body locks up and hot come rushes out of me, filling her and spilling out over both of us.

It's just sex.

And yet . . . it's not.

We're not bodies.

We're pure light, set free for a moment before the universe gathers us and sets us back inside ourselves, particle by particle. Drop by drop.

Slowly, Vanessa pulls the plug from her body. I gather up the toys, wash them in the bathroom, dry them, and place them back in their hiding place. When I come out into the bedroom, Vanessa is on her back in the bed looking out the window at the sky. No clouds, only the smoggy blue-gray of an L.A. summer.

I climb into bed and hold her close. The sheets smell like her and me together. It's a good smell.

"So," I say.

"So."

"How did you enjoy your first . . . ?" I trail off, unsure of what to call what we just did.

She snorts. "It was okay. A little rough, but I enjoyed it."

"Would you say . . . you enjoyed it in the end?"

"Yeah. In the end."

We laugh like dorks. When the laughter fades, I put my arms around her and squeeze her tight. I don't think I've ever felt this relaxed around anyone.

"What you did there," I say, "that takes a lot of trust. I don't take it for granted."

She strokes my face, my neck. "I trust you. You know that." Her sleepy eyes drift over my tattoos. "When we talk, I think we mostly talk about the past. But I've enjoyed talking about who you are now. I think you're smarter than you give yourself credit for. And I'm glad you're trying new things, like this beer program. I think it's really cool." She touches my lips. "The things I've learned about you—you shouldn't be alive, Sal. Most people wouldn't have come out of your experiences alive, much less whole."

"There's plenty missing in who I am."

"Maybe." She looks into my eyes. "But you have what counts. You have pride."

"Pride?"

"Yeah."

"You mean I strut around like an asshole?"

"No, stupid. I don't mean that kind of pride. Not the flashy loudmouthed kind without anything to back it up. I mean, pride in yourself. In who you are. In the man you've built yourself up to be, without much help from the rest of the world."

I look at her pretty face, her lips, her dark, smooth skin. "Pride, huh?"

"Yeah. Pride. I like a lot of things about you, Sal. You work like an ox, and you have more discipline than anyone I've ever met. You're smarter than you pretend to be. Behind the tats and the muscles and the frown, you're just a big teddy bear."

"What? No, I'm not."

She smiles and gives me a squeeze. "You are so. But your

pride—that's what I like best about you. That's what makes you who you are."

When we kiss, I know the truth.

I love her.

No more crushing, no more falling, no more flirting. I love her, and I want her to be in my future as much as I want to be in hers.

New mission.

Do whatever it takes to make myself the kind of man who deserves to be in Vanessa Velasco's life.

So I do something crazy. I call up Barry at Defiance and say I can't make it to work. He asks me if I'm okay. I tell him I'm fine, but I have a family emergency to attend to.

WHICH IS ONLY KIND of a lie.

"No!" Muñeca says. "No, no, no. This is bad."

"What's wrong?"

"I'm stuck. I can't move."

"Why not?"

"I'm on licorice. I can't move."

We're playing Candy Land. An epic battle. She's the red gingerbread man. I'm the blue. She takes the game very seriously.

I'm pretty good with little kids. I played with Regina's kids and I used to have to watch my little sister all the time. Muñeca is a different kind of child. First of all, she's got her mom's clear-eyed stare. She talks a lot, but she always speaks in complete sentences because neither Vanessa nor Chinita can stand baby talk. Sometimes she sounds like a tiny adult.

"Sal, it's your turn."

It's Chinita's bingo night at the church, so I promised

Vanessa I'd watch Muñeca for the evening while she did her last-minute studying upstairs. First, Muñeca and I played on the swings. Then I made Muñeca a grilled cheese sandwich and some soup. Now we're playing Candy Land as a final treat before her bedtime.

As much as I am enjoying exploring Gumdrop Mountains with a five-year-old, I keep thinking about Vanessa.

The way she's opened up to me.

The way she's let me into her life.

Me. Of all people. She trusts me.

Her test begins tomorrow at eight. She wants to go to bed early. We wore each other out this afternoon, so for the first time, we'll be sleeping in the same bed. I space out a little bit, thinking about how perfect it will feel to finally fall asleep with Vanessa in my arms.

"Sal! You're stuck too!"

I look down. My blue gingerbread man is stuck on a black dot. "Oh, look at that. I ain't going anywhere."

"You *aren't* going anywhere."

"Right you are," I say in a fake English accent. "I am not going anywhere, my lady."

Muñeca giggles. When she draws another card, Chancla takes off like a rocket from the kitchen to the front door, growling. He scratches at the wood and barks. I get that strange prickly feeling on the back of my neck and I tense up in my chair.

Trouble's coming.

The doorbell rings.

SEVENTEEN

DEMON AND SPIDER stand at the door, hands in their pockets. They look freshly scrubbed. Their goatees are sharp-edged and their heads are shaved bald.

"Ghost." Spider's nervous. Twitchy. I haven't seen him since Regina kicked us out. "We're here to come get you."

"Sal?" Vanessa comes down the stairs. "What's going on?"

Muñeca skips up behind me but before she can make it to the door, Vanessa sees who's standing outside and scoops her up.

"Take it outside," Vanessa says to me. Her voice is sharp and cold. She turns around and carries her daughter upstairs.

"But what about our game?" Muñeca asks.

Vanessa shuts the bedroom door before I can hear the answer.

Anger boils in my blood, but with Demon's eyes on me, I can't let it out. "What the hell are you talking about?" I say.

"Ruben told you I'd be coming to see you, right?" Spider asks.

"Yeah. Weeks ago."

"Come on," Demon says. "We gotta go. Now."

"Leave your phone here," Spider says. "Wallet too."

Shit.

No phone means no GPS. No wallet means the cops will have a harder time identifying me. Or my body. "Where are we going?" I ask.

"Fuck, no more questions," Demon barks. "Let's go."

I grab my hoodie and keys and lock the door behind me. Outside, the darkness of the streets closes over me. I feel it cling to my skin like humidity. I follow Demon and Spider down the familiar alleys and side streets I used to haunt. After five years, nothing has changed—broken asphalt, forests of dead weeds. We pass mountains of litter, left and forgotten—bent shopping carts and discarded tires and old mattresses.

We walk along the retaining wall that separates the freeway from the neighborhood. Hollenbeck is one of the few gangs that has turf on both sides of the freeway. That's how old this gang is —it was here before the freeway.

Spider moves a plywood board leaning against a chain-link fence. There's a big hole there where the wires have been cut and rolled back. Demon goes through. I follow him. Spider follows me and replaces the board.

Now it's completely dark. I think I know where I am, but I'm not sure. It's been a long time. We walk through the shadows, our path covered with weeds and litter. Dogs bark at us through fences. A car passes a block away, blasting *banda* music. The subwoofers rattle my teeth.

We climb over two low walls into a yard that's packed dirt and clumps of half-dead crabgrass. Empty beer bottles and cans are everywhere, along with cigarette butts. The house itself is dark. Demon opens a grimy sliding door and we enter.

I know where we are. This is one of ESHB's crash pads— an abandoned house we've taken over. Homeboys sleep here when they've got nowhere to go. It's a place to get drunk and

high. This is also our arsenal. The closets and attic are full of
guns.

The smell of mold and rotting food hits me hard. We're
standing in the kitchen. Fast food trash and empty pizza boxes
are piled on the counter. I hear the buzz of black flies. My
stomach cramps. Anxiety tightens the muscles in my chest. I try
to take a deep breath but the disgusting smell makes me feel
worse. I grab the familiar muscle on the inside of my arm and
pinch it, hard.

Focus.

Don't lose your shit.

"Come on," Spider says.

I follow him and Demon through the hallway. There's a
faint light coming from one of the bedrooms. Demon opens the
door. Hollenbeck tags are spray-painted all over the walls.
Someone has run an extension cord through a window and a
single lamp lights the room. The window has been covered with
aluminum foil so none of the light can be seen from the street.

We step inside. Sitting on mattresses are five homeboys, two
of whom I recognize as Demon's minions, Ray Ray and Lil
Man. The other three I don't know, but they're just as young.
Pot smoke fills the air. All of them are high as shit.

Bad to worse.

Demon takes the wheel. "Okay. Just like we talked about at
our last meeting. Hollenbeck Gardens. Ray Ray, Lil Man, what
unit?"

"236," says Lil Man.

"Triste, Lalo. What unit?"

One of the other kids says, "378."

"Flaco, you're with Spider. Flaco, which unit?"

"109," says the skinny kid in the corner.

Demon looks at me and grins. "That means you're with me,
Ghost. Lucky you. We're unit 125."

As I stand there listening, my blood goes cold in my veins. Hollenbeck Gardens is a run-down housing project in our territory. Five hundred units for low-income families. The majority of them are regular people, adults and kids, not gang members. Ever since it was built in the 1940s, ESHB has controlled Hollenbeck Gardens. Most of our drug operations are based there.

Worse to even worse.

He's a scary motherfucker, but right now, Demon is in his element. He goes over the plan in a cold, clear voice, starting with the stolen van parked in the alley. He goes over the route, pointing out where all the surveillance cameras are. He takes his time. When he's finished, he goes over the plan again, just to make sure we understand.

"Everything we need is in the van. Firebombs. Crowbars. Like Ruben said, the goal is to maximize damage. Break the windows first, then light the bombs and throw them in."

My brain is spinning. I've been out of the life for five years. It's been a long time since I've done any of this. Tonight I'm jumping in headfirst.

"Remember: Calm. Coordinated. Nobody lose your heads. Everything has to happen at the same time," Demon says. "Don't give them time to react. Don't give them time to figure out what's going on. All four units at once, then we're out. Understand?"

The kids nod, serious as undertakers. I glance at Spider. He looks just as nervous as I feel. He may be number three in the gang now, but he's never been involved in the heavy lifting.

Demon hands out our supplies. Black sweats to put on over our clothes. Hoodies and black watch caps. He gives us each a cheap plastic lighter. He takes out a box of gloves and hands them around. I take two and put them in my pocket. My hands are shaking. Every part of me wants to turn and run. But I know that if I do, the next meeting they'll be planning is how to take me out.

Trapped in the web. Again.

"No phones. No wallets. Nothing to identify yourself," Demon says.

As the kids empty their pockets onto the mattresses, I watch as Demon takes a semiautomatic pistol from his waistband. He checks the chamber and tucks the gun back in. Unless Spider's hiding something, Demon's the only one of us who's strapped.

When we're ready, Demon takes a quick look at each of us like a drill sergeant doing inspections. "Stay focused tonight," he says. "The people living in these units have been talked to. Warned. They've chosen to stay and disrespect us. Remember. Hollenbeck Gardens is ours. They need to see that."

The kids nod and murmur in agreement.

Demon's wearing a watch. It's flashy and expensive—a banger's watch. He looks at the time. "Let's go."

We head out to the alley where the stolen van is parked. Demon throws me the keys. "Let's see if you're really as good with cars as they say you are."

Everyone piles in and Demon slides the door shut. I start up the van. I haven't driven a car in five years, so the simple action feels good—better than good. In spite of my anxiety, I get an adrenaline rush when I rev the engine.

The interior of the van stinks of gasoline. We are silent as I drive the two short miles to a parking spot one block from Hollenbeck Gardens. I back into the space, facing the van toward our getaway route on the avenue.

I turn off the engine and the lights but leave the keys in the ignition. Spider distributes Molotov cocktails and crowbars, which disappear under our baggy clothes. We exit the van and leave it unlocked. We follow in single file behind Demon through a park to the entrance. It's a simple gate, unlocked, specifically chosen because there are no surveillance cameras here. We enter, leaving the gate wide open behind us.

All the younger homeboys disappear into the shadows except for the one called Flaco, who follows Demon, Spider, and me. Our two units are close together. Like all the other buildings, Building 1 is two stories and houses a hundred units. Each unit has an exterior entrance installed with a metal security door. Rusty metal bars cover all of the windows. Outside, drooping clotheslines stand on a narrow lawn of dead grass. Toys are littered here and there—a deflated soccer ball. A beat-up tricycle on its side. The air smells like a combination of old cooking oil, weed, and piss.

I'm sick to my stomach.

When we're close, we split off. I follow Demon to our unit, 125. The number has been spray-painted with a stencil right in the middle of the door.

"This is it."

Demon motions to the second window from the entrance—a bedroom. Whoever planned this attack has an evil mind. It's the middle of the night, and people are asleep in their homes. Maximum damage. Maximum fear.

I take out the Molotov cocktail I've been hiding inside my hoodie. It's so simple, I feel stupid holding it in my hand. A beer bottle filled with gasoline. A fuse, a piece of torn cotton stuffed down the neck.

The raised crowbar in Demon's hand casts a shadow on the wall like the blade of the Grim Reaper.

"Light it," he whispers.

My shaking hands flick the wheel of the lighter. As soon as the cloth fuse catches fire, Demon shoves the crowbar between the bars and shoots it like a pool stick, shattering the glass.

"Now," he says.

In the split second between the moment I raise my arm to

throw the firebomb and the moment I let go, there's a scream inside the house—a woman's.

And then I hear it.

A baby starts to cry inside.

This is wrong.

I look at Demon. In the firelight, the whites of his eyes are whiter than white. His face is almost ecstatic with expectation.

The two words cut the inside of my mouth like I'm spitting out the nails of my coffin. "I can't."

"*Pinche leva,*" Demon says. "I knew it. Fucking bitch."

Before I can stop him, he grabs the bottle out of my hand and lobs it into the unit. It explodes inside the bedroom in a ball of fire. He's sloppy, though. Glass from the windowpane slices the side of his hand, tearing his flesh. The nitrile glove hangs in two bloody flaps. He pulls it off and stuffs it into his pocket.

"Shit," he says. "Run."

We take off at full speed toward the open gate. Someone yells. Lights come on in the apartments. People come out to see what's going on.

We keep running until we're through the gate. I see the youngsters ahead of us, sprinting across the park toward the van.

I look behind me to make sure Spider and Flaco made it out. They're exiting the gate when it happens.

Two short bursts of gunfire. Some kind of semiautomatic.

Spider falls.

I stop in my tracks. With his pistol, Demon is the only one who can give us any cover. But instead of returning fire, Demon keeps running toward the van, leaving us behind.

No time to think. I see Flaco trying to pick up Spider, but he's not strong enough. I run toward them. The baggy sweats slow me down. With each step I take, the passing seconds grow slower.

More gunfire. I keep going. I hear bullets ripping through the air.

I skid to a stop in the dead grass. Spider is laid out, stunned. He's bleeding—from where? His legs? Flaco is shaking with terror. The kid is as skinny as a pencil.

"Help me get him to his knees," I say.

Flaco and I get Spider up. More gunfire—the kid starts sobbing.

"It's okay, you're okay," I say.

I take Spider's right arm and drape it behind my neck. I grab hold of his bloody thigh. Adrenaline floods my system. I balance Spider on my shoulders and get to my feet.

"Go," I yell. "Go, go, go."

Flaco takes off, flying over the grass. Even more gunshots ring out behind us as I start across the park. There are no trees to hide us, no cover at all. Carrying my friend, I run.

No thinking.

No brain.

All body.

I run.

My lungs burn. My quads are on fire. I hear footsteps behind us. Sirens come closer. We might be leaving a trail of blood behind us, clear as day. Who's behind us? I don't know. I can't turn around to look.

I keep running.

Spider is losing consciousness. "Ghost?" he says.

"Hang on, motherfucker," I gasp. "We're gonna get out of here."

At last we reach the edge of the park. The van is still there and the door is open. Ray Ray is at the wheel and the engine's started up. I know from the expression on Demon's face they were two seconds from leaving our asses behind.

I throw Spider into the van and jump in. The van takes off before the door is closed.

Sweat pours off me. Fire fills my chest. I strip off my cap and bloody hoodie. I turn on the light in the van and look at Spider. His entire lower body is covered in blood. I don't know where he's been hit. I turn him over. There are bullet holes in his thigh, but his entire right leg is soaked with blood. I smell gunpowder and blood, sweet and metallic.

"Hospital," I gasp. "Ray Ray, hospital, now!"

Demon is sitting in the shotgun seat holding his injured hand. "No."

"The fuck?" I sit up. The kids are cowering in the back of the van. They're in shock and now they're even more frightened. No one ever crosses Demon.

"He's bleeding out. He needs an emergency room," I growl.

"I don't give a shit what he needs," Demon says. "We go to the hospital and we're done. They have us. On camera. The van. Everything. Fuck you—I'm not going back inside."

Up front, Ray Ray is scared. "Boss, what do I do?"

Demon turns away from the shitshow in the back of the van. "Back to the safe house."

Rage mixes with the adrenaline in my veins. If it weren't for the scared teenagers in the van, I'd kill Demon for what he's doing. I'd bash his skull in with one of the crowbars. What does it matter? For what happened at Hollenbeck Gardens, I'm already a dead man anyway.

Spider coughs. "What's going on?"

I help him onto his back, roll up my hoodie, and put it under his head. "Everything's good, homes. Just rest right now."

Ray Ray pulls the van back into the alley and the kids pile out. Spider's breathing is getting weaker. Demon turns to me as he leaves.

"All yours, bitch." With a smile, he shuts the door of the van.

The streets are quiet. I drive like an altar boy to County General, hands at two and ten, following the speed limit. I try not to think about what would happen if I got stopped right now. A parolee in a stolen van with a homeboy shot up like a saltshaker? They'd lock me up and throw away the key.

"You still there?" I call.

"Yeah." Spider's voice is weak.

I have to keep him conscious. "You got shot in the ass, *cabrón*."

"I sure did." He coughs.

"Shit, you heavy as fuck too. What your side girl been feeding you?"

"Homes, the usual. Rice, beans, and pussy."

We laugh to hide the fear.

When we reach the emergency room at last, I get out of the van and call over an orderly, who brings a stretcher. We lift Spider onto the gurney and the orderly straps him in.

"What happened?" the orderly asks.

"I was just walking down the street," Spider says. "A car came by and they shot me. I don't know what happened."

It's our standard story, one we practice in case something like this happens. I squeeze Spider's shoulder. "You'll be okay now," I say.

"Ghost," Spider says, "if something happens, tell Regina I love her." They slip an oxygen mask over his face.

"Tell her yourself," I say.

Before anyone can ask me any questions, I get in the van and drive away.

As soon as my tires hit their driveway, Yoda and his mechanics roll open the gate for me. I park in the chop shop and hand over the keys. The mechanics pull down the garage door, hiding us from the street.

"We've been waiting for you," Yoda says. "Where the hell have you been?"

"Don't ask."

Yoda grunts. "The usual breakdown?"

"Yeah."

The mechanics begin the hard work of dismantling the van piece by piece. They'll rip out and torch the upholstery, salvage the parts they can sell, and send the rest to the scrap yard. They'll sand off all the vehicle ID numbers. A witness may be able to describe the getaway van, but the cops will never find it.

I strip off the bloody sweatpants and T-shirt and hose off my shoes. There's a grease-stained shop sink in the back of the garage. I pick up the black nub of soap and scrub Spider's blood off my face, arms, and hands. The sight of red circling the drain shakes me out of my numbness.

This is the second time I've had to wash blood off my hands.

Broken promises—I promised myself I'd never have blood on my hands again. And here I am.

Again.

I turn off the water and brace myself on the sink. I take a deep, shaky breath.

I'm light-headed and cold.

Shock. I'm in shock.

"Hey, you okay?" Yoda asks.

I take another breath and stand up straight. "I'm fine." I force my voice to stay steady. "You got a clean shirt I can borrow?"

In his office, Yoda finds me a dark blue work shirt, faded and soft. The red patch above the front pocket says FRANKIE. The shirt strains against my shoulders but it fits.

Head pounding, I walk the three miles back to Vanessa's house, sticking to dark side streets and ducking into the shadows whenever a car passes. A police helicopter circles endlessly over

Hollenbeck Gardens, its bright spotlight like an accusing finger. Smoke in the air—I can smell it.

Full of self-hatred, I do what career sinners do in times of crisis. I pray. From personal experience, I know God doesn't listen to prayers from people like me. But fuck it. I pray anyway. I pray those families aren't hurt. I pray that the mother and baby I heard inside the apartment were able to get out safe. I pray Spider will be okay.

One mile passes under my feet, then two. The rhythm of my steps calms me down.

I gather up the pieces of my brain and go over the reality of my situation. I literally dodged bullets today. The young homeboys may have been scared shitless, but none of them were hurt. But why were we firebombing families? Why those units? Why were those people threats to Hollenbeck?

One foot in front of the other.

One step.

Then another.

Fear swirls in my stomach. Demon will tell Ruben that I couldn't do what I was told, that I didn't have the guts to stand up for the gang when it mattered.

Fuck—I've seen homeboys green-lit for less.

It happens fast. Shot from dark cars while they walked to the park. While they stood on the corner with their friends. While they came out of the liquor store with a six-pack in their hand.

One step.

Then another.

What have I got going for me?

Not much. I've been in the game for a long time. I did my time. I didn't snitch. Ruben and my father were best friends. That has to count for something, right?

If I get to Ruben first, I might have a chance.

What will I tell him?

I'll say I'm a liability. Unreliable—my anxiety makes me unpredictable. I'll tell Ruben he doesn't need somebody like me around.

Best-case scenario, Ruben will declare me a dropout.

I'd have to leave the neighborhood forever.

Two months ago, leaving this hood would've hurt, but it wouldn't have been impossible.

But now.

After Vanessa.

The idea of leaving the neighborhood—of leaving her—makes my stomach seize up.

I flash back to the steel in her eyes when Spider and Demon showed up at the door. The quiet anger. The way she cut me with her words: "Take it outside."

I flash back to the way she went through the things in the garage. Keep, sell, toss. She never second-guessed herself.

When she looks at me again, will she make the choice to throw me away?

The world is falling down around me. I have to find a way to keep the roof from caving in. I don't have my phone—it's still at the house. As soon as I get there, I'll pick it up and call Ruben. It's my only chance.

Vanessa's street is quiet. Only three hours have passed since I left. Strange that two hours is all it takes to change someone's entire life.

I climb the front porch steps and take out my keys. My phone is just inside the door. I'll call Ruben, convince him to hold back the order to green-light me, convince him to give me time to get out of town.

From there, I'll make things up to Vanessa. I'll find a way to fix this. I see my way out. My fingers twitch to dial his number. I have to get to him before Demon does.

"Hey, big brother."

I jump. It's too late—someone's behind me. I turn and muscle memory puts me in a fighting stance, ready to lash out.

The dark figure jumps backward, hands out. "Whoa, hold up!"

I blink and shake the adrenaline out of my head. "The fuck?"

The stranger lowers his hoodie and steps into the light. "Surprised to see me?"

I'm confused. "What? I thought—"

"You thought I was out in October? I was a good boy. Here I am. *¿Me extrañaste?*"

He holds out his arms. His face is leaner and he's got a beard. He's carrying more muscle, just like I am.

"Motherfucker," I say.

For the first time in five years, I embrace my younger brother Eddie.

He laughs. "Trouble's back."

EIGHTEEN

NEW PROBLEM. I have to find a place to stash my ex-con younger brother.

"How'd you find me?" I ask.

Eddie follows me to the backyard. "I asked around. When they told me Vanessa Velasco had taken in a stray dog like you, I thought they were joking." He laughs.

I smile. "Shh. Keep it down, fucker."

I unlock the garage and turn on the lights. It's a completely different place from the one I moved into. The space is empty and clean, with tools hung up neatly over the workbench and only a few small boxes of photo albums on a shelf. The rollout bed is still inside, made up with clean sheets even though I haven't slept in here for weeks.

I hand my keys to him. "Bathroom is through the back door."

Eddie takes the keys. "It's not the welcome-home party I expected, but I guess it's not bad." He puts down his duffel bag, sits on the bed, and looks at me. "So what were you doing out so late, Frankie?"

I'm confused for a second until he points to the patch on my shirt. My brain is operating in slow motion—I'm coming down from shock. My brother looks at me for an explanation, but the story seems too big and too complicated for me to tell right now. Besides, I have to get to my phone—I have to get to Ruben.

"Get some rest. I'll tell you tomorrow," I say. "You need anything else?"

Eddie kicks off his sneakers and leans back on the bed. "On my first night of freedom in five years? How about two dozen nymphomaniacs and a bottle of Hennessy?"

"We're out of both, homes."

"Well, shit." He shrugs and tucks his hands behind his head. "Then I think I'm all good."

In spite of everything, seeing my brother home again gives me a kick in the feels. "It's good to have you back, Eddie."

"Good to be back, homes," he says.

I go inside the house and pick up my phone where it sits on the dining table next to the Candy Land board. Muñeca has left the pieces and cards where they were.

I pace the living room as I dial Ruben's number. My heart beats itself to shit in my chest.

Four rings, then five. As usual, there's no answer. I leave another voicemail, afraid to leave a recording of the desperation in my voice.

"Ruben," I say, "it's Ghost. I have to talk to you. Things went south tonight. I don't know what you've heard. I want you to hear my version of things. I want to tell you the truth before . . ." I trail off for a second, unsure of what to say. I clear my throat. "I'll call again in the morning. Please. I need to talk to you."

I end the call and think of my options. I could go over to his house—no. No, I can't do that. It's just past eleven. And we aren't allowed to go over to his house without an invitation—that's been the rule for as long as I can remember.

Demon is a scary motherfucker, but he's calculating, not

crazy. I don't think he'd go after me without Ruben's permission. With the heat on, it doesn't make sense he'd stick his neck out tonight.

Even after my scrub-down at the garage, I feel sticky and disgusting. I strip off all my clothes and take a hot shower in the downstairs bathroom. I find a clean pair of sweatpants in the dryer and put them on.

Carefully, I check all the windows and locks. I turn off all the lights. I walk up the stairs, keeping my feet quiet on the steps. Vanessa's door is open a crack. I slip inside and shut it behind me.

In the moonlight, her ironed clothes hang on the closet door. Her purse and briefcase sit on the dresser, packed and zipped. Her phone is plugged in on the nightstand. She's ready for battle tomorrow. Her exam starts at eight, but she told me she's planning on being there an hour early, just in case something unexpected happens.

Pale light falls over the bed. In the middle of the mattress, Vanessa lies curled up under a thin blanket. Her dark hair is spread out on her pillow like a shadow. She's asleep. Her breathing is soft and even.

I stand still for a moment, taking in her beauty.

At twenty-four, I've lived half my life inside a nightmare. I've given and taken beatings, been in and out of cuffs. I dropped five years of my life in the dark hole of the California penal system. The things I've seen and done would break most people in two.

The dull ache in my forearm pulses. I run my fingers over the bruise. It never fades because I never give it the chance.

I realize something.

I've slept alone my whole life.

The shape of my shadow curves around Vanessa's sleeping body, as if even my shadow wants to hold her in its arms.

I lift the blanket and lie down behind her. I'm afraid to touch her, to wake her, even though every atom in my body feels her pull.

But she turns around and her eyes flutter open.

"Vanessa," I say.

She blinks slowly until she realizes I'm here, next to her. "It's you."

"I'm here."

She touches my face. "What did you do, Sal?"

The weight of my actions hits me like a roof caving in. My chest cracks under the guilt.

Do I tell her the truth? Do I tell her what I did tonight?

No—I can't.

I have to protect her. She is too good for me, too good for the ugly reality of who I am.

"I didn't do anything," I whisper.

Her hand on my cheek is soft and warm. "Don't lie to me."

The lie that I'm a good man is the only reason she allows me in this bed. I need her tonight. I need her touch. "It's the truth."

She embraces me and rests her head against my chest. I wrap my arms around her and pull her close.

"I was so worried," she murmurs. "I'm glad you're safe, baby."

I hold on tight. If I find a way to get out of this, I'll never let her go.

"Good night, baby."

Sleep slides over us like another layer of moonlight, slow and silent.

THE DOG BARKS at the front door.

Broken glass.

Laughter.

I raise my head. The clock on Vanessa's nightstand says 4:35.

Tucked up against me, Vanessa rubs her eyes. "What's going on?"

"I don't know," I mumble.

I get out of bed, clumsy with sleep. Vanessa follows me downstairs. Right when we reach the first floor, we hear more glass breaking. More laughter.

Muñeca climbs down the stairs to see what's happening. Chinita shuffles out of her bedroom. "What is going on?" she asks.

"All of you, stay back," I say. They retreat into the hallway, eyes on me.

Without turning on the lights, I peek between the curtains in the front window. In the driveway, six dark figures surround Vanessa's car.

Shit.

"Throw it," someone says. It's Demon's voice.

More broken glass. The interior of Vanessa's car ignites and fills with flames.

I turn around. The three faces—Vanessa's, Chinita's, and Muneca's—look back at me with fear and confusion.

"Go into the kitchen," I say. "Stay there, as far back from the front of the house as you can. Whatever you do, don't come outside."

"Mommy?" the little girl says.

"What is going on?" Vanessa demands.

"I'll take care of this." I pick up Muñeca and hand her to Vanessa. "Go now."

They do as I tell them. I put on my shoes, grab the doorknob, and take a breath.

I summon the gangster I used to be. Like an evil spell, he rises up from the deep shame inside me.

Do you know?

Do you know how I got my name?

They called me Ghost because I appeared and disappeared out of nowhere.

They called me Ghost because I haunted the dreams of the people I hurt.

They called me Ghost because like the dead, I feared nothing.

I burst out of the house.

Without saying anything, I grab the shadow nearest to me— it's the kid named Lalo—and slam him against the side of the car, knocking him out on the doorframe. Two homeboys try to grab me, but I use my weight to throw them off balance. I pin the first one to the ground and whale on him with my fists. The second one tries to put his arms around me but an elbow to his temple stuns him and sends him staggering. A third homeboy runs at me, trying to knock me on my back. I dodge him and take his legs out from under him.

That's when I hear her voice.

"Leave him alone!"

My blood goes cold. I get to my feet. "No, Vanessa! Go back inside!"

She's got one of their crowbars in her hands. Demon tries to take it from her. She gets him in the knee before he grabs the crowbar in his fist and backhands her so hard my own ears ring.

I roar. Three sets of arms hold me back. I strain and pull, trying to get to her. Someone socks me. Warm blood fills my mouth. I surge forward and pull my right arm free.

Vanessa's hurt—she's hurt.

I take one heavy step, then another. Someone tackles me. As

I fall, I grab one of the homeboys and take him down with me, knocking his head against the concrete driveway.

Smoke fills the air. A dozen hands drag me down into the dirt. There's too many of them. I can't get free.

"Vanessa!" I yell. My chest is burning. I can't get air. I kick, I spit. Someone grabs my free arm and pins it to the ground. I can't move. Someone kicks my side, hard. I'm overcome by the urge to vomit.

Suddenly, Demon's face is in mine. There's liquor on his breath. "This is what we do to little bitches in Hollenbeck, Ghost. This is what happens."

The hands let go, but before I can crawl away, the *vatos* start kicking me, hard, all at once. Brutal blows land on my back, my stomach, and my head. Automatically, my arms go up to protect my face and I curl into a fetal position. The pain is intense. But all I can think about is fighting back. All I can think about is Vanessa.

Laughing, Demon runs his mouth while the younger homeboys do his dirty work for him.

"Hey, want to know a secret? Your dad begged for us not to shoot him. Begged, like the little bitch-ass faggot he was. Like father, like son."

I'm gasping. I can't get air. Every time I try to take a breath, another blow sucks it out of me. I'm getting dizzy. I squint my eyes—is Eddie carrying Vanessa into the house? I can't see. I can't move.

"I watched him go down, Ghost," Demon says. "Just like I'm gonna watch you go down."

Someone kicks me in the head.

In the dark shadow of the circle, my brain starts to wander.

I have a flashback to when I was thirteen, getting jumped in by the gang. It was just like this—me on the ground while a group of homeboys beat me up with their fists and feet. As long as I could take the pain and didn't fight back, I was in. I made my body slack. I made my brain go blank. I took it. All of their abuse. When they stopped, they helped me to my feet and congratulated me.

That was the moment I became an official member of ESHB.

I never knew I'd be on the ground like this again.

Police sirens approach. Demon finally tells his boys to stop. The youngsters scatter. Before he disappears, Demon whispers in my ear, "All I'm waiting for is the green light. Then you're dead, motherfucker. Dead, you hear me?"

His footsteps on the sidewalk fade as he runs away.

I lie still on the grass until I'm sure they're gone. I feel like a bag of broken bones and torn muscles. The sirens come closer and closer until they fade again. They're one street down, going in the direction of Hollenbeck Gardens.

Before my eyes swell shut, I see Eddie come down the steps with a fire extinguisher in his hands. He puts out the fire inside the car.

"Come on." My brother helps me to my feet and drags me up the front porch steps. He shuts the door behind us and we stumble into the kitchen.

Chinita sits on a chair at the dining table. Muñeca sits in her lap. The little girl wails—tears stream down her frightened face. Vanessa stands by the kitchen sink. Her cheek is swollen and her eye is turning purple.

I look at all the pain I've caused and take an unsteady step toward Vanessa. "Baby, are you okay?"

"Don't touch me." Her voice is angry and hard. "You lied to me. What did you do last night? Why did they come here?"

The words get stuck in my throat. None of the people in this kitchen—not even Eddie—know the truth. If there's an investigation into Hollenbeck Gardens, I don't want any of them involved. I don't want to risk any of them being questioned by the police or harassed by the gang.

I take another step toward Vanessa and touch her arm. She flinches and shakes me off. The simple motion hurts worse than the beatdown I received outside.

"What the hell did you do?" she demands. "Stop hiding things from me."

"This wasn't supposed to happen," I say through a mouthful of blood.

Tears well in her eyes, but she doesn't let them fall. "No," she says. "I'm not doing this again. I trusted you. I can't believe I fell for your bullshit. I can't believe I fell for you."

Muñeca cries harder.

"Shh. Come on, let's go." Chinita takes her into her bedroom and shuts the door.

I can't bear to see this. "Vanessa—"

"One gangster is another gangster is another gangster." She's sobbing so hard she can barely get the words out. "You're all pieces of shit."

I put my hands on her shoulders. I have to make her see. I have to make her understand. "Listen to me—"

She shoves me back hard enough that the backs of my knees collide with the table. The pieces on the Candy Land board fall down. "Get your hands off me." She looks between me and Eddie. "Both of you—get your things and get out of my house."

I'm back in my nightmare. Everything's falling apart in my hands. "Vanessa. Please."

"Get out of my house!"

Rage, hurt, and fear roll off her like waves. I want to take her in my arms and make her pain go away. I am desperate to make her understand.

"Just listen to me—"

"Get out!"

Eddie takes hold of my arm and pulls me toward the back door. "Come on. Let's go."

SWEAT COVERS MY BODY. The air is hot and still.

Where am I?

I wake up on a sofa in a small living room.

What is this place?

The walls are wood panels hung with paintings of saints. There are bundles of dried herbs hanging everywhere. A statue of Santo Niño de Atocha sits by the door next to a lit candle. Wildflowers in vases sit on every table.

Someone's covered me with a smelly blanket. I throw it off, but I don't feel any cooler. The room is still sweltering hot. I'm too tall for the sofa. My legs hang over the armrest.

When I yawn, I remember how bad I hurt. My head feels like it's been stuck in a car crusher. One of my eyes is swollen shut. My whole body aches. My ribs are so sore, it's hard to breathe.

With my one good eye, I look out the dusty window. All I can see are leaves. Everything is bright green, like a jungle. Sunshine filters through the thick trees.

What is this place?

I lie motionless, listening to the rasp of my shallow breathing.

Wait. Is the room rocking?

Am I hungover?

No—I didn't drink last night.

I look at the shape of the room. For the first time, I realize I'm in a trailer. It's swaying on its foundations.

Why?

And then I hear it.

"Yeah, just like that. That pussy's so good. So good. Fuck."

I cover my head with the blanket and groan.

My younger brother is getting laid in the back room of the trailer.

There's a slapping sound, followed by what sounds like someone opening a closet door and slamming it a couple dozen times. A woman starts moaning.

"Harder," she says. "Give it to me. You're gonna make me come. I'm gonna come, I'm gonna—"

When she screams, I'm not sure who feels more relief—her, for coming, or me, for not having to listen to Eddie get his rocks off.

"Yes, yes, yes. Oh God. That is so fucking good." There's a deep grunt, like a troll passing a kidney stone. I wonder if I sound like that when I come. I hope not.

My head blazes with pain when I sit up. I find my shoes and put them on. I stumble out of the trailer and blink until my good eye adjusts to the sunlight.

I'm standing in a wild green garden. Rows of vegetables, tall trees, and potted plants cover every square inch of dirt. There's hardly room to walk. Through the branches of the trees, the white walls of County General Hospital rise up beyond the garden fence.

A community garden. This must be the caretaker's trailer.

I find an overturned plastic bucket and sit down. The wall of the run-down trailer is hot from the sun. I lean against it, close my eyes, and let the heat slowly bake the hurt out of my brain.

Jesus Christ.

What have I done?

I've screwed everything up.

After a few minutes, leaves rustle nearby. I automatically grab a shovel leaning against the trailer.

A little old gardener comes out of the garden. He's wearing a white button-down short sleeve shirt and some kind of necklace made out of bone. He's got long white hair, a white beard, and the kind face of a longtime stoner.

He sees the shovel in my hands. *"Tranquilo, tranquilo,"* he says. "This is my house, *soldado*. I'm not here to hurt you."

He goes into the trailer. I sit still. A couple minutes pass. The sun gets hotter. The gardener comes out holding a mug full of hot, scary-looking liquid.

"For your injuries," he says.

I'm thirsty and weak, so I take the mug and drink. It's some kind of tea, and it tastes like shit. When I hand the mug back, the gardener says, "No, no. All of it."

"But I don't want—"

"You'll feel better. I promise." He disappears back into the garden.

I sniff the tea and take another sip. It still tastes like shit, but for some reason, my head is getting clearer. I drink it, mouthful by mouthful, until the mug is empty. The tea, plus the sun, makes me almost feel human.

My body has been broken before. I know how to fix it.

But my heart?

What can fix the empty hole in my chest?

A woman comes out of the trailer. She's tall, dark, and skinny. Her black hair is pulled back in a messy bun. She's wearing a chef's outfit—white jacket, checked pants, and clogs. She looks embarrassed. Quickly, she leaves without making eye contact with me and disappears into the garden.

Now Eddie comes out of the trailer. He's barefoot and shirtless, dressed in only a pair of basketball shorts. Tattoos cover his body—he has even more than I do. He's even gotten tattoos to disguise the ugly scars on his chest and arms.

A fresh cigarette dangles from his lips and a copy of the *LA*

Chronicle is tucked under his arm. He sits down next to me on an old folding chair and lights up. After his first drag, he looks like the definition of the word *mellow*.

"Who was that?" I ask.

"I don't know."

"What?"

"I didn't get her name." Another drag. "She was in the garden this morning, picking vegetables. We had a moment." He grins. "So I took her inside and . . . we partied."

Eddie has always had this talent. One of his nicknames used to be the Pussy Whisperer.

"You look like shit," he says. "How do you feel?"

I shrug. "Your gardener friend gave me some tea. It made me feel better. I don't know what was in it."

My brother laughs. "I hope you don't have a piss test soon."

"What? Why?"

"You feel better because that motherfucker puts weed in everything."

Shit. "How do you know him anyway?"

"Rafa? Rafa grows the best *mota*. I've known him for years. And he lets me crash here when I've got nowhere else to go."

The sun beats down on us, horrible and good at the same time. Eddie finishes his cigarette and opens the newspaper. He pulls out the local section, folds it in half and hands it to me.

"Is this what you were up to last night?"

I squint at the newspaper. The text is too small. My vision is blurry and my head aches.

"Read it to me." I hand the paper back.

"'Arson investigators are looking into an attack that occurred late Sunday in East Los Angeles. The blaze started just after ten at the Hollenbeck Gardens housing complex. A group of arsonists firebombed four separate families using Molotov cocktails. Representatives from the Los Angeles Fire Department reported that all residents were evacuated safely. The fire was put down in fifteen minutes. No injuries were reported.'"

I think of the woman and baby in the unit Demon set on fire. "Thank God," I murmur.

Eddie continues, "'Police officials said the attacks may have been racially motivated. All four families targeted are African American. According to witnesses, the arsonists are Latino. Investigators said race is being considered as a possible motive for the attack based on a history of racial tensions between residents and local gang members.'"

"Fuck." I drop my aching head in my hands. "I never saw who they were. They were Black. That's what connected them."

My brother folds up the paper. "I thought Hollenbeck didn't do shit like this anymore."

"I thought so too."

"So why would the big homies order this?" Eddie asks. "This kind of stuff happened, when? 1992? 1993?"

Back in the day, the Organization made it a priority to "clean up" their neighborhoods and keep them Latino. Gang members were ordered to drive out all Black people by using threats, intimidation, and violence. The idea was to control the drug trade in East L.A. With this in mind, brown-on-black crime was not uncommon. Back in 1992, Hollenbeck gang members firebombed seven black families. For twenty years, Black families were afraid to move into Hollenbeck Gardens. Five or six years ago, as the violence died down and gangs focused on business, things started to change. The neighborhood slowly became more integrated.

"I haven't heard about any problems with Black drug dealers in our territory. Why start up this bullshit now?" I ask.

Eddie shrugs. "Only Ruben would know."

I need to call Ruben, but I don't want to get his voicemail

again. I suspect he's screening me out of his calls. "You got a phone yet?" I ask.

"Yeah. First thing I did when I got out." Eddie reaches into his pocket and takes out his burner.

I flip it open and dial Ruben's number by memory. He answers on the first ring. "Who is this?"

I freeze, surprised to hear his voice after so many weeks.

Eddie nods at me. "Ask him," he says quietly.

"It's Ghost," I say.

Ruben's voice turns to ice. "Why are you calling me?"

Why? Where should I start? "Something happened last night between me and Demon. I want to let you know my side of the story before you decide what to do."

"Demon was arrested. Early this morning. I haven't talked to him."

What? Demon's been picked up? "You need to know, I had some problems last night. I couldn't—"

"I don't have time to hear this right now." Ruben sounds like he's driving. He's on edge, about to hang up. So I cut to my second most important question.

"The kids shaking down Slim—shaking down the businesses along the avenue—they weren't Black. Slim said they were from Las Palmas."

"Slim needs to keep his fat mouth shut." Ruben's voice is deadly. My blood goes cold. "You shouldn't have called me. I'm getting rid of this phone after this call."

"But how do I contact you if—"

Before I can finish my last question, Ruben hangs up.

NINETEEN

I'M STUCK.

Stuck in the jungle.

If the police really picked up Demon, it's not safe for me to be seen out and about.

The hippie *curandero* has set up an outdoor shower. In slow motion, I strip off all my clothes. Every time I move my neck, every time I bend my arms, pain screams through my nervous system.

Wincing, I slink naked to the coral tree behind the trailer. I stand on four paving stones set over a thick layer of moss. A tin bucket punched with holes hangs from a branch above my head. I turn on the tap and a garden hose fills the bucket. Ice-cold water drips down on me. My sore muscles seize up. Everything hurts. I'm covered in cuts and bruises, but still my hand creeps to the familiar patch of dark flesh on my forearm. I grab it. I pinch it, hard. Fresh pain floods my brain like fire, but I don't stop.

"Motherfucker," I whisper. "What have you done? What have you done?"

After I get dressed, I send Eddie out for some Advil. I tell him to get me a new hoodie from the discount store and to pick up a six-pack for Rafa for letting us stay here.

When he's back, Rafa makes us lunch. It's fresh tortillas and *calabacitas,* cut-up vegetables from the garden. My mouth is sore, but every bite makes me feel stronger. I clean my plate. So does Eddie. It's simple food, farmer's food, exactly the kind of thing our mom made for us when we were growing up.

After lunch, Eddie and I wash the dishes. Rafa rolls a fat joint, smokes it, and falls asleep in a hammock.

"Homie knows how to live," Eddie says.

Inside the trailer, I take out my backpack. In the outside pocket is the old sock where I keep my money. I take out the roll of cash and count it. It's all there. Two thousand dollars—a deposit, first, and last month's rent on the apartment I was hoping to get for me and Eddie.

Ten months of savings.

I look at it for a moment.

I know what I have to do.

"Take this." I put the roll in my brother's hand. "Go see Yoda. Have him send a tow truck for Vanessa's car. If this covers the cost of replacing the interior and a loaner car for her, do it. If there's too much damage, see what kind of a car he can find her for two grand. A good one. Reliable, not too beat-up."

Eddie looks at the money. "Where'd you get this?"

"I worked for it, *cabrón.*" I think about all the nights I spent mopping floors and scrubbing toilets on my knees. "I had big plans for that. But . . . this is more important."

"Are you sure?"

I think about Vanessa, getting out of her car carrying groceries, her briefcase, her daughter's backpack—carrying the weight of her world, all by herself. Guilt slams me hard. Did she get a ride to her test this morning? Did she make it on time? "Yeah," I say, "I'm sure."

Eddie takes the money. The wad is too big for his wallet so he rolls it up with a rubber band and puts it in his backpack.

"Make sure any car she ends up with is legit," I say. "The last thing I want is for Vanessa to get caught with a stolen car. Papers, transfer fees, everything. Everything has to be legal. Okay?"

"You got it, boss." Before he zips up the bag, he takes out my keys. "I gave Vanessa all her keys back. But here are the rest of yours."

The ring is light. Two keys from work—the back doors for Defiance and Serenity. Plus the three keys Miguel the church groundskeeper gave me at the carnival.

Eddie looks at them before he hands them over. "How did you get a key to the storage unit? Dad never gave me one."

I freeze. "What?"

He points to the small padlock key. "That one. Right there. Dad's storage unit."

Questions flood my aching brain. "Where is it? And how did you know about it?"

"It's under the freeway. Right next to the nursing home on the other side of the park. He took me there a couple times. He used to keep shit there he didn't want Mom to find."

Almost a year has passed since Dreamer died. I didn't know he had left anything behind. "Do you remember the unit number?"

Eddie nods. We both have a good memory. "Yeah. It was 96. I remember because he always used to joke that 69 turns to 96 when you're full."

"Dirty-ass old man." We laugh a little bit. In spite of the ways he let us down, he was our father.

Eddie checks himself in one of Rafa's feng shui mirrors and rubs his beard. He picks up the backpack. "All right. I'm gonna go. How about you? What are you going to do tonight?"

I search my brother's face and realize that he looks like me. Both of us look like Dreamer. The ghost of our dad haunts our faces. I rub the padlock key between my thumb and forefinger.

"I'm going to wait for it to get dark," I say, "then I'm going to work."

After sunset, Rafa turns on his lights. He's rigged a car battery to a few strings of dusty Christmas lights hung in the trees.

"See you tomorrow, Ghost." He raises his beer bottle to me. He's sitting on the overturned bucket, high as shit, enjoying a spiritual journey.

"Good night." I zip up my new black hoodie and leave him and the jungle in peace.

I sit in the back of the bus and take the short ride to the park. I walk in the shadow of the overpass to the public storage units that Eddie told me about. Unit 96 is an outdoor unit at the end of a long row.

No one is here. The orange streetlamps give off weak light. I slip my key into the padlock and turn. The lock springs loose. I grab the handle and lift the metal door. The slats rattle and squeal.

The dark unit is empty except for three boxes.

Except for Eddie, Angel, me, and a sack of misery, heartache, and bullshit, here is everything Dreamer Rosas left behind. All of his worldly possessions. Three fucking cardboard boxes.

I drag them into the light. I take a knee and paw through them. Inside the first are old financial documents—tax returns, pay stubs, receipts for mortgage payments, account statements, and past-due notices. The second box holds copies of police reports, court documents, paperwork for bonds—a slime trail of his time in and out of jail.

Disappointment weighs on me. I don't know what I wanted to find here, but it wasn't this.

Then I open the third box.

Two framed photos and a binder.

I pick up the first framed photo. My sister, Esperanza. It's her third birthday. She's sitting by a Little Mermaid cake and smiling at the camera. She's wearing a purple dress. You can see three sets of hands on the back of her chair—me and my brothers, but we've been cut out of the picture. Esperanza's hair was curly, like mine. Her party hat is crooked, and there's a punch stain around her mouth. She was always running around, trying to keep up with us. My baby sister—tough and sweet and always laughing.

I trail my finger through the dust on her face, as if I can wipe away time and circumstance. I touch the glass and press it gently.

Is there another world, another universe, where she didn't die? Where we're all together, unbroken?

I wipe my eyes with my sleeve and tuck her picture back into the box.

The second framed photo is from my parents' wedding, taken during the reception in the church hall. I recognize the cabinets that line the wall behind them. My dad is wearing a white tuxedo. He's shaved bald—gangster style, before he got a job and grew out his hair. He's tall and built, with that droop-eyed face that made him look either high or menacing depending on the situation.

My mom is dressed in a big white satin gown with puffy sleeves. Her hair is permed and she's wearing blue eye shadow. Her crown of white flowers matches the white flowers in her bouquet. In the bright flash of the camera, she and my dad look happy but nervous. They were only twenty years old.

I look closer. Under the bouquet, they hold hands. You can

tell they're holding on tight from the grip and the way their fingers are pale. It's almost as if they knew what was coming—that their marriage would be a roller coaster. A terrifying one, especially in the end.

Dreamer had found a good woman and gone straight for her. He left the gang. The stress of living drove him back to Hollenbeck. Neither he nor my mom knew how to cope, and it broke them. Even after fourteen years of marriage, it broke them.

Vanessa's words come back to me. "Two months. You can be good for two months, can't you?"

It's almost like she was bargaining with me. Like she knew I would backslide, and the best she could hope for was two months.

I couldn't even give her that.

Few people find love. Of those, even fewer know how to take care of it.

I failed her.

I put the photo back.

There's one more thing in the box. It's a thick black binder, one a kid might use for school. I tip it toward the light and flip it open.

It holds receipts for payments, going back almost fifteen years. The newest one is dated just before my dad passed away.

What is this?

I squint.

The receipts are from Tierra del Sol Board and Care Facility in Sunland, a half hour's drive north of Los Angeles.

Patient's name—Hortensia Rosas.

Who's that?

Her last name is Rosas, but my dad said all his relatives were dead.

I turn through the pages of the binder, looking for more clues, but I can't find any.

A truck pulls up to a unit across the driveway. The slamming doors shock me out of my trance. I take the last receipt from the front of the binder, fold it and put it in my backpack. I close the binder, put it back in the box, and put the boxes back in the unit.

My head is full of fresh questions. I close the metal door and click the padlock back in place.

I MAKE it just in time for visiting hours. Regina is sitting by Spider's bed. When I lower my hoodie, she says, "*Hijole.* That must have hurt."

"It did."

She stands and I give her an awkward hug. Her eyes are red from crying.

"He told me what you did," she whispers. "Thank you, Ghost."

"Homeboy would've done the same for me."

She grabs her jacket from where it hangs on the chair. "I'll let you two have some time." She leaves, closing the door behind her.

I sit down in the chair. There are weird tubes and things attached to Spider's leg. He's hooked up to monitors and an IV drip. He's not as pale as he was when I brought him here, but he still looks weak. I know he lost a lot of blood last night.

"Look at you," I say.

"Shit, look at you. Who did that?"

"My buddy Demon."

"That fucking lunatic." Spider holds up his fist. He's weak as a baby bird. I bump it.

"What did the doctor say?" I ask.

"Well, first of all, I wasn't shot in the ass."

"That's good."

Spider goes on to tell me about his surgery this morning and the thing attached to his leg.

"It's a wound vac," he says. "Supposed to make me heal faster. That's what they tell me anyway. But they could tell me anything and I'd believe them. I'm on really strong painkillers right now. I'm high as fuck. This is some good shit."

We talk. Spider tells me the police came to question him this afternoon, and not just LAPD either. There were guys with badges from other agencies. ATF and LAFD and FBI. Alphabet soup.

"What did you tell them?" I ask.

"Jack shit," says Spider. "Fuckers got nothing to place me at the scene."

Still, we both know this is bad. A multi-agency task force. Because the attacks were racially motivated, everybody's going to crack down hard on this. The spotlight's on Hollenbeck. Everybody will be watching, including the feds.

"Demon's been arrested."

I remember the shredded glove. "He cut himself on the glass. They'll get a DNA sample."

Attempted first-degree murder. No judge is going to grant bail. Demon is fucked.

"What about Ruben?" I ask. "Did he come see you?"

Spider shakes his head. "No. No one can find him."

"What?"

"Regina went over to the house this afternoon. Ruben's wife said he left two weeks ago. He didn't say where. All his numbers are disconnected."

It's worse than I thought. No Ruben, no Demon. The law is

cracking down on Hollenbeck and our leaders are nowhere to be found.

"Wait a second," I say. "It's you."

"It's me, what?"

"You're next in line. Until Ruben turns up, you're in charge."

Spider nods. "I've been thinking about that ever since Demon got picked up."

"What are you going to do?"

"What Ruben would've done. Tell everyone to lay low and wait for word from Pelican Bay."

Hollenbeck takes all of its orders from homeboys inside the prison system—the highest of the high in the Organization are locked up in Pelican Bay, the supermax state prison in Northern California. Those were the leaders who ordered this hit on Black families in Hollenbeck Gardens. They were the ones who green-lit my dad.

For the first time in a long time, I see a crack in the wall. I see light.

"Spider," I say, "I need something."

Homeboy studies my face. "Name it."

"Cut me loose."

"What?"

Spider is loyal to the gang. He'd bleed for Hollenbeck. He wouldn't feel sympathy for me if I told him I've lost my way.

In the last few weeks, Ruben and Demon and the young homeboys have taught me something that I didn't see before.

Gang leaders find the missing piece inside of us and promise they can fill it, but only if we have honor. Only if we're brave. Only if we do what they say.

It's nothing but manipulation. Nothing but older men using younger men to do their dirty work.

But I don't share these thoughts with Spider.

"My anxiety—it's gotten worse," I lie.

I remind him about the attack I had when I first got out of prison. I show him the bruise on my arm. I tell him I couldn't throw the Molotov cocktail because I was having another breakdown. Demon thought I was being a pussy. But I tell Spider it was my anxiety.

I lie.

I lie to save my own life.

Spider listens. After I finish, he's quiet for a long time. We listen to the hum and beep of the machines in his hospital room. People talk quietly outside. The elevator in the hall dings and the doors slide open. I hold my breath.

"All right," he says at last. "You're retired. Give me a week to let all the homeboys know. They'll leave you alone."

Instead of saying thank you, I take his hand and give it a squeeze.

"Motherfucker," he says, and smiles.

MY REFLECTION in the glass door scares me. I put up my hood, get off the bus, and walk to Defiance.

All the lights in the gym are off and the back door is locked. I stash my backpack, change my T-shirt, and start my work.

Everything is sore, so I move slowly through tasks that should be easy. I fill the mop bucket and wheel the vacuum cleaner out of the closet. I open a new trash bag and do my rounds. Like it always does, my routine calms me down.

Spider is going to be okay. Demon is off the streets. I've been retired from the gang and when word gets out, I'll be safe to walk the streets of my own neighborhood without being afraid I'll get taken out.

I should be happy.

But all I can think about is her.

The way she laughs, loud and deep. The way she runs around in those heels, as if it were as easy to chase a little kid as it was to chase a better career. The way she blots her pizza and halves her churros and worries about the way her ass is getting bigger—so weird to me, like worrying about your bank account getting bigger. Why wouldn't you want something awesome to get bigger?

I'm so distracted that I don't notice the laughter until my hand is on the doorknob of the office.

I freeze.

A woman's giggle.

Goddamn it.

Not again.

Through the blinds in the office, I see them. Barry and Chantal. My boss and the little white girl trainer from Connecticut. She's bent over his desk with her tits smashed against the surface. He's behind her, shirtless, with his warm-up pants pulled down to his knees. I've never seen so much spray-tan in my life. They're going at it hard enough that paint chips are flaking off the wall where the corner of the desk is banging against it.

Chantal has gone all porn star. She's squeaking like a mouse. "Gimme that big cock. Yes. Give it to me. Give it to me, you big stud."

"Yeah, take it, you slippery fucking slut. Take it."

My hand drops from the doorknob. As silently as I can, I step backward and leave the hall. Now would probably be a good time to clean the toilets. Conveniently, I could barf in one if I needed to.

In the bathroom, I get on my knees and scrub.

Try as I might, I can't get the image of them out of my head. I mean, not in a perverted way, but in a philosophical way.

What would it be like to be that free? To get it on whenever you wanted, not caring who saw you, and not giving a shit who judged you?

I flush the toilet and move on to the next one.

What would it be like to have a family who could front you the cash to do the things you wanted—to start your own business, to move across the country, to become an actor?

Flush. Next.

I know Barry and Chantal. They're nice people.

And I know what you're thinking—I'm jealous of them.

The truth is, I'm not. They had no more say over where and how they were born than I did.

I just wonder. Who would I have turned out to be if I'd had what they had?

When I finish my shift, I'm exhausted, but I don't want to get on the bus back home. Vanessa isn't waiting for me when I get back. I'm not ready to face that reality yet.

I walk to the beach. The heavy fog wets my hair and skin. I sit on the cool sand and look out as far as I can over the dark water.

I was once locked up with a homeboy who was doing twenty-five to life. I asked him, "What's the first thing you'll do when you get out?"

He didn't hesitate. "Take off all my clothes and jump into the ocean."

I understood that desire. To be surrounded, embraced, taken away on a current, and stripped of all control. Instead of being bottled up and forgotten, to be poured out into the great darkness where we could rejoin the world at last, just another tiny drop in the sea.

The fog lifts slowly. It thins out until, here and there, little rips show patches of blue sky. Then, all at once, the sun burns away the fog and the world is covered in light.

I tried to be a different man. I tried to do the right thing. But I didn't take the steps I needed to take to transform from the inside out. I didn't make the big changes I needed to make for the new life to take hold.

I failed.

I stand up and brush the sand from my legs.

I walk to Bay City Brews and sit in the parking lot like a hobo until Alan pulls up in his Volvo.

"Hey, Sal. This is a surprise." He unlocks the door for me and sees my face. "Holy crap. Are you all right?"

For the first time in two days, I say something honest. "Not really."

"You want to talk about it?"

"Yeah, but . . . maybe not yet."

Alan nods. In silence, we have coffee and toast. His daytime crew trickles in. Alan takes care of some paperwork before we head to the back room.

We don't talk.

We set up the capper and bottle a batch of *saison* he's calling Beach Bonfire. We take samples of a lager we put up a week ago and do an inventory of his supplies before putting in a new order.

"It's time to check your beer," he says. "Are you ready?"

My first recipe—the *Hefeweizen* brewed with fresh *hoja santa* from Vanessa's garden.

I watch as Alan fills two glasses from the tank. Bubbles rush up through the unfiltered golden liquid and form a snowy white head.

"Looks good," Alan says. "Let's see how it tastes."

We clink glasses and drink.

The flavor fills my mouth. It's not like anything I've ever tasted and yet—it tastes familiar. Bitter and sweet, spicy and cold. The *hoja santa* fills my nose and all of a sudden I'm seven, standing in my mother's garden, holding her basket while she gathers herbs.

"*Un poquito de esto, un poquito de aquello,*" she whispers. "A little bit of this, a little bit of that. That's the secret recipe, Salvador."

I put the glass down on the metal countertop. I can't breathe. A sob escapes from my chest, broken and ugly.

Alan puts his arms around me.

"I'm sorry," I say. "I don't know . . . what the . . . what the fuck is wrong with me."

"Nothing is wrong with you, Sal," he says quietly. "Nothing at all."

WELCOME TO BURBANK.

I walk from the bus stop to my corner store and pick up some eggs and a bunch of bananas. On my way home, I pass house after house with identical floor plans, little cottages built in the '50s. They all have bright green lawns.

I'm copying my brother and growing out a beard. My hair is longish now. With the curls I look like a cross between Jim Morrison and a Mexican Jesus.

This is a nice neighborhood, quiet and well behaved, but just to be safe, I always wear long sleeves and keep my tattoos covered up. I don't know any of my neighbors. I'm just a stranger here. To be honest, I like it. Being alone doesn't bother me.

The days are getting colder. The wind blows through my hoodie. I have to buy a real jacket soon.

My apartment complex is small, twelve units total. There's a courtyard with a palm tree. My apartment is on the second floor.

I live alone even though I have two bedrooms. For a week, Eddie tried to live with me, but he got bored and took the bus back to East L.A. At first I was angry with him, but I've come to realize he's his own man. He has to find his own way.

Today was leg day at Defiance, so I make myself an omelet and a protein shake with two bananas. I eat my breakfast at the counter, then wash my dishes and put them away.

Surprise, surprise—my place is neat and tidy. Not that there's much to keep clean. I've got a new mattress and one armchair from the Goodwill store. That's it.

Instead of going straight to bed, I take off my shoes, open my blinds, and sit in the armchair. In the light from the window, I open one of the books Alan gave me about the history of beer. I read a chapter about Trappist monks.

Would I make a good monk? Shit, I'm living the life of one right now. Minus the prayer, I guess.

I doze off with the book in my hands.

Someone knocks at the door.

Who's visiting me? No one visits me.

I get up and look through the peephole.

It's Vanessa.

What the fuck?

I look again, just to make sure.

Yeah, it's her.

I run a hand through my hair.

What's she doing here?

Get a grip, Sal.

I unchain the door and open it.

I haven't seen Vanessa since the night of the fire, but she's lived in my head nonstop for the past eight weeks. Night and day, thoughts of her push out all my other thoughts. For the luxury of every memory, every wet dream, I pay a high price— regret for the mistakes I made. Regret for the way I lost her.

But thoughts of Vanessa can't compete with the reality of Vanessa, standing here at my front door.

My whole body wakes up from its two-month nap. My blood heats up, melting my heart until it starts beating again.

She's wearing boots and jeans and a soft sweater that rides her curves. Her long dark hair is loose and she's wearing her red lipstick, I think, to kill me.

"Hey." My voice sounds far away. Nervous and scared.

"Hey." She looks at my chest and my beard and my hair and the apartment behind me, but she avoids making eye contact. "I'm just here . . . to . . . uh, give you this. It was sent to the house by mistake."

She reaches into her purse and takes out a thick envelope. It has my name on it but her address. It's from Greenbriar University in Glendale.

"Oh, shit." The words escape my mouth before I realize I've said them.

"Exactly." She holds up the envelope higher. "Take it."

When I take the envelope, she turns to leave.

"Wait," I say quickly. "Can you stay while I open it?"

"What?"

"You helped me write the application. I don't think I can do this alone."

She looks at the envelope in my hands and then up into my eyes at last. Pain flashes between us for a moment before I open the door wider and say, "Just for a second. Come inside."

She brushes past me and the scent of her strawberry shampoo goes straight to the pleasure center inside my brain. That's the smell of lying naked in bed with a beautiful woman. That's the smell of three orgasms a day. That's the smell of soft skin and wild mornings and falling asleep on her pillow after she goes to work.

Just like that, I'm hard as a crowbar.

I adjust my boner so she doesn't see it.

She looks around my apartment. "So this is your place?"

"Yeah, yeah. My friend Alan loaned me the money." I try to see it from her perspective. No one would be impressed by this. "Uh, I got a chair." I point out the boring beige armchair. "It's really comfortable. Have a seat." I move the book out of the way.

Vanessa looks at me with an eyebrow raised and sits down.

I look at her for a moment and try not to feel what I'm feeling, but it's hopeless.

This is my apartment. This is my chair. Vanessa is sitting in my chair in my apartment just like she sits in my heart. There is only one seat in my heart, and it's hers. It will always be hers.

"So," she says.

"So."

"Are you going to open it?"

Carefully, I tear open the envelope. Inside is a full-color folder of the university and a group of smiling students clinking beer bottles. The folder is stuffed with flyers and documents, but right on top is a letter from the director of the hospitality management program.

"Read it," Vanessa says. She's excited for me, which means way more than whatever is written in this letter.

"'Dear Salvador Rosas, Congratulations on being admitted into the Brewing Science program at Greenbriar University. It is my pleasure to welcome you to this innovative program and to offer you a full scholarship. We were impressed by your application. You placed among our top group of applicants, and we are excited to have you join us.'"

I blink. "Hold up. I have to read that again." I read the letter to myself a second time. At the bottom of the letter is a hand-written note from the director. *We enjoyed your beer. Well done.*

Vanessa's smiling. "You got in."

"I got in."

"With a full scholarship."

"With a full scholarship."

I look at the letter, front and back. This has to be a joke. Why would they want me? I didn't hide that I dropped out of high school. They know I got my associate's degree in prison. I'm a fucking lowlife. And yet . . . they're going to pay me to attend their school?

Vanessa takes the letter out of my hands and reads it to herself.

"You sent them a beer?" she asks.

I smile. "Yeah."

"What kind of beer?"

Alan and I bottled the second batch two days ago. He's selling it as a special edition at Bay City Brews, but he says the recipe belongs to me. "Do you want to try some? I have a bottle in the fridge."

She glances at her watch. "It's nine o'clock in the morning."

"You mean it's beer o'clock." I go to the fridge and take out the bottle. I put it on the edge of the counter and smack it. The cap flies off.

"You make beer and you don't have a bottle opener?" she says.

"What?" I say. "It's open, ain't it?" I pour a glass for her, complete with a foamy head.

She takes the glass and clinks it against my bottle. "Congratulations, Sal."

We drink. I watch her as she takes a sip. She smiles and takes another. "What is this? It's delicious."

"This is a *Hefeweizen* flavored with *hoja santa*. I got the idea sitting in your backyard. The flavors complement each other. Spicy, not bitter."

Vanessa takes a third sip. "What do you call it?"

Alan had his graphic designer make up a special edition label using the Old English font from one of my tattoos. I hand Vanessa the bottle. "You gave me the idea for the name too."

She reads the label aloud. "Eastside Pride." She turns the bottle back and forth in the light from the window. Golden sunlight fills the brown glass.

"I can't stop thinking about you," I say quietly.

"Sal—"

"Every moment, Vanessa. Every moment is filled with you. With regret over what I did to you." My arms ache to embrace her but I hold back.

She puts the bottle and glass down on the windowsill. "Why? Why did you lie to me? I'm a big girl. I grew up in the hood, same as you. I can handle the truth. Why didn't you respect me enough to tell me the truth?"

I kneel on the carpet in front of her. "I didn't want to lose you," I say. "If you knew the truth about me, you'd kick me out of your life. If you knew the truth about how scared I was, what a fucking coward I was, you would have made me go."

"People can't leave gangs," she says quietly. "Can they?"

"Not really. If you drop out, if you stop taking orders, any homeboy has the right to take you down if he sees you on the streets. That's what happened the night of the fire." I look into her sad eyes. "I thought I could figure out a way to cut myself loose. To convince Ruben to let me go. But I wasn't brave enough or strong enough to do it. By the time Demon and Spider showed up at the house, I was too late."

I decide to tell her everything that happened the night of the firebombings up to my visit with Spider in the hospital. If the police come to question her, she can tell them whatever she wants—it's her choice. But she deserves to know the truth.

When I finish the story, I'm sitting cross-legged on the floor.

"If you're retired from the gang and Spider tells the homeboys to leave you alone, why did you move away from the neighborhood?" Vanessa asks.

"After everything that happened," I say, "I knew I had to

leave. To start over. The guilt and the regret were too strong." I look up at her. "Every time I thought about how I hurt you—it was like stabbing a knife into my chest, again and again."

Vanessa is quiet for a long time. I don't know what to say, so I just sit there, waiting. At last, she wipes her eyes with her fingertips and shakes her head. "My mascara," she says. "Can I use your bathroom?"

"Sure," I say. "Down the hall."

I hear the door close and the water run. When it opens again, there's silence.

"Sal?"

I stand up and join her in the hallway. "What's wrong?"

"What's that?" Vanessa points. The door to the spare bedroom is open and spread out on the carpet is an old bedsheet. There's a toolbox and steel wool. The little bicycle that used to belong to Vanessa is upturned on the sheet where I've been removing some rust from the frame.

"Oh, yeah," I say. "Uh, about that."

I follow her into the bedroom. She examines the bike. "I thought I told you to throw this away."

"Right. So technically, I didn't steal it." I smile at her but she doesn't smile back. "When Yoda towed your grandfather's truck, I put this in the bed and told him to hang on to it for me. I don't have much to do in the afternoons. Restoring this has been a good way to pass the time."

"Were you going to sell it?"

"Sell it? No." I turn the wheel. "I was planning on having it ready by Christmas. I was going to have Eddie deliver it, Christmas morning, all dramatic. The tag would say, 'To Muñeca. From Santa.'"

Tears fill her eyes. "Motherfucker," she says.

"Do you mean motherfucker in a good way . . . or a bad way?" I ask.

"I was so lonely. You have no idea how lonely I was, every day with nothing but work and my kid and bills. Then you come into my life, and Sal, it was like I came alive again." She sobs. I want to wrap my arms around her, but still I hold back. She slips into Spanish, the language we use for our deepest feelings. "It's like you woke me up after I'd been asleep for five years. Every part of me, awake and alive. But now, without you, I'm twice as lonely as I was before. As if being happy for a short time only magnified my loneliness instead of weakening it."

I watch as she runs her fingers over the dusty streamers on the sheet.

"I heard you passed your test," I say. "I'm proud of you. I knew you would."

She nods but says nothing.

"I'm sorry, Vanessa. I'm sorry for that night, for everything."

"I know."

"You and me, we happened real fast," I say.

Vanessa smiles sadly. "When it comes to guys, I don't really know how to go slow."

For the first time in two months, I reach forward and cup her cheek in my hand. Her tears are warm. The touch of her soft skin turns my willpower to dust. My heart pounds against my rib cage.

"How about we try it now?" I ask.

"Try what?"

"Going slow."

"Slow, huh?" She looks up at me. "I'd like that."

Vanessa lets me lead her into my bedroom. As I remove each piece of clothing from her body, I run my hands over her exposed skin. My nerve endings drink in her softness. Down to her pink lace bra and panties, she lies down in my bed—technically, my queen-size mattress on the floor—and holds out her arms.

"Come here," she whispers.

I lie down over her, pinning her hips to the mattress with mine. She runs her fingers through my hair and pulls my head down into a soft, sweet kiss. I nip at her red lips. She parts her teeth and I slip the tip of my tongue between them. She licks me and a jolt shakes my entire body.

"Your beard—it's rough," she whispers against my lips.

"Should I shave it?"

"No. I like it."

Her hands slide underneath my clothes and soon she's stripped me down to my boxers. With a clever wrestling move, she flips me onto the mattress and straddles me. Through the lace of her panties and the cotton of my boxers, I feel her heat.

She runs her hands all over my chest as she takes a slow ride, grinding down on my hard cock. I rest my hands on her hipbones and look up at her.

This girl—this woman—drives me crazy.

So smart and sexy and tough.

She took a chance on me once and she's taking a chance on me again.

I will not let her down a second time.

It's my turn to pull her down into another hot kiss. The last of our clothes melt away and I hold her feverish body against me. Pinned against her soft stomach, my dick is hard and wet. She is so perfect I wonder for a moment if I'm dreaming, sitting in my armchair nudging a book about Trappist monks off my lap with my steel-hard cock.

Vanessa breaks the kiss and starts a slow journey down my body. She kisses my neck just below my beard. She kisses my shoulders, my collarbone, and my chest. With the tip of her tongue, she swirls my nipples. My head drops back on the pillow and I close my eyes. This feels too good to be real. Too good to be anything but a dream.

Her hand slides down my abs. She grabs the base of my cock in her little fist and gives me a hard pump. With a happy sigh, she wraps her lips around the head of my cock and starts to go down on me. She sucks me hard while teasing the head of my cock with little flicks of her tongue. At the same time, she kneads my shaft in her fist, stroking in time with her mouth.

It's too much. I have to hold back as I push her back gently.

"Not yet," I whisper.

I lay her on her back and cover her neck with kisses. I knead her tits and suck on her dark nipples until the hard, pretty tips turn rosy from my tongue.

When I reach down between her legs, my fingertips drown in her wetness.

"I'm still on the pill," she whispers. "I haven't been with anyone since you."

I kiss her full red lips and swirl my fingertip around her hard little clit. "I haven't been with anyone since you either."

She spreads her legs for me. I take my dick in my hand and slide it up and down her swollen lips. She's slick and hot. My whole body aches to dive in but I massage her clit with the head of my cock until she's trembling, grasping on to my forearms like she's falling off the edge of a cliff.

"Please," she says.

I press the head of my cock against her opening and push. Her tight lips stretch to crown me. She shuts her eyes tight and holds her breath. I lift myself up on my arms and swing my hips forward, slamming my dick into her so deep I can feel her wetness on my balls. We moan. I pull back and slam into her again. She arches her back. Goosebumps break out all over her body. I pull back once more—this time almost to the tip—and thrust hard.

"Whatever you want in a man," I whisper in her ear. "Whatever you need. I want to become him."

She opens her eyes and touches my face. "Don't be stupid," she whispers. "You are already what I want in a man. You are what I need."

Hot blood races through my veins. I lose myself in Vanessa—her touch, her voice, her scent. The way her pussy milks me, urging me on with each thrust until I can't hold back. I grab her hips and with the tip of my dick, thrust hard against her sweet spot again and again and again until her entire body locks up.

"Sal," she whispers, "I'm going to come."

When her orgasm rips through her, I let go. We come together, grabbing on to each other and cursing, the pleasure so strong it binds us together like fire fusing two pieces of glass into one.

Afterward, we hold each other. Our legs are tangled together under the covers. Vanessa strokes my arm from shoulder to wrist and back again. When her fingers rest on the fading bruise, I flinch.

"Tell me about this." She looks into my eyes. "Tell me the truth."

One of the hardest things I've ever done is return to therapy. For a long time, in my head, admitting I needed help was the same as admitting defeat. But now I know this isn't true.

I hold my arm up to the light where we can both see the bruise. "This—this is my anxiety," I say. "I self-harm."

As I explain what I've learned, Vanessa listens. I tell her about my therapist. I tell her about negative thought patterns and coping skills.

"At first, I thought therapy was complete bullshit," I say quietly. "But then I gave it a chance. It helps."

"How often do you see your therapist?"

"Once a week for one hour."

Vanessa takes my wrist and gently brings my arm to her lips.

I hold my breath. When she kisses the bruise, my soul cracks open.

"I'm proud of you, Sal," she whispers.

For the first time in weeks, the anger and regret and sadness in my chest go silent. Now I feel a deep sense of peace. Even stronger than that, I feel a sense of possibility—Vanessa and I have a future together. It's as bright and beautiful as she is.

Right before she falls asleep, she says, "I missed you."

I kiss her forehead and stroke her hair.

I wish I could bottle up this moment and save it for a million years.

"I missed you too, *hermosa,*" I whisper.

EPILOGUE

CHRISTMAS MORNING

RED IS Muñeca's favorite color. I painted the bicycle candy-flake red and her mom got her a matching helmet. I sit on the back porch steps with my brother and Chinita, who holds the evil wiener dog in her arms. Together, we watch the little girl ride circles around and around on the driveway. Sunlight glitters on her helmet.

Eddie is enjoying a big plate of tamales, courtesy of Chinita. I hand him an ice-cold bottle of Eastside Pride.

"Yes. Break out that opener, homes."

I reach into my pocket for my keys.

On the ring are the three keys from Dreamer and the key for my apartment in Burbank. But there are also keys to Vanessa's house, where I spend two days a week. I've been upgraded from "Mommy's Special Friend" to "Mommy's Boyfriend," which, I have to say, is pretty tight. I've given notice at both of my jobs in Santa Monica, so I'll be turning in my keys for Serenity Day Spa and Defiance Gym next month when I start my studies at Greenbriar.

It's unreal, the way my life has shaped up.

On my keychain is a new metal bottle opener, engraved

with a rose—my last name, Rosas. Even cooler than that are the words engraved below it.

"From Vanessa. With Love."

She gave the bottle opener to me last night after midnight mass, all wrapped up with a bow.

With my new baller-ass bottle opener, I pop open Eddie's beer. The bottle releases a satisfying hiss. I watch my brother as he takes a long drink.

"Damn. That's some good shit," he says.

"Watch your language around my great-grandbaby, Eduardo," Chinita scolds. She turns to me with an annoyed look on her face. "I like you, Sal, but your brother? I'm not so sure."

Vanessa comes out of the house. "Are you guys ready to go?"

I stand up and give my girlfriend a kiss on the cheek. "Almost ready."

Eddie shotguns the beer and puts his plate in the sink. I put on my jacket and pick up the poinsettia plant on the kitchen table.

"Okay, let's go," I say.

Chinita and Muñeca wave us off.

"Good luck!" Chinita calls as we back out of the driveway.

The Tierra del Sol Board and Care Facility is an orange stucco building on a busy street in Sunland. It's not fancy, but the small garden by the front door is neat and the parking lot is swept up. I open the door for Vanessa and my brother and we walk to the reception desk. I hold the poinsettia in my hands.

There's an Asian woman in scrubs behind the counter. "Good afternoon," she says. "How may I help you?"

"Hello," I say. "We're here to visit Hortensia Rosas."

The woman looks surprised. She searches our faces. "Oh," she says.

"Is something wrong?" Vanessa asks.

"No, not at all. Mrs. Rosas doesn't get many visitors, that's all." She pauses. "None, in fact." She pushes a clipboard across the counter and asks us all to sign in. She checks our ID cards and gives us visitor stickers to put on.

"Follow me," she says.

As she leads us down a long, sunny corridor, Eddie tries to chat her up. "So, working on Christmas, huh? That's rough."

"We're a twenty-four-hour facility," she replies.

"Are your patients all seniors?"

"Not all. But they are all adults. Many are living with Alzheimer's disease and dementia. We have a trained medical staff and a doctor on call."

The woman stops at the room at the end of the hall. "Wait here, please." She knocks and goes inside. After a minute, she steps out and opens the door. "Okay. You can go in. If you need anything, just press the button by the side of the bed." She turns and walks back down the hall.

I look at Vanessa. "Here we go."

We step inside. It's a simple bedroom, with a chest of drawers and a closet. There's a private bathroom with a shower you can sit down in. Instead of a regular bed, there's a hospital bed. There are no decorations in the room—no photos, no paintings.

By the window is a woman in a wheelchair. She's dressed in a jogging suit. There's a blanket over her lap. Someone has brushed and arranged her gray hair into a braid. She's wearing lip gloss.

"Hello?" Eddie says.

She doesn't move.

I put the poinsettia down on the nightstand.

We stand in a half circle in front of the woman. Her eyes are fixed on the wall behind us, as if we are aren't there.

"Señora? Hortensia?" Vanessa says.

No response.

The woman's hands are crossed in her lap. Her expression is not happy, not sad. She looks like she's in deep concentration, lost in her own thoughts.

I study her face. She's familiar—she has a square jaw, like mine. Her hair, where it escapes from the braid, is curly.

"I think," I say, "I think this might be our grandmother."

"But Dad said she died," Eddie says. "Way back when he was sixteen."

"The receipts in the binder went back fifteen years. He kept the binder in the storage unit where he didn't want Mom to see it. Why?"

I look at Eddie, who shrugs.

"And an even bigger mystery—these places aren't cheap," Vanessa says. "Who's been paying for her care since your dad passed away?"

We look at the woman in the wheelchair. I get down on my knees, reach forward and put my hand over hers. Her skin is warm. Because she hasn't moved, I thought she'd be cold—cold like a statue. But she's very much alive.

"Señora," I say quietly, "my name is Salvador Rosas. This is my brother Eddie, and my girlfriend, Vanessa Velasco. My dad was Dreamer Rosas." I struggle to remember my dad's real name. He's always been Dreamer to me. "José-Luis. Did you know José-Luis?"

The woman blinks, but she can't see me. She says nothing.

Before we leave, Vanessa puts the red poinsettia on the chest of drawers where the old lady can see it. She straightens the blanket and lightly touches the woman's shoulder.

"What a mystery," Vanessa whispers.

With more questions than ever, we walk in silence back to the reception desk. We take off our visitor's passes and put them in the trash. Before we leave, Vanessa stops and turns to the nurse.

"Excuse me," she says. "Would it be possible to add my name as an emergency contact for Hortensia? I believe the primary emergency contact will be out of the country for a few months and you might not be able to get ahold of him."

"Of course," the woman says. "Let me pull up her file."

Her fingers fly over the keyboard. An input form appears on the screen.

"Is the account paid through the next six months? Or through the next year?" Vanessa asks. She's a genius, my girlfriend.

The woman scrolls down. "Uh, no. This particular account is paid month-to-month. Looks like by cashier's check, received on the first." More keyboard clacks. "Okay. What's your phone number?"

Vanessa gives her number.

"And your email address?"

"Uh, it's kind of complicated," Vanessa says. "Can I type it in?"

"Yeah, sure. Enter it right there." The woman slides the keyboard to Vanessa and turns the monitor so she can see it. Behind her, I sneak a peek at the existing emergency contact number and burn it into my memory.

"Thank you so much." Vanessa returns the keyboard and turns the monitor back. We exchange a glance.

"Of course," the woman says.

If someone has taken all this effort to care for Hortensia Rosas without leaving a trail of information, they will probably pick up the phone if Tierra del Sol calls. I clear my throat. "Sorry to be such a pain," I say. "My phone ran out of battery. Could I borrow your phone really quick?"

The woman looks at me suspiciously. I can see what she's thinking. Why not borrow Vanessa's phone, or my brother's phone? But her politeness wins out. She hands me the phone behind the desk.

"Dial 9 for an outside line," she says.

Eddie and Vanessa watch me as I dial the emergency contact number. My heart is beating hard. My hands are cold.

On the second ring, someone picks up. "Hello?"

I shiver like a ghost just walked over my grave. I'd know that voice anywhere. "Dad?"

He hangs up on me.

I put down the phone.

Eddie and Vanessa stare at me.

"He's alive," I say. "Dreamer Rosas is alive."

AN EASTSIDE BREWERY PLAYLIST

"The Town I Live In"—Thee Midniters
"One Time One Night"—Los Lobos
"Forever Mine"—The O'Jays
"Handful of Water"—Sofia Valdés
"Ojos Del Sol"—Y La Bamba
"Rayito de Luna"—Los Panchos
"You Don't Know Me"—Caetano Veloso
"Put Me In Jail"—Sunny & The Sunliners
"Andar Conmigo"—Julieta Venegas
"Devil or Angel"—The Clovers
"That's All"—Thee Midniters
"El Chico del Apartamento 512"—Selena
"Angel Baby"—Rosie and the Originals
"Nobody's Clown"—Los Yesterdays
"Oh My Angel"—Bertha Tillman
"Un Millón de Primaveras"—Vicente Fernández
"I'm So Proud"—The Impressions
"I Wish You Love"—Joe Bataan
"Tu Cabeza en Mi Hombro"—Enrique Guzmán

"When Somebody Loves You Back"—Teddy Pendergrass
"Las Golondrinas"—Mariachi Vargas De Tecalitlán
"Por Mujeres Como Tú"—Pepe Aguilar
"Saint Behind the Glass"—Los Lobos
"Always and Forever"—Heatwave

NOTE TO READERS

In 2014 and 2015, I volunteered at a gang intervention and reentry program. During my time there, I spent many hours conducting in-person interviews with trainees. Their stories of trauma and transformation inspired the characters in *Thirsty*.

ACKNOWLEDGMENTS

To Jennifer Haymore. Your kindness and mentorship have formed the basis for my entire career. How can I thank you for all you've done? Let's start with a beer. I definitely owe you a beer.

To Deidre Knight and Heather Tebbs. Thank you for believing in Sal (and in me).

To Lindsey Vargas, Berenice Escobedo, Oscar Ramirez, Nicholas Marrone, and Cheryl Klein. What a dream team! Thank you all for your time, patience, and expertise.

To Art Laboe at *The Art Laboe Connection*. I'd like to dedicate "Just Don't Want to Be Lonely" by The Main Ingredient to Brent Hopkins. Please tell him I love him. Could you send him some kisses? Thanks, Art.

To the staff and trainees at Homeboy Industries, my heartfelt thanks always.

And most of all, to my readers. Thank you for picking up this book and giving me the gift of your time. I'll never take it for granted.

ALSO BY MIA HOPKINS

The Eastside Brewery series

Thirsty

Trashed

Tanked

The Cowboy Cocktail series

Cowboy Valentine

Cowboy Resurrection

Cowboy Player

Cowboy Karma

Cowboy Rising

The Kings of California series

Deep Down

Hollywood Honkytonk

ABOUT THE AUTHOR

Mia Hopkins writes lush romances starring fun, sexy characters who love to get down and dirty. Her award-winning books have been featured by many publications including *The New York Times, The Washington Post, USA Today* and *Entertainment Weekly.* She lives in Los Angeles with her family.

For more information...
www.miahopkinsauthor.com

@miahopkinsxoxo

Read on for an excerpt from
Trashed
An Eastside Brewery Novel
by Mia Hopkins

ONE

At sunset, I ride across the bridge. Behind me is my hood. In front of me, beyond the river and the rail yards, downtown Los Angeles rises up with its tall buildings and cranes like giants.

For Valentine's Day, pink and red lights flash along the top of the US Bank Tower. I'm a romantic. You wouldn't know it by looking at me. My friend Rafa teased me before I left the trailer.

"Going to see your Valentine, Trouble?" he asked.

"Shit, I wish," I said.

My lonely ass passes warehouses and factories, homeless camps and fancy remodeled apartment buildings. In the jewelry district, traffic gets heavy, but I weave through the cars.

The place I'm looking for sits on the ground floor of one of the big glass skyscrapers. White light floods its sign, no missing it.

Giacomo's.

I ride my bike down a narrow alley until I find a pair of Dumpsters and a back door.

The cold wind between the buildings is so strong, I almost fall over when I stop. I catch myself and carefully lock my piece-of-shit bike to some exposed pipes. My ears are still ringing from the wind as I open the heavy metal door. It slams shut behind me.

I stand there, blinking in the bright lights.

I've never been in a restaurant kitchen before. It's big. Red tile floor. Everything is steel—countertops, shelves, refrigerators, ovens, pots and pans. There's an army of cooks dressed in striped pants and white jackets and aprons, cutting vegetables or butchering meat or mixing up weird-looking things in bowls as big as sinks.

I'm supposed to find the general manager. For a second, I study the faces of the staff. A couple of them are white, but most of them are brown. Are any of these guys the general manager?

I take another step into the kitchen. Some of the cooks raise their heads from their work. A few of them look surprised before they turn their faces away.

This reaction is nothing new to me.

I'm not exactly Mickey Mouse.

A cook pushing a cart full of boxes crosses my path. He's got a big black mustache and that ageless look the *veteranos* in my neighborhood sometimes have. He could be twenty-eight or fifty-eight—hard to tell.

"Excuse me," I say to him, "I'm looking for the general manager. Do you know where he is?"

"The GM? Dino?" The cook looks too busy to ask who I am or what I want with the general manager. "Check the office. Over there." He gestures to some doors on the other side of the kitchen.

The other cooks give me the side eye as I cross their territory and enter the swinging doors. On the other side across a hallway is a tiny office where a white dude in a navy-blue suit and a pink shirt sits at a desk.

"Hello?" I ask.

The man swivels in his chair. He's got narrow shoulders and

a little paunch. His gray hair is wavy and carefully styled. His reaction to me is exactly what I expect. He sits up straight and his eyes widen. We're alone in the office and he's scared.

"Can I help you?" he asks.

"Uh, yeah, hi," I say in a quiet voice. "My employment agency sent me. They told me you need a dishwasher tonight." I take my papers out and hand them over to him, along with my ID, just to save time.

The man looks at my ID and eyes me suspiciously. "Eduardo Rosas."

It's my real name, but I still feel weird when I hear it. "Yes, sir," I say. "Eddie."

He hesitates slightly as he puts his hand out to shake mine. "Dino Moretti."

We get some paperwork done together as I stand in the tiny office. I see shelves of binders, a corkboard pinned with receipts, and an old timecard machine. A split-screen monitor shows the six security cameras set up around the restaurant.

Dino studies me without trying to be obvious about it. What's he thinking? Has he hired anyone like me before? Do the tattoos on my neck scare him? From his reaction to me, they might.

Dino types my information directly into the computer. "Are you available to work full time?"

"Yes, I'm looking for full-time work."

"Are you able to lift twenty-five pounds?"

When I don't answer, he looks up from the screen and we make eye contact. I know he has to ask this question, but let's face it, I'm a gorilla. Six-foot-two, two-twenty. "Uh, yeah," I say, and for the first time, the guy cracks a smile.

"Emergency contact information?"

"My older brother. Salvador Rosas." I open up my cheap flip phone and find Sal's number. I read it out loud.

Dino taps in the number and clicks the mouse a few times. Then he turns back to me. "Let me tell you a little bit about us. Giacomo's is a fine dining establishment, open only for dinner. We do one hundred and fifty covers a night."

I don't know what that means so I just nod.

"We specialize in regional Italian food. My brother Giacomo is the executive chef. He's the head of the kitchen. When he is on a book tour or traveling to promote the restaurant, like right now, his sous chef Carmen Centeno is in charge." He looks sideways at me. "As a heads-up, her word is law. She runs a very tight ship. No slacking. No shortcuts. I've seen her throw staff out of her kitchen at the height of service. Understand?"

I nod. "Yes. Got it."

"Have you washed dishes in a commercial kitchen before?"

"Yes, sir." It's a lie, but I need this job.

"Good," says Dino. "The other gentleman you'll be working with is also new. He has never worked dish. You can show him the ropes. Go ahead and get set up."

With that, Dino turns back to his computer and picks up the phone. I stand there for a moment before I realize we're done.

When I find the employee restroom, I stash my bag and hoodie in an empty locker. I don't have a lock, but I don't have anything worth stealing either. I walk over to the dishwashing area and slip a plastic apron on over my head.

A kid comes toward me through the busy kitchen. He's white, a little younger than me. He's got plugs in his ears and a pierced nose. He's got tattoos too, dragons and flowers up and down his arms. His tattoos are the colorful, expensive kind, done in a shop. Compared with his, mine look rough and sloppy. But they should. They're prison tattoos.

"Hey," the kid says. "Are you the other dishwasher tonight?"

"Yeah." I pause, reminding myself to use my real name. "I'm Eddie."

"Nice to meet you," he says. "Boner."

"Boner?"

"Yeah," he says, like it's no big thing for me to call him Boner. "Dino told me you've done this before and that I should listen to what you say."

Because he's from my employment agency, I figure it wouldn't hurt to tell him the truth. I say quietly, "Listen. I haven't really done this before."

The kid's bright blue eyes get wide. "You haven't?"

"No."

"But—"

I fake a confident smile. "It's just washing dishes, right? We'll figure it out."

Together, we examine our station. On one wall, there's a sink with three sections. On the other wall, there's a bigger sink with a silver sprayer and a weird silver box-thing with two doors that slide down on both sides. I assume this is the dishwashing machine. A stack of plastic racks sits underneath on its own shelf. A conveyor belt slides through the machine, kind of like a mini carwash.

I'm pretty good with cars and fixing things, so after messing with the buttons, I think I know how this thingy works.

Boner and I make a plan. We figure he'll organize the dishes on the countertop as they come in. Then I'll stack them in the racks and run them through the machine.

No problem, right?

All of a sudden, the noisy kitchen goes quiet. Boner and I watch from our corner as an army of servers comes in through the swinging doors and stands in a circle by the line. They're dressed in black from head to toe. They're wearing long black aprons that fall down past their knees. Someone is standing in the middle of the group.

"Who is it?" Boner whispers.

"The chef, I guess," I say, but I can't see.

"Okay, here we go," says a woman's voice. It's deep, loud, and steady—the voice of a federal judge or the captain of a ship full of nuclear weapons. "Valentine's Day specials. Listen carefully and hold all questions until the end, understood?"

"Yes, Chef," the staff says.

She says something in Italian and then translates it to English. "Farmer's market vegetable salad, organic rose petals, pancetta, and vinaigrette." She says something else in Italian. "Seared scallops with blood orange and salsify." She says one more thing in Italian. "Wagyu beef two ways, served with polenta and roasted red beets." I hear a ruffling of papers. "Tonight's fresh pasta is tagliatelle with *sugo di carne* and parmesan. Special dessert, mascarpone *semifreddo* with crushed amaretti and candied flowers. Questions?"

The wait staff asks a few questions, and for some reason, I find myself zoning out, wishing I could listen to more of the chef's voice. It's sexy, a little rough.

Man, it's been a long time.

A long time.

Before my mind wanders back to that morning in the garden, the meeting ends. The waiters all clear out and the staff gets back to their stations. The chef has disappeared, the kitchen settles in. Boner and I watch as the cooks check all their ingredients and make sure all their equipment is in the proper place. They look calm and happy.

"See?" I elbow Boner. "They're chill. This'll be cake."

The kid smiles nervously and reties his apron. "Do you think we should ask someone, just to make sure we're doing the right thing?"

That would expose my lie and put me out of a job. I wave my hand, all casual even though I feel anxious too. "We'll be fine. Don't worry."

At that exact moment, the ticket machine at the end of the metal counter screams to life.

Two hours later, Boner and I are in deep shit.

Not only are busboys dropping off endless tubs of dirty dishes, prep cooks are dropping off stacks of sauté pans and saucepans faster than we can wash them. Our dish pit is a clusterfuck.

I'm cranking, but as soon as I put one rack through the machine, another five appear next to me. Boner is stacking the dishes as fast as he can, but the kid is in over his head. The machine takes a minute and a half but even that isn't fast enough to keep up.

A busser takes pity on us. With a disgusted look on his face, he shows Boner how to separate the plates and the glasses into the correct plastic racks. Then he has to go—he has his own responsibilities to take care of.

Goddamn.

What have I gotten us into?

All around us, the kitchen is a blazing hell of fire, food, knives, hot pans, and cooks busting their asses to get their dishes done. I can hear the female chef barking orders at her staff. "Two *sugo*, one branzino, fire four beef specials!" Each time she says something, all the cooks yell back at her in unison, "Chef!"

A busser drops off another tray full of dirty dishes. I curse under my breath. All of a sudden, the conveyor belt stops.

Boner and I look at each other.

"What the—?" There's absolute fear in his eyes.

I've been in prison riots. I've been pepper-sprayed and Tasered. I've had my balls kicked in by rival gangsters. Hell, I've even been shot.

Still, panic hits me when I realize the dishwashing machine has stopped working.

"You check what's going on. I'll clear off the dishes on the other side." Boner wipes his hands on his pants.

"Okay." I squirt some water on an extremely dirty sauté pan covered in what looks like fresh blood. The water hits a big metal spoon in the sink and sprays Boner's face. Now there's a huge puddle all over the floor.

"Shit, I'm sorry," I say.

"It's okay, it's okay." The kid wipes his face with his arm. He's a good sport, considering how I've fucked us both over in a big way. On the other side of the machine, he picks up a full tray of dishes and hauls it over his skinny shoulder.

Then it happens.

Like a palm tree in a hurricane, he bends to the right and bends to the left. He catches himself and a feeling of extreme relief hits me—until he takes one step backward, slips on the wet floor, and falls over completely. His feet fly up toward the ceiling.

The kitchen is loud, full of yelling chefs and clanking pots and pans. But when the tray of dishes crashes to the floor, smashing into a million expensive pieces, everyone looks up from their work at us.

I'm helping Boner to his feet when we both hear her voice cutting through the silence.

"What the hell is going on back here?"

Boner opens his mouth to say something, but I step out in front of him and cut him off. "It's my fault. I dropped the dishes, Chef."

"What?" Boner says. "No, it was—"

"My mistake." I put my hand on the kid's chest and push him behind me.

Everyone is staring at us. I notice the whites of the cooks' eyes as they watch from their stations, simultaneously working and enjoying the free show. My heart is beating hard. I am about to lose yet another job. But I can't let Boner take this fall. We're in this mess because of me.

I face the chef at last.

Tall and slender, she's got high cheekbones, full lips, and brown eyes that tilt upward at the corners. Her skin is smooth and dark, and her hair is tied up in a black, glossy bun.

Jesus Christ.

It's her—the woman in the garden.

The moment we recognize each other lasts less than a second. She blinks and I blink, and now we both have to make a decision about how to proceed with all these people watching. Acknowledge that we've met before? Or ignore that we have any history at all?

She makes the decision for both of us.

"What is going on back here?" she asks again. Her dark eyes ricochet between me and Boner before taking in the broken dishes, the dish pit, the broken dishwashing machine, and the dirty dishes piled up to heaven.

"What's your name?" She's looking straight at me, completely ignoring Boner, who whimpers like a puppy behind me.

"Eddie Rosas, Chef." I keep my voice steady. I try, anyway.

"Dino said you've worked as a dishwasher before." Her voice is icy and hard. "Did he lie to me?"

"No, Chef."

"So you lied to Dino."

Instead of saying anything more, I begin to take off the apron. It's about eight o'clock. I can be back at Rafa's before nine, get to bed early, and return to the employment agency tomorrow to see if any new assignments turn up.

"What are you doing?" she says. "You're not going anywhere." She points to the floor. "These dishes are from an artisan potter in Ojai. Unless you have a couple thousand dollars in your locker, you owe us some labor."

I look up. No way in hell is she going to admit she knows me, not in front of her troops. But when we lock eyes, her chest rises and falls sharply, like she's catching her breath.

And that's when I know.

She remembers. That morning—our morning.

The heat, the wildness.

I read the embroidery on the front of her white chef's jacket. Carmen Centeno, Sous Chef.

Six months I've been trying to find this woman. She never told me her name.

"Chef Centeno," I say in a calm voice, "I'm not the kind of person to run away from something I've done."

I'm taking a jab at her, and she knows it. She was the one who ran away after...well, after we did what we did.

When she narrows her eyes at me, my body catches fire.

"Okay, Eddie," she says. "So how do we fix this?"

Made in the USA
Middletown, DE
01 July 2024

56626303R00175